Ben Elton is one of Brtaining writers. From ce
First World War to the e
unique perspective on
topics of our time.

He has written twelve major bestsellers, including *Stark*, *Popcorn* (winner of the Crime Writers' Association Gold Dagger Award), *Inconceivable* (filmed as *Maybe Baby*, which he also directed), *Dead Famous*, *High Society* (winner of the WHSmith People's Choice Award) and *The First Casualty*.

He has also written some of television's most popular and incisive comedy, including *The Young Ones*, *Blackadder* and *The Man from Auntie*. His stage work includes three West End plays and the hit musicals *The Beautiful Game* and *We Will Rock You*.

He is married with three children.

Dead Famous

Inconceivable

'Extremely funny, clever, well-written, sharp and unexpectedly moving . . . This brilliant, chaotic satire merits rereading several times' *Mail on Sunday*

'Extremely funny without ever being tasteless or cruel . . . this is Elton at his best – mature, humane, and still a laugh a minute. At least' *Daily Telegraph*

'A very funny book about a sensitive subject. The characters are well-developed, the action is page-turning and it's beginning to seem as if Ben Elton the writer might be even funnier than Ben Elton the comic' *Daily Mail*

'This is Elton doing what he does best, taking comedy to a place most people wouldn't dream of visiting and asking some serious questions while he's about it. It's a brave and personal novel' *Mirror*

'A tender, beautifully balanced romantic comedy' *Spectator*

'Moving and thoroughly entertaining' *Daily Express*

'Anyone who has had trouble starting a family will recognize the fertility roller-coaster Elton perceptively and wittily describes' *The Age*, Melbourne

Blast from the Past

ction is tight and well-plotted, the dialogue is punchy whole thing runs along so nicely that you never have to feel you're reading a book at all' *Guardian*

beginning, and the reminder that it is fear itself that ou jump wouldn't be out of place in a psychological *Blast from the Past* is a comedy, but an edgy comedy ick moral satire that works as a hairy cliff-hanger' *Sunday Times*

Also by Ben Elton

STARK
GRIDLOCK
THIS OTHER EDEN
POPCORN
BLAST FROM THE PAST
INCONCEIVABLE
DEAD FAMOUS
HIGH SOCIETY
PAST MORTEM
THE FIRST CASUALTY
CHART THROB

and published by Black Swan

BLIND FAITH

Ben Elton

BLACK SWAN

TRANSWORLD PUBLISHERS
61–63 Uxbridge Road, London W5 5SA
A Random House Group Company
www.rbooks.co.uk

BLIND FAITH
A BLACK SWAN BOOK: 9780552773911

First published in Great Britain in 2007 by Bantam Press
a division of Transworld Publishers
Black Swan edition published 2008

A CIP catalogue record for this book
is available from the British Library.

Addresses for Random House Group Ltd companies outside the UK
can be found at: www.randomhouse.co.uk
The Random House Group Ltd Reg. No. 954009

The Random House Group Limited supports The Forest Stewardship
Council (FSC), the leading international forest certification organisation. All
ourtitles that are printed on Greenpeace approved FSC certified paper carry the
FSC logo. Our paper procurement policy can be found at
www.rbooks.co.uk/environment

Typeset in 11/16pt Giovanni Book by Falcon Oast Graphic Art Ltd.

Printed in the UK by CPI Cox & Wyman, Reading, RG1 8EX.

2 4 6 8 10 9 7 5 3 1

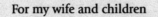
For my wife and children

1

Trafford said goodbye to his wife, kissed their tiny baby on the forehead and began to unlock the various bolts and deadlocks that secured their front door.

'And a very good morning to you *too*, Trafford,' said the voice of Barbieheart.

'Yes, of course, good morning, Barbieheart,' Trafford replied nervously. 'Good morning indeed, I mean goodbye . . . I mean . . . well, I mean I don't want to be late, you see.'

'I'm not holding you up, Trafford.'

'No. Absolutely.'

'Well now, you take care to have a great day.'

'Thank you. Thank you very much. I will.'

Trafford's wife looked at him angrily. He knew that Chantorria suspected him of deliberately not greeting Barbieheart, as some kind of protest, some bizarre bid for independence. She was right, of course.

'Sometimes he doesn't even say good morning to *me*,' Chantorria volunteered apologetically, waving at Barbieheart's face on the wallscreen.

She was only trying to suck up; Trafford knew Chantorria hated Barbieheart as much as he did. But trying to keep her sweet was the right thing to do, the safe thing to do. At least one member of the family had a sense of what was proper.

Barbieheart extracted her hand from the huge sack of cheesy snacks on which she was breakfasting and waved back. She was moderator of the tenement chat room and, having grown too large to leave her apartment, she was scarcely ever absent from her post. A constant presence in every household, Barbieheart was an extra member of the family and one whom Trafford deeply resented.

'Go, go! Run, Trafford!' Barbieheart said with exaggerated cheeriness. 'It's a brand new day, praise the Love.'

Trafford left his apartment and began to descend the many litter-strewn, rat-infested staircases to the street below. The lift worked but Trafford never used it. He claimed he liked to walk down for the exercise but really it was so that he could enjoy a few brief moments away from communitainment screens. He could never admit that, of course: it would look dangerously weird. After all, what was not to like about a news and entertainment video on the wall of a boring lift?

Out on the pavement Trafford headed for the tube station, picking his way carefully through the cellophane, the filthy pink ribbons, the rotting blooms, the little photographs, the scribbled-on scraps of paper and the gilt-edged cards:

Gathered unto the Lord.

One more star in the zodiac.

A new heartbeat in Heaven.

He knew better than to tread on a single kiss-laden message or wilted flower; he had seen men beaten senseless for less. They missed nothing, those keening women who gathered on the pavements in the heat of the morning to mourn their dead and broadcast to the street the age-old songs of grief.

I will always love you.

The heart must go on.

One foot wrong, one petal defiled, and that weeping, hugging huddle would without doubt consider themselves to have been shown disrespect. And disrespect was something for which, even in their grief, these women were constantly vigilant. Even a suspicion of disrespect would turn public sorrow instantly to public rage. The fuse was short, the tinder dry; it took almost nothing to summon forth the mob from the surrounding apartment buildings and spark an orgy of People's Justice which the police would regret but not condemn. Many who fell victim to the righteous fury of the mob never understood what offence it was that they had unwittingly given, just as many who rushed to join the frenzied mêlée could only guess at what outrage the object of their fury had committed. Something to do with children, no doubt, because nobody dissed the people's kiddies. Least of all the dead ones.

And there were so many dead ones.

Death was everywhere. In the buzz of insects' wings, in the splashing of the dirty water and borne on the whisper of the wind. It stalked everybody, old and young alike, but it was the young who were the most vulnerable and they suffered most.

Libra Divine: Heaven has a brand new superstar.

Tyson Armani: Simply the best.

Malibu: A candle in the wind.

So many dead children. Millions and millions of them. No stretch of pavement without its shrine. No personal web page without its catalogue of tiny faces that had looked upon the world for such a short time but lived on now only in Heaven and in cyberspace.

My little sister.

My tiny cousin.

My boy. My girl.

All safe now in the arms of Jesus. And Diana. The Love Spirit and the Lord. Dead but safe. Safe, thank God, from paedophiles.

Sagiquarius: Pure for ever. Defiled, never.

Child mortality was the burning cross that branded the souls of the nation, the pain that the people must bear in repentance for the sins of their faithless forefathers. No child was safe: the plagues which swept through the community affected rich and poor alike. God's great plan was no respecter of wealth or rank, although without doubt the more crowded the district, the more severe were the epidemics that afflicted it. Bumps and sores, boils and

14

pustules, aching bones, running eyes and infected chests, these were the dangers that an infant must negotiate before it had even learned to walk. The mother who brought six babies into the world could only hope to take three of them to McDonald's to celebrate their fifth birthdays. For half of them at least, the party sacks would never be filled.

Chantorria had recently given birth to their first child, a time of joy but also a time of grim trepidation. Like all new parents, she and Trafford had spent the weeks since their daughter's arrival listening out for telltale coughs, watching for rashes and testing constantly for sensitivity to sound and light.

Now, however, it was time for Trafford to return to work and this particular day was a Fizzy Coff. Fizzy Coff was short for 'physical office' and meant that it was a day when Trafford's personally adapted work structure required him to attend his actual workplace, as opposed to the virtual version which existed online and which he could get to without leaving his bed.

Fizzy Coffs were a statutory requirement; the law expected each person to spend at least 25 per cent of their working hours in the company of real, physical colleagues in a real physical space. It was intended at some point to increase this proportion to 50 per cent and the transport system was supposedly being updated to cope with the extra travel hours, but Trafford doubted that it would ever happen. All future planning for the transport system seemed to him to focus on the modest ambition of preventing it from grinding to a complete halt.

Fizzy Coffs were a relatively recent development. Twenty solstices previously, when Trafford had first entered employment, he had not been required to go out to a physical workplace at all. Few people did, except those whose job was serving food and drink or lapdancing. That had been in a time when the virtues of the virtual had gone unchallenged. The public health advantages of keeping people apart had been obvious and it was generally assumed that at some point all work would be done at home. But the growing trend towards social dysfunction had alerted both the Temple and the government to the human need for Face Time. Care workers and spiritual counsellors had concluded that people who dealt exclusively with virtual individuals tended to be at an emotional disadvantage when confronted with the real thing. Unable to relate to fellow members of the community, they were awkward, tongue-tied, and would occasionally shoot at random as many people as they could before turning their guns on themselves.

It had also become clear that it was impossible to meet a series of sexual partners while sitting alone in a tiny flat in front of a computer screen surrounded by pizza boxes. This had of course brought the Temple into the debate. With one in two children dying in infancy, the first and foremost spiritual duty of the people was to produce more children and you cannot produce children without sexual partners. The High Council of the Temple had therefore let it be known that the government must enable the people to interact more regularly, and so Fizzy Coffs became mandatory.

It was therefore principally in order to produce children and to prevent them from developing into deranged killers that Trafford found himself picking his way through the emotionally charged litter of a permanently traumatized society in the burning heat of a stinking Sagittarian morning.

2

Trafford was a civil servant of sorts. Most people who were not in catering and hospitality were civil servants, the government being by far the largest employer in the country. In fact, since almost everything that people consumed or used came from somewhere else, the principal activity of the government was finding people something to do.

Trafford worked for NatDat, the National Data Bank, which existed to collect and store information about the population. Historically NatDat had been a branch of the Home Office but it had long since grown so huge that the Home Office had become a branch of it. Every single recordable fact about every single person in the country was logged at NatDat. Every financial transaction, every appearance on a CCTV camera, every click on every computer, every quirk of every retina, every filling in every tooth was captured and entombed in the mainframes of NatDat and subsequently encrypted on to the little black strips on the back of people's Temple membership cards.

This was not an exercise in mass observation, nor was it sinister evidence of an all-knowing police state. The police had their own data bank with which to combat terrorism and terrorism continued unabated anyway, it having long since become clear that no matter how much information was stored about people they would still be able to detonate themselves in public places if they were really determined to do so. In fact the vast majority of the population (including most potential terrorists and random killers) published every possible detail of their lives on their Face Space pages anyway and lived in hope that somebody would read them. In a world where a desire for privacy was proscribed as a perversion and a denial of faith, there was little point in government-sponsored mass observation.

Yet NatDat continued to grow, employing more and more people, simply to record and to store more and more information. To the best of Trafford's knowledge, nobody ever looked at any of the information he stored. He had never been called upon to supply any of it to anyone. He merely processed it, as did a million others like him, moving it from machine to machine like a great shifting sea. Sometimes, in his dreams, Trafford imagined a sudden information tsunami, a moment when all the electronic movements, the As and Bs of a trillion zillion micro-communications, would coalesce into one vast unstoppable tidal wave and drown the population in the virtual version of their own lives.

Despite the clarity of this vision and the fact that the recounting of dreams was a major element in both social intercourse and spiritual worship, Trafford did not share this dream with anyone. When invited to describe a dream at Community Confession or over chocolate lattes at social hubs on Fizzy Coffs, Trafford never told the truth. Instead he made up dreams, taking elements from other people's interminable sagas and stitching them together – a startled rabbit from one, a sense of falling from another, a sudden overwhelming awareness that it was 'all good' from a third, until he had enough to make an acceptable tale which would see him through until he could legitimately pass on the microphone.

Nobody ever noticed. Most people were simply itching to tell their own tales. Trafford did not keep his dreams a secret because he thought they were in any way significant; they were meaningless to him and hence must be doubly meaningless to anybody else. He kept them a secret simply in order to enjoy the sensual pleasure of *having* a secret. Of not emoting. Any secret was exciting to Trafford, no matter how banal. Something which he alone knew. Something which he did not share.

3

With weary resignation Trafford joined the crowd that was attempting to get into the tube station. No matter how much tidal planning the authorities imposed upon the commuting population, there was always a crowd at the entrance. There was a crowd at the entrance to everything and a crowd inside everything and as often as not a crowd assembled separately, in a holding area, awaiting access to the crowd that was waiting at the entrance to join the crowd that was inside. People spent so much of their lives shuffling forward at a snail's pace that it had become part of the physical characteristics of the population; they shuffled even on those rare occasions when there was not somebody jammed up in front of them and another person pushing them from behind. The authorities often ran public health campaigns urging people to straighten their backs and to take proper strides instead of pigeon steps. This would, they assured everyone, be good for their spines and enable them to look to the horizon with clear-eyed zeal. Nobody took any notice, sensing perhaps that there was little point in taking proper strides when it simply meant that you would arrive more quickly at the next people jam.

Trafford hated people jams. He had heard stories from his mother (who had perhaps heard them from her mother) of a time when it was possible to find solitude, when even in the cities there had been green places where one might sit and not smell the sweat of half a dozen other human beings. But that had been in the wicked years BTF. Before the country had shrunk under the vengeance of the Love and all the population had been forced to squeeze into half the space it had previously enjoyed.

Trafford shuffled forward, watching the gates opening and closing as the platforms beneath them emptied and filled. He knew that he should not complain, that he was lucky to live near a functioning tube line with an effective pumping system. But he didn't feel lucky, crushed in among the shuffling crowd, struggling towards the start of his utterly pointless day. Exhausted after a night spent in a tiny room with his even more exhausted wife and a screaming baby, he did not feel lucky. He felt numb.

A voice called out his name. 'Trafford. Trafford Sewell. Come share with me!'

Trafford knew the voice well. He also knew that he would have to go share. He would have to relinquish his place in the mass shuffle (despite being no more than two gate closures from the entrance) and go where he was summoned. It would make him late for work, of course, but this would not lead to his being counselled and encouraged to reconsider the decisions he took about what time he left the house. No employer would ever expect a person to disobey their Confessor's invitation to share.

Trafford turned and began to push back against the human tide.

And there was so much tide to push against. So many people and so *much* of each person. And almost all of it on display. So much flesh. So much sweating near-naked flesh. Huge women in the tiniest of crop tops and panties, combinations that were basically little more than bikinis. Some were bare even at the bosom, the big, baby-sucked nipples pointing accusingly at Trafford as he struggled past, pink and brown signposts reminding him that he was going in the wrong direction. Men in short shorts and trainers, in vests, or bare to the waist. It was often the largest bellies that were the most exposed, thrust forward like great battering rams, proud bellies, bellies of size, topped off with pendulous, quivering, hairy man breasts.

Trafford held his arms aloft as he attempted to penetrate the almost solid mass of flesh that faced him. He did this for fear that his hands might accidentally brush against a breast or, worse, get lodged in a crotch as he attempted to prise his way past. The merest touch could so easily be wilfully misinterpreted.

'Are you fiddlin' with me?' a voice would shriek. 'Did you disrespect my booby?'

Always it seemed to Trafford that the larger and more naked the woman, the more likely she was to scream that her breasts had been disrespected. Yet in such a crush and with breasts so very, very large it was difficult to avoid disrespecting them. Breasts like beach balls, bursting out of tiny triangles of shiny cloth, with great burned-brown semicircles of half-revealed nipples loomed inches from his face.

The inevitable happened.

'Pervert!' someone shouted. 'The fucking station's behind you.'

Trafford did not attempt to find from whom the voice had come. He knew that the last thing an outraged person wanted to hear was reason and so instantly he turned ninety degrees and pushed sideways against the crowd. He had to get away from that voice: the word 'pervert' was but a short step from the word 'paedo', and once that word was uttered in a restive, sullen crowd the stakes mounted. It was astonishing how, in crushes where there was scarcely room to scratch one's nose, space could suddenly be found to kick a man to death.

'Sorry, sorry. Excuse me,' Trafford muttered, his arms raised and his chin on his chest, touching nobody's boobies, catching nobody's eye. 'My Confessor called me, I have to get through.'

The angry voice receded behind him and then, all in a rush, as if breaking through a dense jungle canopy,

Trafford popped out of the wall of bodies and almost into the arms of his community spiritual guide, Confessor Bailey.

'Hey, hey, hey!' Bailey laughed, big and jovial as always. 'Steady there, steady. More haste less speed, Trafford, as a wise man once said.'

'You called me, Confessor. Was there something?' Trafford asked, trying to look as cheerful as the Confessor was pretending to feel.

'Something? Something! Of course there's something, Trafford!' Bailey shouted, enfolding him in a fierce bear hug. 'Congratulations is what there is, brother! Congratulations and love salutations! I understand that the Lord of Life has blessed you and your lovely, lovely, sexy, sexy lady with a beautiful baby girl kiddie. Am I right?'

Confessor Bailey continued to hold Trafford in his huge embrace. The preacher was a big man; the top of Trafford's head came barely to his chin, Trafford's cheek was pressed against Bailey's chest and the smell of expensive designer perfume and scented toilet products mixed with sweat was nearly overpowering. Bailey wasn't naked, of course: he was dressed quite modestly, as befitted his senior position in the community, in tight, pure white satin hot pants, white kneesocks and a white Lycra cycling jersey. The jersey was emblazoned with a glittering golden cross spotted with winking pin lights. Above the cross was a rainbow, also illuminated, and within the rainbow a hologram of a dove in flight. On his head Confessor

Bailey wore a tall mitre studded with costume jewels and bound with more strings of lights.

'You are right,' Trafford stammered into Bailey's chest, trying not to breathe in too deeply, 'we've had a baby.'

'All good, I hope. Chantorria well? Strong? Proud? In control? Working on getting her figure back?'

'Yes, yes, of course.'

'Then I say Go, girl! Praise the Lord. Praise the Love!'

'Praise the Love,' Trafford echoed dutifully.

'Kiddie doing fine?'

'Yes, very well, thank you, Father,' Trafford replied. 'She's gorgeous.'

'Of course she is. Made in the image of her precious sexy mother and as such in the image of our Creator. And does the gorgeous darling have a name?'

'Well, we thought perhaps . . . Caitlin.'

Confessor Bailey frowned. Formal, traditional names were not fashionable any more. The past itself was not fashionable. Everybody knew that it was in the past that society had made its mistakes. The past was a place of ignorance, heresy and dark, dark sorcery. The past was a place where man was taught that the ape was his brother and where Christian ministers claimed that God was not a real person at all but merely a metaphor for goodness.

'We haven't absolutely decided yet,' Trafford continued hurriedly, his courage deserting him. 'Chantorria thought perhaps Happymeal.'

'You should listen to your lady,' Confessor Bailey replied firmly. 'She has a clever head on those strong, womanly shoulders. Cute too, and great boobs for naturals. Big and proud.'

'Thank you, Confessor Bailey, I shall tell her that you said so.'

The Confessor smiled but his mood did not lighten.

'I checked your Face Space page, Trafford,' he said sternly. 'I also checked your board on the Community Space site.'

Trafford looked at the ground, knowing what was coming. There could be no other reason for Confessor Bailey to summon him from the crowd.

'I even Goog'ed you up on the WorldTube and yet . . .' Bailey continued, his voice getting sterner by the syllable, 'I found no birthing video.'

Trafford's head remained bowed. He had only hoped to keep the secret for a short time, just while he and Chantorria got to know their child. He had intended to post the required video that very evening. It had been just his luck to bump into Bailey. He stared fiercely at a rotting remembrance card that lay between his feet.

Fanta: Gone to Heaven but always in our hearts.

'Problem with your broadband, Trafford?' Confessor Bailey asked icily. 'I find if you just turn it off at the wall and wait five minutes . . .'

'I didn't actually post a birthing video . . . yet,' Trafford admitted. It was always better to confess, the Temple knew everything anyway. Everybody knew everything. 'Chantorria reminded me to but . . . well, I just haven't got round to it.'

The priest smiled but it was a hard, joyless smile. 'You just haven't got round to it?'

'No.'

'You did not feel moved to share this beautiful and most special Lord-given event, which is like no other and after which you will never be the same, with your community? With the world?'

'I announced it,' Trafford protested weakly. 'I put it on my blog.'

Now Bailey was not even bothering to smile.

'You *announced* it? You put the *birth of a kiddie* on your *blog*? And that is *all*?'

'I wrote about it! I described how beautiful—'

'You *described it*!' The priest was angry now. 'The Lord has blessed us with digital recording equipment with which we can capture, celebrate and worship in diamond detail the *exactitude* of every nuance of his creation and yet you, you in your vanity, think that your *description*, the work of your lowly, humble, inadequate *imagination*, can somehow do the job better! You believe your description, your *fiction*, to be a better medium for representing God's work than digitized reality!'

Suddenly Trafford was scared. He had not expected Confessor Bailey to put this spin on his excuse. Fiction was not a word that was used lightly. Fiction was a sin, fiction was sacrilege. Everybody knew that invention, the act of creation, was the prerogative of the Love and only of the Love. God created reality and man worshipped it, that was the way of truth. Men created only lies.

'No!' Trafford protested. 'Not fiction! Just . . . a description, that's all. A description of reality . . . reality in words.'

'Why didn't you record it? Why didn't you broadcast *real* reality instead of your own paltry efforts to *describe* it? When you shave in the morning do you use a mirror?'

'Well, yes, of course I—'

'Exactly, you do not rely on a *description* of your face. You do not apply the razor to your flesh guided only by the printed word! Because if you did you would soon cut yourself to pieces.'

'Well, no . . .'

'So *real* reality is fine when it comes to your own personal comfort but when it comes to celebrating the divine gift of life, a *description* of reality will suffice. Is that it?'

'No!'

'*Why* did you not Tube a birthing video, Trafford?'

Trafford knew the answer but he could never say it. He could not possibly confess that his decision to delay posting the birthing video on the net had been the result of a strange force deep within him which desired a moment of *privacy*. A longing to keep something to *himself*, even if only for a short while.

He could not say that. Nothing was more offensive to the Temple and to the community in general than privacy. Why would anyone wish to hide any aspect of themselves from the gaze of others? Was it not their duty to celebrate themselves? Perhaps Trafford was ashamed of something? Or perhaps he thought he was in some way special? *Better* than his fellow men and women, *too good* for them?

'Privacy,' Bailey stated with quiet menace, 'is a blasphemy, Trafford. Only perverts do things in private.'

'I know that, Confessor.'

'If you have nothing to be ashamed of, you have nothing to hide.'

'I just didn't think anybody would be interested,' Trafford stammered. 'You know, there's so much going on in our tenement besides us. Goodness knows, Galaxy Starlight at Number 8a is having sex with her husband's dad but her husband still loves her big time so now it's a threesome and they're streaming it live 24/7. Why would anybody want to look at—?'

'Is something wrong?' the Confessor broke in, his face suddenly a picture of desperate concern. 'Is the kiddie deformed?'

'No!'

'Thank the Love.'

'Thank the Love.'

'Say hallelujah!'

'Hallelujah!'

'Was it a difficult birth?' the priest went on. 'Did Chantorria tear?'

'A little but . . .'

'If so, all the more reason to share and to emote. Tragedy and pain are lordly creations too, sent to test our strength and try us. Be proud of your pain! When we share our suffering we learn and we grow and we share our connection with God.'

'Everything's fine, really . . .'

'Say Love!'

'Love!'

'Say *Everlasting* Love!'

'Everlasting Love!'

'Let me hear you say Ev Love!'

'Ev Love!'

The Confessor had raised his face to Heaven for these ringing incantations but now his fierce glare returned to Trafford.

'Then *why* have you not done your duty by your community and posted a birthing video?'

There was simply no answer. The truth would have resulted in a public denunciation at Confession, perhaps even a whipping. Once more Trafford stared at the ground. A new thought occurred to Bailey.

'Is Chantorria *ashamed* of her cooch?' he asked suddenly.

'No, Confessor! Certainly not! It was me who . . . forgot to post the vid.'

'Eve had a cooch! Mother Mary had a cooch! Diana had a cooch! Cooches make kiddies. Chantorria should be proud to be a strong woman with a kiddie-making cooch.'

'She is! Of course she is, Father. Very proud. Proud to be a woman.'

'A strong woman! A woman of faith.'

'Yes, of course. Faith is at the centre of our lives. Nothing

31

is more important to us than our one-on-one relationship with the Love. We talk to him all the time.'

'Then why has she not shown the cooch the Love gave her to the world in its time of greatest creativity? Does she not wish to be a role model? To empower others? To help them to celebrate and to learn from her Lord-given experience? Does she not think that she is beautiful and that everybody should watch her, share with her? Applaud her?'

'Well, of course she does. Of course, she thinks all of those things.'

Confessor Bailey stood back and solemnly laid his hand upon Trafford's brow. 'Then you will share the birthing video forthwith?'

'Yes . . . yes, I will, Father. Of course. I'm sorry,' Trafford replied.

'Good,' said the Confessor, smiling once more. 'You send my big love big time to Chantorria and to little Happymeal. Don't forget now.'

4

Trafford bid Bailey an obsequious farewell, hugely relieved
to have got away without the prospect of official censure
from the pulpit, and turned once more to face the crowd
that was attempting to enter the tube station. A wall of
gleaming, sweating, half-naked and occasionally entirely
naked bottoms confronted him. Bottoms hanging over
shorts, bottoms clamped around thongs. All or a part of
every single buttock in the crowd was on display. Huge or
petite, saggy or pert. Hairy, waxed, deep cleavages, mottled
cheeks. Stretch marks, surgical scars, extravagant tattoos
and love bites. Proud bottoms. In-your-face bottoms.
Bottoms that were as good as anybody else's bottom.

Trafford knew that never in his life would he get used to
the casual display of so much flesh. He did not want to see
these bottoms; he did not want his vision busied with the
endless quirks of other people's bodies. No matter how

hard he tried not to notice, small details kept forcing themselves to the forefront of his consciousness and they made him queasy. He wished that these people would cover themselves up.

It wasn't that he found nakedness objectionable in itself. It was only that something in him felt that flesh should be presented artfully, with mystery even, not forced upon a person. It was the same with breast enlargements. He knew the logic: if boobs were attractive, surely then the larger the better. What was not to like? It was undeniable, and yet somehow he suspected that sometimes less might be more.

He never said this to anyone, not even to Chantorria. He knew only too well how threatened and uncomfortable people would feel if he were to reveal to them that he had a problem with looking at their naked buttock divisions. They would denounce him on the web boards; they would say that his failure to applaud the pride that they took in their body images was sacrilegious. Had they not all been made in God's image? Therefore anybody who had a problem with a person's appearance must also have a problem with God. They would hint darkly that only those who believed that the apes were man's brother had any reason to be ashamed of any aspect of humanity. It was dangerous enough that he was himself excessively modest in his dress. Declining to expose his own body an inch more than the heat and stern social convention dictated, he always wore a T-shirt rather than a vest and his shorts stretched almost halfway to his knees. Indeed so overdressed was he in comparison to the norm that it was not uncommon for people to accuse him of being a Muslim and tell him to get back to the ghetto or better still, to where he came from, if it was still above water.

Trafford attempted to put these thoughts from his mind and, fighting down the nausea that was mounting in his stomach, began for the second time that morning to shuffle his way towards the gates of the tube station. A news and infotainment loop was playing on the screens which hung above the gates. It was the same loop that had been playing on the lamp posts that lined the streets along which Trafford had walked to get to the station. It was also flickering, unbidden, on his travel card and had without doubt been playing in the lift that he had avoided that morning. All the same loop. So many platforms on which to view, so little to be viewed.

In *Entertainment News* various stars were engaged in ferocious struggles with their personal demons, struggles which with the help of God they were determined to win. In *News News* more huge bombs had gone off in crowded places. The army was doing a tough job under very difficult circumstances in the various peacekeeping zones around the world, and also in policing the walls of Christendom as a billion cholera-ravaged infidels massed at the gates pleading for a glass of clean water. In more mundane domestic news there had been a number of instances of vigilantism and People's Justice (with which the authorities sympathized but which they could not officially condone) and the government appeared to be standing idly by while a highly organized fifth column of paedophiles infiltrated the community.

In *Weather News* there were the usual broken sea defences, collapsed pumping stations and floods everywhere.

Trafford wondered why they did not simply play the same tape each day. It was always the same news and by 9 a.m. everybody had learned by heart the small variations in personalities and locations anyway.

Two more loops, he reckoned, and he'd be through the gates.

Hundreds believed dead . . .

He couldn't hear the soundtrack any more, not deep within the crowd. The commentary had merged with the cacophony created by the personal communitainment devices that hung from every neck.

The bomber, who was seventeen . . .

Uh! Uh! Duf duf! Duf duf!

Died when his . . .

Girl, you truly could be a star . . .

Trafford stuffed his own muted earphones deeper into his ears to try to shut out the noise. He was always trying to shut out the noise, along with the sight of people's bodies, and the smell. Sweat, perfumed toilet products and food. Above all, food.

The majority of people were eating as they shuffled forward, listening to their communitainers, staring at the video loop and pushing food into their mouths. It seemed that not a single sensory organ was in repose. It would be worse on the train, of course. Trafford was dreading it: a packed, baking hot tin can full of people eating pizzas and burgers and chicken and healthy chocolate-and-cereal brunch bars. He took out an extra strong peppermint, the only thing that got him through his journey without being sick. Unfortunately it was becoming increasingly difficult to track down peppermints that were not coated in chocolate. Shop assistants found it inexplicable that he asked for them. What was not to like about chocolate?

5

In some ways Trafford enjoyed Fizzy Coffs. He loathed crowds but he was not averse to company, not least because he sensed that one or two of his colleagues at NatDat kept, as he did, a part of themselves private. He would never know for sure, of course. That was the point about privacy: it was private, which was what made it so special. The pressure to share and to emote was so all-encompassing it was exhausting.

A banner hung from the roof of Trafford's office. *How do you feel?* it asked. *Tell someone right now!* This was a slogan promoted by the Ministry of Well-being, alongside *Sharing. What's not to like?*

All day long on the TV, the radio and over the web the community was constantly cajoled to ring in and emote.

'Tell us how you feel,' the DJs demanded. 'We want to hear from *you*! What's making you angry?'

Every health worker and spiritual adviser had the same message: 'Deal with your issues. Be proud of your feelings. Confront your demons. *Talk about yourself!*'

Above all, this was the message of the Temple.

'Man is God's work!' Confessor Bailey thundered to his congregation. 'Everything we are, everything we do, everything we say is the creation of the Lord and the Love. Therefore, when we talk about ourselves we are *actually* talking about God! Each thought we have, each word we say, each part of the bodies in which we exult is a gift from the Love and should be held up high for all to see! A desire for privacy is a denial of the Love and he who denies the Love *has no faith!*'

Trafford wanted privacy, or even just a bit of peace. Every day he wanted to shout, 'Here's an idea: why don't we all shut up for five minutes?' But it was a very serious crime to have no faith.

It had not always been a crime. The Temple liked to imply that it had been but it had not. Trafford knew this because the change in the law had come about in his own lifetime. The statutory obligation to have faith was the very first of the Wembley Laws, or People's Statutes to give them their legal title.

As all laws were now Wembley Laws, it was increasingly difficult to recall a time when there had been any other form of legislation, but there had been. When Trafford was a boy, laws had still been the creation of a misguided, corrupt, out of touch, elected élite who called themselves Members of Parliament.

The change had come about due to the growing frustration within the community and particularly within the High Council of the Temple that the elected lawmakers were not 'listening to the people'. No matter which group of politicians was elected to govern, they always found themselves immediately out of step with the 'will of the people' and, what was worse, they refused to listen to it and learn. It seemed almost to be a function of government that it existed to frustrate the clear-sighted common sense of men and women of faith.

Strangely, this problem bothered the politicians as much as it did the people themselves. Of course it was in a politician's own interest to legislate for whatever it was that the people wanted. The question was how best could the elected representatives hand back power to the electorate?

The first solution they tried was the instant plebiscite. Major issues were put before the people online and the people were then invited to vote and, if they wished, suggest alternatives and amendments. This had been a disaster, promoting as it did not the will of the people but the will of the *person*, the individual. For it was very soon discovered that while crowds can be controlled, individuals often act independently, and in the great democracy of the net any computer-literate paedophile or ape lover could communicate with the entire world and any number of points of view could be exhibited and canvassed. Anarchy ensued and, astonishingly, it became increasingly difficult to define what the 'will of the people' actually was.

It was the Confessors of the Temple who came up with the solution. Physical laws would be made by physical people. It would be a return to the very definition of democracy. The Temple had access to the people, the Temple regularly organized vast gatherings of the people. What could be more obvious than to grant these gatherings law-making powers? The Holy Order was announced at the weekly Wembley Stadium Faith Festival. These were the celebrations at which charismatic believers from all over the capital convened to share their heartache, rejoice in the Love and testify to their faith. The stadium held 250,000 people and so it was decreed that any gathering of that number who could be seen to speak with one voice should be able to make a law.

Since it was only the Temple who were in a position to stage such events and also the Temple which controlled the New New Wembley Stadium, the only venue that could hold so vast a crowd, it followed that the Temple would henceforth make the laws and government would become merely an organ of administration. This development, besides being solid common sense, was also *legal* in every way, even under the old laws. For even in the time of ignorance BTF, it had been a crime to incite religious hatred and what could be more calculated to incite religious hatred than to deny the will of the faithful?

The first Wembley Laws passed were inevitably the Faith Laws and the most important Faith Law of all was the one that made it illegal to have no faith. This statute also drew legitimacy from the old laws BTF, for even then it had been an offence to denigrate another person's religion. The Temple simply argued that if a person had no faith themselves then clearly that person did not believe in the faith held by others, and if you did not believe in something then how could you possibly respect it? A person must therefore, by law, have faith.

6

The one thing about Fizzy Coff days that Trafford loathed with a passion was the Gr'ug. The Gr'ug, or Group Hug, was a compulsory part of the communal working experience. Trafford tried to avoid them as often as possible by being absent on little office errands or feigning sickness in the lavatory, but he had to be careful: repeated absences could provoke severe censure and even denunciation at Confession. Therefore on the majority of occasions the Gr'ug had to be faced.

'Gather round, everybody,' a cheery voice shouted.

It was Princess Lovebud. Princess Lovebud always initiated the Gr'ugs, though she had no specific authority to do this since there were no ranks or degrees of seniority among Trafford's immediate colleagues. Officially hierarchy was kept to a minimum in government workplaces in order to avoid damaging people's self-esteem and making them feel uncomfortable. Personal aspiration was of course statutory. It was a Wembley Law.

Any person who is prepared to dream the dream can be whatever they want to be. By law.

This law was one of the many inconsistencies of life that Trafford noted every day and which troubled him deeply. Just as it was against the law to denigrate a person's faith, it was also illegal to doubt or deny the practical reality of their ambitions and aspirations, or 'dreams' as they were popularly known. Trafford could not understand this. Everybody he had ever met wanted to be hugely rich and famous and yet not one of them had ever become so. In fact, as things got progressively harder, hotter and more crowded in the city, people's lives were quite clearly getting worse. Nonetheless the concrete certainty that each person could have everything they ever wanted simply by wanting it was a statutory human right.

Trafford could see that reality contradicted official dogma every day and in every way. Yet still people believed (or claimed to believe) that dreams could and would come true and it was legally required of Trafford that he believe in their belief. Something simply wasn't making sense.

To Trafford's mind, nothing made sense, particularly God. Once he had heard a woman shouting on a street corner. She had insisted that if God, the Love, the Creator, the Supreme Being, cared so much about kiddies, why were so many of them dying in pain? She had been holding a baby to her lactating breast as she spoke and when the police finally prised it from her it was discovered to be dead. The woman had voiced a contradiction that had occurred to Trafford many times. It must, he felt, have occurred to everybody. Yet the woman was arrested for incitement to religious hatred and Trafford never saw her again.

So many laws contradicted actual personal experience, which was why, despite the absence of official rank in the workplace, there was nonetheless a strict pecking order. It was based on the conspicuous public display of spiritual orthodoxy and in Trafford's little world Princess Lovebud was top dog. Princess Lovebud was so filled with faith that Trafford wondered how there was any room left inside her for the doughnuts which she consumed throughout the day.

Princess Lovebud believed in everything. First and foremost, of course, she believed in the Lord and the Love and the law of the Temple. It also went without saying that she believed in Baby Jesus and that Baby Jesus wanted Princess Lovebud to dream the dream and to be anything and everything that she wanted to be. But Princess Lovebud's all-consuming faith went further. She was a trained astrologer, a tarot reader, a white witch and a departmental Slimmer of the Year (using the power of faith). She practised only tantric sex and claimed to be a Buddhist in that she believed absolutely in the power of love and the healing strength of being her own person. All these faiths were entirely consistent with the teachings of the Temple, since it was assumed that all faith was simply a faith in the Love by another name. The obvious exceptions to this law were the designated 'false faiths', Islam, that great 'other', and of course the dirty Jews.

Princess Lovebud certainly had faith. She was (as she constantly reminded people) a deeply, deeply spiritual person. She was also as dangerous as a pit bull if crossed and would diss you big time on the office blog if she detected, even for a moment, a lack of respect for her or her family.

Trafford suspected that she was an informer for the Inquisition.

'Group Hug!' Princess Lovebud shouted, smiling broadly and throwing wide her arms, and then, in a grating imitation of a little girl, she added, 'Wanna hug, need a hug, got to have a hu-u-u-u-g.'

Trafford and his colleagues dutifully assembled in the centre of the open-plan office and formed a circle with their arms entwined and heads bowed solemnly towards the centre. Trafford, to his horror, found himself standing next to Princess Lovebud, laying his arm across her naked back, or at least as far as it would go, for Princess Lovebud was proud to be a woman of size and Trafford's arm was not long enough to hook itself around her waist. He was instead forced to leave it resting across the great folded muffin top that bulged over her satin thong. This position was agonizingly ambiguous. How much pressure to apply? Too little would indicate a lack of joy and commitment to the communal experience, while too much might bring forth an accusation of harassment and disrespect. Princess Lovebud was terrifyingly unpredictable and a charge of abuse from one rumoured to have contacts in the Inquisition was too alarming even to think about.

'O Lord, O Love, O Lord of Love,' Princess Lovebud chanted loudly as Trafford struggled to keep his arm from shaking, 'grant us the serenity to be ourselves and to love ourselves and to be everything that we want to be. To dream the dream and to live the dream as you want us to do, O Lord. Each day is an open door; let us have the courage to step through it and not to close it behind us, that others might step through it also. You made me in your image, Lord, and so it is my duty to love myself as you love me. I believe that children are the future. Amen.'

'Amen,' the circle echoed at the top of their voices.

'And speaking of children,' Princess Lovebud shouted, like some holiday-camp master of ceremonies about to announce the raffle prize, 'I believe Trafford has some news for us!'

All eyes turned to Trafford. He should have seen it coming, of course; obviously a woman like Princess Lovebud would never allow a big cake moment like the birth of a kiddie to pass un-caked, and yet he was at a loss what to say.

'Yes,' he stammered, 'that's right . . . Chantorria has had a baby girl.'

'Well, don't sound so *happy* about it!' Princess Lovebud shrieked with steely-edged good humour, adding, 'A little *girl*! A girly girl! May she have enormous proud boobies and may her daddy buy her even bigger ones!'

Everybody laughed heartily and then cheered. People

47

shouted, 'Way to go' and 'Bring it on' and Trafford was high-fived and hugged and kissed.

After this Princess Lovebud assumed an expression of agonized empathy and invited any previously bereaved mothers in the group to use the occasion of Trafford's happiness to share their grief.

'I'll go first,' she added and began to weep.

For five long minutes Princess Lovebud confessed loudly and extravagantly to a sorrow that would never end and a pain that would never heal. The agony was real: Trafford did not doubt that Princess Lovebud missed the babies that she had lost with the same intensity as any other bereaved parent. It was simply that she was so much louder than any of the other mothers. Everybody shouted, of course; even intimate conversations were conducted at the top of a person's voice. The Temple believed firmly that volume was a reliable benchmark of sincerity and that those who spoke quietly were not sufficiently proud of whatever it was that they had to say. The Temple expected those of faith to make a joyful noise unto the Love. Everybody was loud but Princess Lovebud was somehow always louder and the harsh, twisted vowels and wilfully misplaced consonants fell like hammer blows on Trafford's eardrums.

'I know,' Princess Lovebud concluded, 'I know absolutely that my little kiddies ain't dead but with Jesus, safe in the Love and nestling in the tender arms of Diana. What don't kill me makes me stronger, every journey begins with a single step and I have been made a more empowered and a better woman through the pain that the Love has seen fit to visit upon my woman's breasts.'

When Princess Lovebud had finally ceased to emote and the cheers and whoops which greeted her speech had died down, two other women followed in similar noisy vein but a third, a young black woman who had only recently lost a five-year-old to the pustules, spoke briefly and, Trafford sensed, reluctantly. She certainly did not express sufficient outward fervour to satisfy Princess Lovebud.

'Let it out, Kahlua,' she demanded brutally. 'Lean on us. Share with us. Let us feel your pain.'

Kahlua raised her face and opened her mouth but no sound came. She did not cry – her eyes were dry – and yet as Trafford looked at her he felt as if he was looking through an almost impenetrable veil of tears.

'Tell us how you feel,' Princess Lovebud demanded. 'I would have thought that as an African British woman of beautiful colour you'd want to emote big time and get it all out so as you can grow stronger and us can too and all.'

The silent, invisible, dry tears fell in torrents; to Trafford the room was awash with them and he could almost taste the salt of Kahlua's secret sadness.

'When Duke died,' she said quietly, 'I died.'

Princess Lovebud's expression showed that she was not impressed with Kahlua's testification but she realized it was all she was going to get and so she led the applause. After that, the celebration of Trafford's happiness began in earnest.

It was a celebration at which Trafford found himself

extremely reluctant to emote in a socially appropriate manner. This was not just because, like Kahlua, he found the moral obligation to broadcast his deepest and most complex feelings at the top of his voice difficult but also because the sadness of the bereaved mothers who had just testified had brought back memories of Phoenix Rising.

She had been Trafford's first child, with his first wife. Phoenix Rising had died of tetanus at the age of four and no day passed when Trafford did not mourn her. Fortunately for him, he was rarely called upon to testify to this because the suffering of fathers did not form a major part of the emotional fabric of the community. Nor did it feature significantly in the liturgy of the Temple. It was alluded to in passing during Mourning Mass but the grief was considered to be mainly the prerogative of the mother. As serial marriage was considered the most appropriate structure within which children might be got and the Love perpetuated, fathers were transient figures in most homes. Fathers constantly moved on while mothers remained with their children. The Temple approved of this; it was in fact suspicious of long marriages since they seemed to deny the natural duty of every man since Adam to spread the Love. The elders of the Temple reserved for themselves the right of polygamy, conducting their own serial marriages in a parallel rather than a vertical fashion (Confessor Bailey had eight current wives), but they expected the wider community to marry often. After all, Jesus had blessed the marriage at Cana and what Jesus blessed must be perpetuated until death.

Trafford was therefore thinking of Phoenix Rising even as he celebrated the birth of Caitlin Happymeal but fortunately, as he was among civil servants, the party was not as loud or as prolonged as it might have been in another workplace. There was much screaming and shouting, of course. A huge cake was wheeled in covered with sparklers, and boxes of assorted iced doughnuts were also produced. There was a video card in which everybody appeared wishing Trafford the best, and another cake for Chantorria which Trafford was expected to struggle home with on the tube. Nobody, however, suggested that they all take the afternoon off to get hopelessly drunk and, to Trafford's relief and Princess Lovebud's loudly professed disappointment, there was no karaoke.

'What are you like?' she chided loudly. 'This is supposed to be a party!'

But after little more than forty-five minutes the celebration was over and people began to gather up a final doughnut or two, grab another frothy, syrupy latte from the social hub and begin the day's work.

7

Trafford's job title was Senior Executive Analyst. Everybody on his floor was a Senior Executive Analyst. Despite the fact that there were very few ranks within government departments, those which there were had, for the purpose of promoting positivity and self-esteem, the most wonderfully empowering titles. A Senior Executive Analyst was an elevated status position, which meant that the person holding that title was one rung up from basic, which for purposes of positive self-imaging was designated 'senior'. In an idle moment, of which there were many in Trafford's working day, he had looked up the words in his job title in his computer dictionary so he knew that in fact he was neither senior nor an executive nor an analyst. After using a thesaurus he had concluded that he was in fact a clerk and in his private thoughts that was what he called himself.

He worked in the DegSep Division of NatDat. DegSep was short for Degrees of Separation and it existed in order to establish and catalogue the connections (no matter how tenuous) between every single person, every other person and every single thing that happened.

It was Trafford's job (along with his many thousands of colleagues) to establish new links upon which degrees of separation could be calculated. The DegSep computers had long since been programmed to link automatically all those who watched a certain television show with all those who favoured a certain salt-reduced ionizing energy drink, but unless a special program was written for it the computer would not necessarily link those who drank that particular drink *while* watching that particular show. Trafford helped to write such programs.

Trafford's department had recently been astonished to discover that the DegSep computers were not linking preference in pre-cooked meals with parental star signs; hence the fact that an individual with at least one Taurean parent had a very slight statistical likelihood to eat lasagne more often than a person with two Sagittarian parents had lain completely hidden.

Once a new link had been established, then that link had to be cross-linked to all the other links. What, for instance, was the data on the frozen lasagne-eating children of Taureans and their weekend travel habits? The DegSep computers at NatDat knew the answer and although no one would ever again ask the question the information was available should they wish to do so.

At the previous election for civil administrators, the Prime Minister had boasted proudly that the amount of 'information' stored in the NatDat digital archive doubled almost daily and the number of 'facts' in existence about any single citizen had long since surpassed the number of atoms in the universe. The opposition complained that while these statistics were certainly encouraging, not enough was being done and what *was* being done was too little too late.

Trafford was hard at work designing a program that would link choice of nail polish to the number of consonants in a person's middle name when he heard a voice behind him.

'Care to join me for a bite of lunch? You know, just to wet the baby's head.'

Trafford knew the voice: it was Cassius, the oldest employee on Trafford's floor. Cassius did no actual work; he was employed to ensure that the government targets for eliminating age discrimination were met. His job description required him to sit in the corner and be old, next to the woman in the wheelchair. It was not that either of them was incapable – they were both intelligent, computer-literate individuals – and the work, like all NatDat activities, was childishly simple and utterly pointless so it did not matter how efficiently it was done. It was simply that inputting data was not their job. Their job was to meet government targets.

'Well,' Trafford replied without any great enthusiasm, for he had never spoken to Cassius before, 'I'm not sure.'

'Or perhaps you don't want to celebrate, brother?' said

Cassius, and he seemed to Trafford to be staring at him in a vaguely significant manner. 'After all, one out of every two babies dies before its fifth birthday. What's to celebrate?'

Cassius spoke quietly. Kiddie death was not a subject to be discussed lightly, certainly not with a new parent, and had Cassius made the same remark to most fathers his reward would have been a punch in the face.

'All right,' said Trafford, rising. 'I'll come.'

He did not know why he agreed to go except that Cassius had voiced his own unspoken thoughts. One in two. What, indeed, was there to celebrate? Better perhaps to let the public celebrations wait until the child had reached at least the age of five.

To Trafford's surprise, Cassius did not take him to the nearest burger franchise, which was at the far end of the open-plan office, nor did he stop at the one next to the elevator or the one in the lobby of the building.

'Got to stretch my legs,' Cassius explained loudly as they passed the CCTV camera bank at the entrance. 'Getting old. Still, can't complain about that, it's my job.'

In fact Cassius did not take Trafford to a burger joint at all but led him to a small felafel shop in a murky, semi-submerged backstreet.

Trafford stopped on the duckboards outside the entrance.

'You want to eat here?' he asked.

'You don't like felafel?' Cassius enquired.

'No, it's . . . well . . .'

'That this isn't a Felafel House.'

That was it exactly. The grubby little café outside

which they were standing might sell felafels but it was not part of the mighty Felafel House chain, nor was it a part of Felafel House's slightly less popular 'rival', Felafel Munch (which was owned by Felafel House). This was an independent business that catered to the local immigrant underclass. It would normally serve only illegals and the police. The implications of a respectable citizen eating in a place like this were clear. By choosing to ignore the felafel choice of millions of their fellow citizens, they were setting themselves apart from the people's choice of felafel. Clearly they thought themselves too good for Felafel House, a cut above Felafel Munch, and anyone who considered themselves too good for the choices of the people was a posh snob elitist and they had better watch out.

'Please, it's my treat,' said Cassius. 'I really do love a proper home-made felafel.'

Surprised at his new companion's audacity, Trafford allowed himself to be led into the building, up the stairs from the waterlogged ground floor and into a little room above where there were three tables, all unoccupied. Cassius chose one and motioned Trafford to sit. This Trafford did, making a point of looking about himself before carefully positioning his chair so that he had his back to the camera.

'Do you know,' Cassius continued in a friendly, casual tone, 'I rather find that if one wishes to go unnoticed the thing to do is not to *try* to go unnoticed.'

'I wasn't . . .' But Trafford knew it was useless to protest; his manoeuvring had been too obvious.

Cassius smiled. 'We in our department know that almost no information that the authorities collect is ever scrutinized. How could it be? We are all of us under constant surveillance. They'd need police officers for every person to watch all that material and those officers would never be able to sleep. The only time that information is scrutinized is when attention is drawn to it. Therefore, clearly the best way to avoid scrutiny is not to invite it.'

'We are sitting in an independent café, mate,' Trafford replied a little acerbically. He did not like being patronized.

'It's not illegal.'

'No, but only illegals come to places like this.'

'We might be sightseers, researchers for a documentary. Why, we might be police officers ourselves searching out foreign rapists – as long as we sit proudly and with confidence. If, on the other hand, we make obvious, self-conscious efforts to keep our faces from the camera then we are clearly up to no good.'

'Or we could have gone to eat at a Felafel House,' Trafford replied drily. Nonetheless, he straightened up a little and made some effort to look relaxed.

Cassius ordered two felafel and salad wraps.

'Good?' he enquired as Trafford bit into his.

Trafford grimaced. 'No. It's bitter.'

'Not bitter, savoury.'

'Bitter.'

'Give it a chance.'

Trafford tried another bite and as his taste buds became more accustomed he found it strange but not entirely unpleasant to eat something that wasn't sweet.

'All right,' he admitted, 'it's . . . interesting.'

'No corn syrup,' Cassius explained. 'Takes a moment to get used to, but worth it, I think. They make them themselves, just chick peas and seasoning. They don't think that felafels should be sweet.'

Once more Trafford looked about himself nervously.

'Everything should be sweet,' he said, slightly too assertively, as if speaking for the benefit of a third party. 'That's obvious. Sweet is a treat. So the sweeter things are, the more we'll enjoy them.'

'Nobody's listening, Trafford,' Cassius said. 'For Heaven's sake, you yourself work for the National Data Bank, you're a professional busybody. You must have keyed in a billion hours of Citizens' TV. Have *you* ever listened to any of it?'

Trafford smiled. It was a fair point. 'No.'

'Of course you haven't. Nobody listens. This isn't *Nineteen Eighty-Four*.'

'1984? What are you talking about?'

'It's a year from Before The Flood.'

'I know that.'

'And it's the title of a story.'

Trafford's eyes narrowed. Was he being entrapped? Everybody knew about entrapment. It was always in the news: young policemen wandering the canal banks luring sodomites to their doom, drug dealers who turned out to be narcotics agents, and of course ape-men sites on the net that purported to offer proof that life on Earth was many millions of years old but which were in fact Temple-sponsored mind traps.

'You mean . . . fiction?' he asked cautiously.

'Yes, *Nineteen Eighty-Four* is a story about a society where—'

'I don't care, mate!' Trafford interrupted. 'I do not want to know! Stories are blasphemy and fiction is a sin, full of pretend people created by men. I am a person of faith and I know that only the Creator can create people.'

'Goodness,' said Cassius, 'you seem to think that I am a congregation that must be enlightened . . . or perhaps you think I'm a police officer?'

'I don't think anything,' Trafford replied evasively.

He wanted his position clearly on record. Everybody knew that Before The Flood it was fiction that had been the principal corrupter of men. Confessor Bailey reminded them of it week in, week out. Of that terrible time when society had been colonized by *made-up people*. When the television channels had teemed with people *pretending* to be people that they were not! People who were the creation of a third party, *fictional characters*. A time of books, and not the sort of books that were still read in the Enlightened Age, not good books, books of faith, of personal enlightenment, aspiration and self-improvement, books that told you how to get rich, make friends, have great sex and dominate your social group. Not those kinds of books but *stories*, thousands and thousands of stories piled high on shelves. A whole nation obsessed with what was *not true*, corrupted by the delusion that what man could invent was more beautiful, more interesting than what God had created. Then, thankfully, even Before The Flood, a time had come when man slowly began to turn away from stories in favour of *reality*. A time when, mercifully, a new generation began to celebrate only *itself*, to watch only itself on television, to read about only itself in books and magazines and in so doing to celebrate the reality of what God had created.

'Please, Trafford,' Cassius said, 'I'm not a policeman. Why would a policeman sit in the corner of your office for years trying to trap *you*? Are you more important than I had imagined?'

'No, of course not,' Trafford replied, feeling slightly embarrassed. 'But you mentioned *Nineteen Eighty-Four*. You said it was a . . .'

'A story?'

'Shut up, for Love's sake!'

'I don't think that stories are a sin,' Cassius said.

'They are!'

'Why?'

'You know why. Everybody knows why. Because once man had begun inventing stories his pride and vanity grew so great that he thought he could write the story of life itself – and so came about the greatest sin of all, when man wrote the story of the Earth and left out God!'

'My, my,' Cassius replied with a patronizing sniff. 'You must have been an excellent pupil at faith school, Trafford. Do you really believe all that rubbish?'

Trafford rose to leave. Idiots who wanted to get

themselves arrested for blasphemy could do it without implicating him.

'Goodbye, Cassius,' he said loudly. 'Thanks for lunch but I don't think I'll bother again. If you want to speak to me you can do it at the office.'

'One in two,' said Cassius quietly. 'One in two will die, Trafford.'

Trafford remained where he stood. This grim statistic was the reason he had agreed to lunch with Cassius in the first place.

'Stop saying that!' he snapped. 'Are you pleased about it or something? Are you a pervert? If you don't watch it I'll blog you up.'

'Sit down and stop shouting,' Cassius commanded. 'If you denounce me the first question they'll ask is why you were having lunch with me at all. Why did you allow yourself to be brought to a place like this? Guilt by association is not a stain that washes off. You'd be a marked man and Princess Lovebud would eat you alive.'

Trafford hovered for a moment and then sat down once more in silence.

'And for goodness' sake stop pretending that you're a true believer,' Cassius went on. 'It's very boring.'

'I am a true believer,' Trafford protested, but he knew that there was hesitation in his voice.

'If you say so,' Cassius said.

'Why have you asked me here?'

'I wanted to get to know you. I thought that perhaps you might be a little . . . different, that's all.'

'We're all different; we're all individuals, unique and strong, special and proud.'

'Yes, yes . . . but apart from that,' Cassius replied, and for the first time it seemed to Trafford that he sounded a little nervous, 'I mean *actually* different. I wondered if you had any . . . secrets.'

Trafford knew instantly that his face had given him away.

'Please don't worry,' Cassius hurried on. 'You are not the only one. I have secrets too. I have a very special one.'

Trafford shrugged as if to indicate that he was prepared to listen but that he admitted nothing.

'You accused me of celebrating the kiddie mortality rate,' Cassius continued.

'Yes, I did.'

Suddenly Cassius's eyes flashed with anger.

'Don't you think it's the government and the Temple that celebrate it? Glory in it? *Do nothing about it?*'

'I try not to think about it at all.'

'Well, it's time you damn well did, Trafford!' Cassius retorted furiously. 'And it's time you asked yourself what *you* are going to do about it.'

'What do you mean? What can I do? I shall pray and we'll put lavender oil on her pillow and—'

'Pray? *Pray!*'

Trafford was astonished. He had never in his whole life heard that word uttered in a tone of contempt.

'Did you know,' Cassius went on, 'that the diseases which kill the children are preventable?'

What Trafford knew was that he should leave

immediately; the conversation was becoming more dangerous and subversive by the minute. But he did not leave.

'I . . . I know that people once believed that to be the case,' he said, 'but we know now that it's not true.'

'It is true,' Cassius replied.

'How could you possibly know that?'

Cassius ordered coffee.

'Espresso,' he said loudly. 'No milk, no froth, no sugar and absolutely no whipped cream or Jelly Tots.'

The two tiny cups that were brought to them were the smallest cups of coffee Trafford had ever seen, scarcely a thimbleful apiece, and the cups were made of china. Trafford was used only to coffee served by the litre in cardboard buckets.

'Cheers,' Cassius said, raising his cup with a forced smile and adding, 'if I were a policeman and if by the most extraordinary coincidence I happened to be watching now, I would probably not imagine that a man who was about to speak a blasphemy punishable by death would be so boldly unconventional as to order an espresso and, what's more, one with no candy on it.'

Trafford understood the point and also raised his cup, grimacing horribly as he tasted its bitter contents.

'You'll get used to it,' Cassius assured him.

Trafford did not wish to discuss coffee.

'How do you know that there was a time when more children survived?'

'Because,' Cassius replied, 'I am a Vaccinator.'

8

Trafford had heard of them, of course. A sinister secret sect, who practised dark arts that could be traced back to the Age of Lies. An unholy brotherhood who believed in brutalizing children in the name of ancient and discredited 'science'.

'You stick poisoned spikes into kiddies?' Trafford whispered in horror.

'The word is "inoculate" and yes, that is exactly what I do, when I can. If the opportunity arises and if I have the vaccine available. Many big healthy families for whom the Lord is given credit are in fact my work or the work of my brothers and sisters. We seek out those whom we believe may have the strength to think for themselves and help their children to live. That is why I have approached you.'

'Why . . . why me?'

'I've been watching you for some time,' Cassius

answered. 'I told you, I sensed that you keep secrets.'

Trafford did not reply.

'You lost a child, did you not?' Cassius continued. 'Phoenix Rising, to tetanus?'

'Yes. Who hasn't lost a child?'

'You wrote about it most movingly. I archived your blog. It was beautiful, I thought, though distressing. I presume that you have no desire to suffer like that again.'

'You want to inoculate my baby?'

'It is my duty. I am sworn to save children. That is the solemn pledge of every Vaccinator.'

'I should report you to the police,' Trafford said.

Everybody knew that vaccination was nothing less than an attempt by man to deny God his prerogative over fate. Treating illness with medicine was acceptable to the Temple in that it was merely a reaction to God's work, but the theory behind vaccination was that it was possible to *anticipate* God's plan and to change it. To prevent something ever happening. That was black magic, pure and simple. Only God could know the future and only God could *make* the future. Immunization, be it of a child or an adult, was self-evidently an effort to restrict God's options, to *cheat* God, and it was therefore unarguably blasphemous. The Temple reserved some of its most violent invective for those who followed this cult.

'You wouldn't be the first,' Cassius replied with bitterness. 'Many of my brothers and sisters have disappeared for ever into the cellars of the Inquisition when their activities were reported by the very parents whom they sought to help.

Some have been lynched or burned by the mob. Socially a Vaccinator is an enemy of faith and may expect to be dealt with as such. Interesting, isn't it?'

'Interesting?'

'Well, not dissimilar science is required in many legal parts of what remains of medical practice. In implant surgery in particular. What are anti-rejection drugs but an immunization against tissue rejection? What is cosmetic medicine if not an effort to pervert God's plan? Yet beautification, as you know, is the moral duty of the female of the species.'

Trafford shrugged. He was used to the myriad contradictions of the Temple's teaching.

'It's all hypocrisy anyway, of course,' Cassius continued. 'My personal belief is that the elders of the High Council use vaccination to ensure the survival of their own families. They would not be the first despots in history to secretly enjoy that which they deny to their subjects.'

'But vaccination doesn't work. It never did,' Trafford protested. 'I've studied it enough to know that.'

'So you have looked into it then?'

'I've Goog'ed it. I admit that. And even Before The Flood people started to realize that vaccination caused more childhood problems than it claimed to prevent.'

'I agree, that's what they thought.'

'I've read articles on it. It caused everything from autism to obesity. They rejected the practice even before the Enlightenment. Before the Temple.'

'That's right. So spoilt were they in that happy time

66

when childhood death was scarcely known that in their sloth and stupidity people turned away from vaccination. By the time of the flood and the coming of the so-called Enlightenment, even intelligent people had concluded that there was something suspect about the process. They were, of course, utterly wrong.'

'How do you know?'

'I have a feeling,' said Cassius, smiling. 'It's my faith.'

There was no answer to that. Feelings were always legitimate. Even in the middle of a highly dangerous conversation such as this one, Trafford's social instincts meant that he did not wish to make Cassius uncomfortable by challenging his feelings.

'Trafford, I save children,' Cassius said in a firm, clear voice. 'I could almost certainly save your child. In the time when inoculation was generally accepted, at its peak in the third quarter of the twentieth century BTF, all society understood its blessings and scarcely one child in a thousand died in infancy.'

'It's a lie!'

'Now the figure is five hundred.'

'It's a lie. I've *seen* the figures, the statistics. I looked them up. They're recorded, we have the information handed down to us, and infant mortality was as bad in the age of the monkey men as it is now.'

'I have seen the statistics too.'

'Are you saying they are false?'

'No.'

'I personally have never programmed a false statistic in

my entire career. Nor has any departmental president ever asked me to.'

'With statistics it is never necessary to lie to get them to tell you what you want to hear. It is only necessary to reinterpret. Come on,' Cassius said, rising to his feet. 'We've had a long lunch, we should return to work. Even the designated old person is expected to put in an appearance occasionally.'

9

Yet another office celebration was under way when Cassius and Trafford slipped back into the room. A new team member had just joined their DegSep unit and Cresta Fiesta, a young girl fresh out of college, was being hugged in.

Everybody shrieked, everybody embraced the new girl, everybody beamed. Cresta Fiesta babbled that she was utterly made up to be joining such an incredible and amazing crew and everybody assured her that they were equally made up that she should be joining them. The general conviction was expressed that this was the most exciting and happiest of encounters and one that would no doubt lead to lifelong friendships all round.

Hugging in was an important ritual at any new encounter and it was a big mistake not to be seen to join in enthusiastically. Rigid social convention demanded that fervent, near-hysterical joy be professed at the endless laughs and intense sharing of emotions that the new relationship promised, and any individual's lack of enthusiasm was seen as damaging the positivity of the whole group and deeply resented. The entire office therefore crowded round, hovering with arms stretched wide, awaiting their chance to prove their emotional openness and eagerness to big up the whole crew in the name of the Love.

Trafford sensed that most of the assembled workers would have been happy to allow the hugging-in to conclude after everyone had had the chance to embrace and kiss the new girl and emote fulsomely, but inevitably Princess Lovebud had organized a cake.

'You're so *young*! You're a *baby*!' she exclaimed in her loud, honking voice, made even uglier by the incongruous assumption of her favourite 'little girl' character. 'Come here, you. Come here right now, Miss Cresta Fiesta, and give me another *hug*! Wanna hug. Need a hug! Got to have a hug!'

Cresta Fiesta did as she was told, stepping forward to be enfolded in a close, bosomy embrace. There were cheers, whoops and more applause.

'This is a happy crew,' Princess Lovebud continued without releasing Cresta Fiesta from her crushing grip. 'A happy crew and a strong, proud crew. We are all happy, strong, spiritual people. But we don't hold with snobs or loners, OK? We don't like false bitches either and we don't mind telling them so. If you ain't real, you ain't the deal. Right, babes? But that's just us, take us or leave us because we won't change. Can I get a cheer here?'

Dutifully the circle of people, including Trafford and Cassius, erupted into yet more whoops and cheers.

'Now I know a lot more about you than you think, Miss Cresta Fiesta,' Princess Lovebud continued. 'And isn't that a *beautiful* name by the way!'

There were more cheers at this, during which Princess Lovebud and Cresta Fiesta squeezed and hugged like lovers despite having known each other for less than five minutes.

'Oh yes. I know you, babes!' Princess Lovebud shouted into Cresta Fiesta's hair. 'Because I've Goog'ed you up, girlfriend! Oh yes, I've Tubed you big time and let me tell you now, girl, *I liked what I found*!'

'Oh my God!' the new girl shrieked, her mouth speaking through one of Princess Lovebud's huge hoop earrings. 'You ain't Goog'ed me up, babes? You *ain't*! I'll *die*!'

'Yes, I did! I Goog'ed you up big time, babes! And what's more I only went and downloaded some of what I found, didn't I? So, listen up, Cresta Fiesta, babes, because this is your life!'

'Oh my God!' Cresta Fiesta shrieked. 'Oh – my – GOD!'

'Remember your fifth birthday, with the cake on your nose? How funny is *this*! This chick is *cute*!'

Princess Lovebud touched a key on her laptop and the download of a five-year-old's birthday party appeared on the video wall. Everybody cheered and once more Cresta Fiesta shrieked in mock protest.

'Wait, wait, wait!' Princess Lovebud commanded. 'That isn't the best bit! Here it comes.'

On the screen the little girl got cake on her nose and the office erupted into cheers. There followed various shots of Cresta Fiesta growing up. There she was having fun at burger restaurants, riding her bicycle, numerous attempts at karaoke, of course, and then all dressed up in a pink bikini for her high school prom.

'Oh yes, little girls get bigger, don't they, Cresta Fiesta,' Princess Lovebud teased, 'and what a very special prom night that was for you!'

'No!' Cresta Fiesta screamed. 'You're never gonna!'

'I am gonna,' said Princess Lovebud as once more she touched her laptop and brought up a video of two naked teenagers making love. Cresta Fiesta shrieked and screamed and buried her face in Princess Lovebud's bosom while everybody clapped and cheered and assured her that their Cherry Popper downloads were equally embarrassing.

'You look lovely! *So* sexy, babes,' Princess Lovebud assured her. 'I hadn't even had a bikini wax on the day I got sorted out! Check it out on my Face Space page, babes, I've done a montage, you'll die!'

Next came Cresta Fiesta's breast enlargement.

'I was only sixteen,' Cresta Fiesta explained in a serious voice, 'but I pleaded and I pleaded and Mum let me have 'em done early.'

'Go, Mum!' Princess Lovebud screeched. 'It's such a special thing when a mum takes her girly to choose her first boobs.'

'I just knew it was right for me and I just wanted it *so*

much! You know? Just to be as beautiful as I could. For the Lord and the Love. As beautiful as the Love wanted me to be.'

There was much applause and more whooping at this and everybody watched the home video of the sixteen-year-old Cresta Fiesta, unconscious on an operating table, having her breasts cut open, the flesh stripped back and implants inserted.

'At *sixteen*, people!' Princess Lovebud shouted, punching the air. 'How much respect to the Lord is that! So come on, girl, let's see them!'

The group whooped and applauded as the blushing young woman lifted her tiny crop top, unhooked her lace and satin brassiere and proudly displayed her naked quadruple-D-cup breasts.

'They've really empowered me as a woman,' Cresta Fiesta said, 'and taught me to love myself and to grow and believe in myself and my Creator even more and give him big respect.'

'Way to go, girl! Way to go!' Princess Lovebud shouted. 'Because remember! We are the face and body of the Lord and when people look at us, they are looking at God!'

There were yet more cheers but this time they were reverential; heads were bowed and amens said.

'Isn't that right, Sandra Dee?' Princess Lovebud added, a nasty tone entering her voice.

All eyes turned to Sandra Dee.

Sandra Dee looked about twenty-five years old. She had recently joined the team and had instantly become a major target for Princess Lovebud's venom. In part, this was because Sandra Dee had not had her breasts enlarged. The Love had blessed her with only moderately sized breasts and yet that was how she had allowed them to remain. Technically she was within her rights to do this; breast enlargement was not a legal obligation for female citizens. It was, however, something that the Temple very much expected of small-breasted women and it was therefore shockingly unconventional to forgo it. In some ultra-orthodox families, if a woman of slight figure did not wish to have her breasts enhanced her male relatives would impose surgery on her by force. Young women would be drugged by their brothers, father, uncles and cousins and then taken, while unconscious, to hospital where they would later wake up with enormously increased breasts, as befitted them as modest women. These were called 'honour enlargements'.

Sandra Dee returned Princess Lovebud's angry stare but said nothing. Trafford was impressed. Few people dared to face out Princess Lovebud when she was 'on one'. Princess Lovebud was fierce, she was radical, she was proud of the fact that she took absolutely no shit and didn't care who knew it. She was sorry, but that was the way she was and if you didn't like it, deal with it.

'I wonder what the Creator thinks when he looks at you, Sandra Dee,' Princess Lovebud continued in her most sneering manner.

'We cannot know the mind of the Love,' Sandra Dee replied quietly.

'Hallelujah!' said Trafford, punching the air.

All eyes turned to him. It was obvious that his interjection had been made in support of Sandra Dee; on the other hand it was not something that Princess Lovebud or her cronies could object to, as a hallelujah was always appropriate.

'Hallelujah!' the group echoed. They were, after all, in a hug circle and joyful praises must always be echoed.

'Praise the Love!' Trafford shouted, punching the air once more.

'Praise the Love!' the group repeated and Trafford noted that Kahlua, Cassius and one or two other, usually quieter members of the group joined in with more than their typical muted enthusiasm. Sandra Dee, on the other hand, merely went through the motions, continuing to quietly face down her tormentor.

Princess Lovebud was seething; she was not used to being interrupted in full attack mode. 'Oh, I think we can make a pretty good guess at the mind of the Love on this one, girl,' she spat.

'Really?' Sandra Dee replied, raising an eyebrow.

Trafford was thrilled at her courage; nobody crossed Princess Lovebud, ever. He had only interjected under the guise of religious fervour. He thought about repeating the gesture and offering up another hallelujah but he did not quite have the courage. Most of the hug circle were staring angrily at Sandra Dee and it was not healthy to emote in an opposite direction to the majority. Once had been acceptably ambiguous but twice would clearly be evidence of disrespect. People who disrespected the mood of a mob hate invariably turned out to be its next victim. All he could do was look at Sandra Dee in what he hoped was a subtly sympathetic manner.

'It seems to me, Sandra Dee,' Princess Lovebud shouted, 'that the Creator has given you a challenge and that you are not rising to it, girl! He has given you a womb and a cooch that you might be known as a woman and a daughter of Eve and a sister of Diana who loves all babies, but he wasn't so generous in the booby department, was he, girl?'

'Well, I suppose I shall just have to live with it,' Sandra Dee replied.

'Yeah! And the rest of us 'ave to live with 'em too, eh! Except of course you don't 'ave to live with 'em, do you, Sandra Dee? You *choose* to live with 'em and it seems to me that it's time you raised your game, Sandra Dee! It's time for you to become the woman God wants you to be.'

'I think God wants me to be me,' Sandra Dee replied quietly. 'That's why he made me the way I am.'

There was an audible gasp at this. Trafford thought that it might have been Kahlua but, whoever it was, they gasped for the whole hug circle. Sandra Dee was in the process of ensuring that her life would be a misery from that moment on.

'Are you a practising lesbian, Sandra Dee?' Princess Lovebud enquired viciously. 'Do you practise lesbianing?'

Princess Lovebud was following her usual bullying method of random denunciation. Trafford did not imagine that she had any evidence for such a suggestion; lesbianism was, after all, a serious crime.

'No,' Sandra Dee replied.

'Well, in that case get some decent boobies, woman, and stop insulting God and letting down the whole office!'

Sandra Dee did not reply this time, taking refuge in silence. The mood, which had previously been celebratory, was now tense and highly uncomfortable. Cresta Fiesta, whose welcome gathering it was, clearly felt obliged to say something.

'You've got lovely hair, Sandra Dee. Hasn't she got lovely hair, everyone?'

'What a *lovely* thing to say, Cresta Fiesta, and so *like* you,' Princess Lovebud announced. 'And now – let's have some cake!'

Trafford was most surprised that Princess Lovebud was prepared to let the matter drop. Sandra Dee's failure to buckle under the weight of her invective had clearly thrown her. His mother had always told him that the way to deal with bullies was to stand up to them, but since standing up to bullies like Lovebud might easily result in smear campaigns and denunciations to the Inquisition he had never seen the theory put into practice.

Meanwhile the party cranked up another notch. The large welcome cake was brought out along with boxes of variously iced doughnuts and chocolate-chunk muffins. Sandra Dee, however, simply returned to her desk to resume work. This provoked looks of shock and outrage from Princess Lovebud and her cronies. To refuse to break cake with your crew was posh snob behaviour of the worst kind, but Sandra Dee didn't seem to notice the violent anger that she was provoking. As she passed him, Trafford once more attempted to convey some level of sympathy but she gave no sign of being aware of it, perhaps because he had a mouth full of caramel doughnut at the time.

10

When the welcoming celebration finally ended and Trafford had found himself a desk, Cassius strolled over and pulled up a chair beside him.

'I would so love you to show me a little of what you do on those big screens all day long,' Cassius said cheerfully. 'After all, I may be old but I know that I can still learn and grow and do my best to be a better me.'

'Way to go!' shouted Princess Lovebud from where she was introducing Cresta Fiesta to the mysteries of the office paintball league. 'Praise the Love!'

'Praise the Love!' Cassius echoed, putting his hands together as if in prayer and then punching the air.

Trafford glanced across the room to where Sandra Dee was sitting quietly at her machine; her eyes had flicked towards Cassius as he made his obsequious display of piety. Trafford thought he saw a tiny sneer pass across her normally impassive features.

After a little while, when Cassius was satisfied that he and Trafford were being ignored, he leaned over Trafford's shoulder and began to click away on his keyboard.

'Is this how you do it?' he asked innocently, while expertly navigating the computer into the deepest recesses of the NatDat archives. 'Is this where every second of our lives is kept?'

Cassius steered the search program towards the year 15 BTF.

'2014 as it was known then. I've chosen it at random,' he murmured. 'Happy with that?'

Trafford nodded and Cassius pressed the enter key.

In an instant the figures from almost a century before were crowding the computer screen. Numbers, places, dates, all representing tens of thousands of children who had died before they had ever lived and before Cassius and Trafford had been born.

'You see?' said Trafford. 'Two months . . . a week . . . a day. If anything these children from Before The Flood died sooner even than kids these days. Most of those that died didn't even make it to their first birthdays. Old science,' he whispered, 'didn't save them.'

'Apparently not,' agreed Cassius in a loud, assertive voice, before leaning forward once more and applying himself to Trafford's keyboard. 'But what if I do this?'

Trafford tapped the enter key and in an instant all the figures changed.

'Do what?' Trafford asked.

'I have moved the goalposts,' Cassius replied through a mouthful of muffin. 'I have subtracted nine months from all the ages displayed. You will notice that the majority of the figures are now shown as being in the negative.'

'And your point?'

'As you can see, those infants who were recorded as dying at four and a half years old are now listed as having died at the age of three and three-quarters. A child who previously was listed as having died at three months now seems to have died at *minus* six months.'

'Well, of course, you've just knocked nine months off all the figures,' Trafford said.

'Exactly. And, as you can see, those children who were listed as having died early in their first year are now represented by *negative* figures. Look: four months becomes minus five months. One month becomes minus eight. Thousands and thousands of negative figures representing dead children who apparently *died before they were born.*'

'Which is clearly ridiculous. You can't die before you're born. What are you trying to show me?' Trafford asked. He was getting annoyed. Cassius had a rather superior schoolmasterly manner about him which would have been irritating even if he had been making any sense.

'That in fact these children *did* die before they were born.'

'I don't understand. All you've done is subtract a figure . . .'

'Not any figure. Nine months. A woman's term. The mortality figures for the years Before The Flood are not based on the infant's date of birth. They are based on the approximate date of *conception.'*

'I still don't—'

'Don't you see, these figures include abortion and post-coital contraception.'

'What is post-coital contraception?'

'It was a pill a woman could take on the morning after sex. It would effectively cause her womb to reject any bonded cells.'

'You mean chemical abortion?'

'If you wish.'

'It's against the law.'

Trafford had been well enough educated and knew that, in the years BTF, inducing the chemical rejection of a pre-foetal cellular formation had been seen as a different matter to aborting a foetus. The Temple made no such distinction. Abortion was abortion from the first second of conception and it was murder. The so-called 'morning-after pill' had been a not insignificant factor in causing the Love in his anger to bring forth the flood.

'All I am pointing out to you, Trafford,' Cassius continued with the same fixed smile on his face, 'is that whoever compiles the infant mortality statistics does so on the assumption that a child's life begins at the very moment of conception.'

'Which of course it does!' Trafford insisted, looking around nervously.

'Which it may or it may not, whatever you wish,' Cassius replied. 'But these days the Temple does not allow abortion, nor even post-coital contraception, and therefore current mortality figures are calculated from the date of *birth*. In order to compare like with like you need to count only the *positive* numbers on these statistics from Before The Flood, which represent only those babies that died *after* being born.'

Once more Cassius's fingers danced across the keys and with a click he removed all the minus numbers from the chart. The screen was suddenly almost empty.

'As you can see,' he continued, 'the truth is that there was a time when only a tiny, tiny minority of infants failed to reach maturity. In Britain perhaps one in two hundred, not one in two as it is today. This was because of vaccination and that is why I am a Vaccinator. Saving children's lives is my calling and my sworn moral duty. It is, if you like, my faith. I have no doubt that one day I shall pay for my beliefs with my own life but nonetheless I must continue.'

Cassius gathered up their paper plates and cups.

'You know, Trafford,' he said quietly, 'there was once a routine vaccination for tetanus. Had your first daughter been born in that ignorant, wicked age Before The Flood, she would have lived to be an adult.'

11

Trafford arrived back at his flat to find Chantorria breastfeeding their baby. She was beached upon the couch, naked save for slippers and a tea towel draped across her two-day pubic growth.

'Hello, darling. Hello, little baby,' Trafford said to his family. 'Hello, Barbieheart,' he added, nodding towards the wallscreen. 'All well in the chat room?'

'Fine, thank you, Trafford,' the digital image of Barbieheart replied through a mouthful of nachos.

Trafford leaned forward over the video games table to kiss his wife. The room was tiny and very cluttered and it was something of a struggle to find a way to connect his lips with Chantorria's proffered cheek. Trafford had to support himself as he stretched over the table by placing his hands on Chantorria's curled-up legs.

'Ow. My veins!'

'Sorry.'

The couch was a small two-seater, only very slightly bigger than the flat-pack it had arrived in; nonetheless it ran the entire length of one wall. Despite this, Trafford and Chantorria knew that they were fortunate to have so much space. There were only three of them in the flat, which, with its separate sleeping and living spaces, could legally house six. The real rates of occupancy in most similar dwellings were even more crowded than that. Any number of extended families with as many as ten or twelve members were living in apartments smaller than Trafford's. The wrath of the Love had made London so very, very small. And it was getting smaller all the time.

'Anybody sharing the joy?' Trafford enquired.

'Three,' Chantorria replied, giving a rather unenthusiastic wave at the webcam that she had placed precariously on the arm of the couch so that it might cover her feeding her infant.

Trafford touched the key on his wrist top.

The faces of the three podcasters who were sharing Chantorria's joy sprang into view on the wallscreen. Two were mothers from elsewhere in the tenement, both naked of course, one breastfeeding like Chantorria while the other, who had recently lost a toddler to whooping cough, was just there to emote. Trafford turned up the volume on his wrist top.

'I just have to accept that all things are done for a purpose,' the bereaved woman was saying. 'My baby is in a better place, warm and safe in the love of the Love.'

'Hello, Tinkerbell,' Trafford said in as empathetic a tone as he was capable of. 'You OK?'

'Coping. Thanks, Trafford. Trying to stay strong,' Tinkerbell replied, dabbing at her eyes with pink kitchen towel. 'I've just been saying how I know that in the end I will be made a better me by this experience, as the Love intends. I've been speaking to him a lot since I lost little Gucci KitKat and he definitely wants me to be stro . . . stron . . .'

The strength that the Love had wished upon Tinkerbell deserted her. She broke down and wept. Trafford could hear a background chorus of sympathetic voices offering comfort.

'Babes . . . babes . . . *babes.*'

'Be strong, girl. The Lord will protect little KitKat.'

'The pain passes. It always does in the end.'

Trafford clicked on the share counter and a figure appeared in the corner of the screen telling him that, including him and Chantorria, there were forty-seven people online sharing in Tinkerbell's pain.

'Forty-seven friends,' Chantorria said brightly. 'Lovely, Tinkerbell, we're all really getting behind you.'

Chantorria did not add that this number stood in marked contrast to the mere three people who were sharing her joy, but Trafford knew that this was what she was thinking. He knew that Chantorria felt their lack of popularity keenly. They weren't despised particularly, they were merely not popular, and having only three people wanting to watch her breastfeed made her feel vulnerable.

People who were neither popular nor notorious were easy targets for bullying. It hadn't happened yet, not to any significant extent, but if any of the key players in their tenement *did* take it upon themselves to have a problem with them, they would be defenceless. In such a tight-knit community as theirs, isolation was not healthy.

This was why Chantorria constantly nagged Trafford to be more solicitous in his attentions to Barbieheart. Barbieheart was the principal eyes and ears of the building, an enormous, globular, housebound sentinel who, although too big to leave her apartment, occupied every room. Barbieheart could be a powerful ally but she could also be a dangerous enemy, and which she became depended entirely on the amount of flattery and face time she was accorded. Despite his best intentions Trafford found it almost impossible to bring himself to give her the respect she considered her due.

'I've only got three,' Chantorria said with a forced laugh, before adding in a stage whisper, 'and one of them's a perv.'

The third spectator on the wallscreen, a middle-aged man, pretended not to hear. Like Chantorria, he had a tea towel on his lap.

Chantorria completed Caitlin Happymeal's feed while Trafford defrosted two lasagnes and chilled a three-litre bottle of Pepsi. They shared their meal over the video game table. Trafford had tried to put a cloth on it to block out the never-ending cycle of adverts for new games that would shortly be available for download. He found it hard to focus on his food among all the leaping, cavorting, fighting, pixilated figures but Chantorria insisted that the game table remain uncovered.

'We're online, Trafford,' she admonished him. 'Let's try not to look any weirder than we have to.'

Trafford, knowing the logic, acquiesced. If video games and leaping pixilated figures were fun, then clearly the more of them that a person experienced the more fun they had. What was not to like?

They ate in silence, silence at least inasmuch as they did not speak to each other. The room was anything but silent, of course. There was a karaoke reality show playing on both laptops and the news was being streamed to the various phones and communitainment devices that lay about the room. There was an ad for a current blockbuster movie running on the back of the Rice Krispies box and of course the local community on the wallscreen were all emoting. On top of this, the noise from all the other laptops, communications devices and cereal boxes in the tenement could be heard through the plasterboard walls of the apartment.

The heat was oppressive, as it always was. Trafford watched the sweat beading on Chantorria's upper lip as she ate. It ran in rivulets down between her breasts. The baby began to scream, testy in the heat as they all were.

'You two are quiet,' the voice of Barbieheart barked. 'Join in, why don't you?'

Chantorria jumped like a startled bird and instantly turned up the volume on Tinkerbell's face on the screen.

'I just feel lost and totally sick and numb,' Tinkerbell said as her voice rose above the semi-muted babble. There was such pain etched across her youthful countenance, sufficient pain even to carve lines of anguish across the rock-smooth solidity of her heavily Botoxed brow. 'Like a piece of me has been cut out. I don't know what I'd do if I didn't know God was there for me.'

'I'm here for you too!' Chantorria blurted and Trafford winced at the obvious neediness of her tone. Did she not understand that bullies feasted on weakness? If Chantorria did not wish to be treated as a victim then she should not advertise herself as a victim waiting to happen.

For a moment Trafford found his thoughts flitting to Sandra Dee, the natural-breasted young woman whom Princess Lovebud had tried to bully at the office. She was not a victim. She had returned Princess Lovebud's stare and in that small act of defiance she had effectively defended herself. Trafford had noticed this phenomenon before. The mob could be confused by displays of individual courage. But it was very hard to be brave.

'Thanks, Chantorria, that's really, really awesome,' said Tinkerbell through her tears. For a moment Chantorria smiled but then Tinkerbell added nastily, 'Although I'm not sure a young mum with a healthy baby to put on her booby is exactly who I need to be there for me right now.'

Chantorria recoiled as if she had been slapped. She reddened deeply. Trafford watched as not only her face but her shoulders, arms and whole chest throbbed with blotchy mortification, her nipples almost disappearing as her skin around them burned with the colour of fear and embarrassment.

'I didn't mean . . .' Chantorria stammered.

But Tinkerbell had moved on; she had so much that she needed to say. It was her grief, after all.

'One good thing is my psychic,' she was saying. 'You know, Honeymilk? She's been channelling my little boy since he left me and he's told her he's happy where he's gone. Honeymilk is sure of that, he's happy and he's waiting for me with his big sister who went before.'

'Has KitKat learned to talk since he went to Heaven then?' Trafford asked.

He said the words without thinking. He was furious with Tinkerbell for the brutal way she had dismissed Chantorria's efforts to bond. What was more, he was also hugely irritated by the ridiculous notion that Honeymilk had special powers. It was obvious to Trafford that Honeymilk, the self-appointed neighbourhood psychic, was a stupid, cloddish woman, a busybody, a gossip and a liar to boot. The idea that this moronic creature was having conversations with toddlers who had died before they learned to speak was simply absurd.

Trafford certainly knew *why* he had made the comment but nonetheless he wished that he hadn't. Chantorria's face had gone from bright red to ghostly white. She was terrified. Trafford had dissed a bereaved mother about her departed kiddie. Nothing, literally nothing, could be more calculated to offend the community.

Barbieheart, who seemed capable of listening to forty conversations at once, was on it like a shot.

'*What* did you just say?' she thundered.

'I . . .' Trafford struggled for a reply.

'Are you suggesting that Honeymilk *hasn't* been channelling little KitKat?' Barbieheart asked in horror.

'He didn't mean that!' Chantorria bleated.

'Honeymilk . . . *feels* what my baby's thinking,' Tinkerbell protested.

Tinkerbell was confused. After all, it was so unlikely that anybody would publicly diss an emoting dysfunctional that she was not entirely sure she had heard Trafford correctly.

'Of course she feels it,' Barbieheart shouted furiously. 'Honeymilk is a brilliant psychic. She's the dogs. Honeymilk is so there for all of us—'

'Yes, yes, that's right,' Trafford butted in, knowing that he must extricate himself from this potentially lethal faux pas before the other forty or so people sharing Tinkerbell's pain began to take an interest in what he had said. 'That's exactly what I *meant.*'

'What? What did you mean?' Barbieheart demanded suspiciously.

'How . . . how . . . wonderful it is that, through Honeymilk, Tinkerbell has the comfort of knowing her baby's feelings.'

'Then what did you mean by asking if KitKat had learned to talk?' Barbieheart asked, still far from convinced.

'Well, I meant that the fact that Gucci KitKat could not

talk when he was alive must make the feelings of his spirit all the more intense. *Like* talking . . . but even better! An innocent baby can say in *feelings* so much more than we could ever say in words, and thank the Love we have Honeymilk to . . . to interpret that for us. It's as if Gucci KitKat *could* talk.' Trafford smiled at the webcam, his face a picture of pious innocence.

Barbieheart bought it completely.

'Aaaaah,' she said, all anger gone now and replaced with sugary empathy, 'isn't that a *lovely* thing to say, Tinkerbell?'

Tinkerbell smiled on the screen, confident now that she had not been dissed, happy to be loved up.

'Yes, thanks, Trafford,' she said, 'that's lovely. Yeah. Thanks for being there for me.'

'Any time,' Trafford replied, smiling, pleased to see the colour returning once more to Chantorria's face.

12

'I don't know what I'll do if I lose Caitlin Happymeal,' said Chantorria.

Their dinner was nearly over now. Chantorria had passed what remained of the meal in the virtual conviviality of the tenement chat room, declaiming and emoting furiously in a self-conscious effort to socialize and ingratiate herself with Barbieheart after the near debacle of Trafford dissing Tinkerbell.

Now, after almost half an hour, when Trafford could stand the stilted conversation and extravagant professions of faith no longer, he had logged out. He and Chantorria could still be seen and spoken to but their own conversation was muted. The Temple considered this level of privacy socially and spiritually acceptable, even desirable at this time of the evening. As each day drew to a close, men were encouraged to go one-on-one interactively with their current wives in order to nurture their relationships and recommit to each other and to a love of the Love.

'I know I'd rather die myself,' Chantorria continued.

'Yes,' Trafford replied, staring into the congealed remains of his ready meal. 'When Strawberry Lovebliss and I lost Phoenix Rising that was how we both felt. I still do feel that way sometimes, when I think of her. How much better it would have been if I had died. Except that then, of course, I would never have met you and we would never have had Caitlin . . .'

Just then Caitlin Happymeal giggled. She laughed a lot, much more than she cried. Most things seemed to amuse her and the little rope of coloured shapes and rattles that hung above her cot was a particular source of pleasure. She was punching at them and spinning them wildly with her fat little arms and legs, and the more they spun the more she laughed until Trafford and Chantorria could not help laughing too, and for a moment the three of them laughed together over nothing more than a few bright cubes of spinning plastic.

'I think I'd do anything to protect Caitlin,' Trafford said, still gazing at his little daughter.

'Well, of course you would. We both would,' Chantorria replied.

This was the opening that Trafford had been hoping for, a chance to introduce the subject of vaccination, but he hesitated. He did not doubt Chantorria's absolute commitment to their child but he knew that life in the tenement had made her timid and fearful. She would not be an easy person to inveigle into heresy.

He missed his chance. Chantorria's attention had been drawn back to the screen on which Tinkerbell continued to silently emote. That was the hell of those screens: even when the sound was muted, it was almost impossible to avoid one's eye becoming fixed on them.

'Both kids gone,' Chantorria said. 'Poor Tinkerbell will have to begin all over again, although not with that bastard Sabre, Love willing.'

Like everybody else in their building, Trafford and Chantorria were familiar with the detail of Tinkerbell and Sabre's stormy marriage, thanks to the numerous times she and her aggressive, unstable partner had emoted. They were serial emoters, proud victims of every sort of dysfunction. Their violent quarrels and sexually charged reconciliations had never been offline and had of course featured noisily at the Community Confessions. They could also be followed blow by blow and orgasm by orgasm, live, through the thin walls of the building.

Sabre was a serial adulterer.

Tinkerbell was a pill-popping pothead.

Sabre kept trying it on with Tinkerbell's mates.

Tinkerbell never gave Sabre any anyway.

There had of course been numerous public reconciliations too, with Confessor Bailey reminding the snarling combatants that only the Lord and the Love could show them the way to learn and to grow. Then, to the cheers of the group, Sabre would enfold Tinkerbell in his arms and sort her out on the floor of the confessional and all briefly would be well.

'He's going to prison anyway,' Trafford said, not that he was remotely interested in discussing Sabre.

'You really think they'll bang him up?'

Sabre was currently on remand, awaiting trial for driving a vanload of thugs into a Muslim ghetto. The gang had kidnapped two youths and beaten them to death with baseball bats.

'He'll get a year for sure.'

'Even after they bombed our shopping precinct? Surely not.'

'It wasn't the kids that Sabre killed who bombed our precinct.'

'You don't know that.'

'Yes, I do. The kids who blew up our precinct went up with their own bomb; they're in a billion pieces.'

'Well, I hope Tinkerbell finds a better fella for her next husband,' Chantorria said. 'She'll need all the strength she can get after losing KitKat.'

Once more Chantorria had provided Trafford with the opening he needed. This time, tentatively, he began to speak what was on his mind.

'I met a man today,' he said. 'Well, not met exactly, I've met him lots of times, at work, over cake, you know, and doughnuts. But today I actually talked to him. Or rather he talked to me. He took me to lunch. We had felafels.'

'I can't *believe* what you said to Tinkerbell about Honeymilk,' Chantorria exclaimed suddenly. 'What got into you? That kind of comment could get you blogged up big time.'

'I didn't like the way she dissed you when you offered to be there for her.'

'She's lost a *kiddie*.'

'I don't want to talk about Tinkerbell. I'm telling you about this man.'

'What man?'

'The one who took me to lunch. His name's Cassius. He's quite old.'

'What about him?'

'He seemed . . . he seemed to know me.'

'What do you mean, know you?'

'I mean he guessed that . . . that sometimes . . . I like to keep things to myself.'

For the second time that evening the colour drained from Chantorria's face.

'I *told* you people would work it out!' she hissed. 'You and your stupid secrets. Why do you have to be so *weird*! Why do you have to keep things to yourself? What's the point of it? Where does it get you?'

'It doesn't get me anywhere, love,' Trafford replied patiently. 'It just helps me through the day. You've done the same thing yourself.'

Trafford looked across the room to where an old Palm Pilot lay on the kitchen bench. It was what they used for shopping lists and keeping their accounts but Trafford knew that occasionally Chantorria used it as a notepad, jotting down little thoughts and observations, things that she did not then copy to her laptop or include in her public blog, things that only she would ever read or know about. Sometimes she even put her secret thoughts in rhyme. There had been a time when Chantorria had shared these little jottings with Trafford. When they had laughed and cried together over the strange and inconsequential things that she had felt the need to write and which he had thought were beautiful and she said were rubbish. Those days were gone now. Only the power of young love had briefly given Chantorria the strength to share a secret.

'I hardly do that any more,' she protested.

'I know,' Trafford replied sadly.

'Besides I don't mean any disrespect to my maker,' Chantorria went on. 'Where's the harm in a little poem?'

'If there's no harm in them why do you keep them private?'

'I don't *keep* them private! I just don't . . . I just forget to blog them, that's all. I'm not weird. I don't think I'm special. And now look, you've been caught and we're in trouble. They know you keep secrets.'

'Cassius isn't *they*,' Trafford assured her. 'He's just *him* and we have nothing to fear from him either.'

'How do you know he's not a policeman?'

'A policeman sitting in the corner of my office for years trying to trap me?' Trafford replied. 'Perhaps I'm a bit more important than I had imagined.'

He felt a little ashamed, directly quoting Cassius's withering response to his own identical paranoia. But it also felt good to say it, to come out with a response based on logic and evidence. Chantorria *felt* that he might have been entrapped by the authorities; he had *deduced* that this was enormously unlikely.

'Besides,' Trafford continued, 'Cassius has a much bigger secret than you or I could ever have. If anyone needs to be worrying about the cops it's him.'

'Well, that's even worse then. What were you talking to him for? Is he a Muslim terrorist? A sodomite! What does he have to worry about?'

Trafford told Chantorria how he had been offered the services of a Vaccinator. Chantorria listened in silence but horror was written clearly on her face. When Trafford had finished she angrily demanded that he denounce Cassius to the Temple immediately.

'Do you think I should?' Trafford asked.

'I think,' Chantorria whispered urgently, 'that if he's a Vac— one of those awful people and he gets caught, which he will be, and then they Tube him, which is the first thing they'll do, and then they find a vid of you sitting *having a felafel* with him, you are going to have a lot of trouble explaining why you *didn't* denounce.'

'I think we should look at this logically.'

'I *am* looking at it logically and don't talk to me like I'm a bloody idiot. You always do that and actually it's you who's being an idiot. Logically it's bloody obvious that when they catch this bloke, *logically* they'll want to talk to the people he's talked to. That's you, Trafford, and *logically* what do you think will happen then?'

'I'm not talking about me, or you for that matter. I'm

talking about Caitlin. Supposing this man really can help her survive?'

'He can't.'

'Well, all right, how about we say there's a hundred-to-one chance. Would you accept that?'

'I don't know what you're talking about. I don't want to discuss it.'

'Just *think* about it for a minute, for Lord's sake. Chantorria! Say the odds are a hundred to one that he can help. Shouldn't we still take them? Shouldn't we take any remote, tiny chance to help our daughter grow up healthy? Even a thousand-to-one chance is better than nothing at all! Chantorria, I don't want to go through again what I went through with Phoenix Rising. I don't know if I can.'

'Trafford, they *burn* Vaccinators.'

'Only when they catch them. He doesn't think he will be caught,' Trafford replied. 'He doesn't think they notice things.'

'They notice everything.'

'We've always assumed that they do. But maybe they don't.'

'Trafford, you have to denounce him.'

'I'm not going to denounce him.'

'He's an enemy of faith. Protecting him puts us all in danger.'

'I think we should put Caitlin's safety before our own.'

'Of course we should! We do, always!'

'Then I think we should have her inoculated.'

'Is this a terrible sick joke?' Chantorria asked furiously.

'No, of course it isn't.'

'Well, stop fucking grinning then!' Chantorria shouted into Trafford's face.

Trafford had indeed been grinning, following the policy Cassius had suggested of not provoking attention by appearing furtive. He relaxed his face, reflecting that it was in fact Chantorria's expression which was least likely to draw attention from any web spies who might be snooping. It was far more common for the residents of his little rabbit warren to be screaming at each other than smiling.

'I think we should allow this man to inoculate Caitlin,' Trafford repeated.

'I don't believe I'm hearing this. Please tell me you're not serious.'

'I think . . . I think that we have to do everything we can to protect our daughter.'

'You want to allow a total stranger to stick dirty needles into her? I don't call that protection.'

Chantorria went to Caitlin Happymeal and picked her up and hugged her, as if she expected Trafford to produce a great spike there and then and murder the infant with it on the video game table. Perhaps Caitlin somehow sensed Chantorria's fear, for mother and daughter both now seemed to be staring at Trafford accusingly. Physically Caitlin was much more Chantorria's daughter than her father's; she had the same lovely olive-toned skin and huge dark eyes. Now all eyes were on Trafford and for a moment he felt like a stranger in his own family.

'I don't think the needles they use are dirty,' he replied quietly.

'You said yourself they're filled with the same poison they are supposed to protect the child from! Trafford, they fill those needles with *disease*.'

'You're not stupid, Chantorria. You know the theory as well as I do,' Trafford replied, angry now that he was being forced on to the defensive.

'It's not a theory, it's witchcraft.'

'A small dose of the bacteria educates the child's immune system.'

'And you believe that?' Chantorria asked incredulously. 'It's voodoo, Trafford, black magic. It's—'

'All I know is that I've analysed a decade's worth of figures from a period just Before The Flood . . .'

'Monkey time.'

'Call it what you like but the fact is that in those days all the children survived.'

'I don't believe it. It just couldn't be. The Love gathers the children unto him, that's all. It's a fact of life, it can't be changed.'

'It *was* changed, Chantorria! And not by God but by man. Before The Flood almost no children died in infancy.'

'Yes! Yes, Before The Flood! And why did the Love visit the flood upon the monkey men? Because of their vanity! Because of their arrogance! Because of their stories and because they thought they could obstruct the purpose of the Lord by sticking needles full of poison into their children like the witches they were!'

'You don't *know* that the flood was a result of God's anger with man. You've only been told it.'

'We know there was a flood. We know half the world drowned. We know the Muzzies got it worse than we did. Who else do you think sent it but God? And why, if not to punish man for forgetting and denying him?'

'The world got warmer, that's all we know. It's still getting warmer. Ice melted, the seas rose. That is *all we know*.'

'We know that we deserved to be punished.'

Trafford did not believe her. He knew that she was intelligent, that she had an enquiring mind. He did not believe that she accepted without question the orthodox teaching of the Temple any more than he did. Nonetheless, faced with the fear of being accused of heresy, she had become as pious as any Princess Lovebud or Barbieheart.

In the end that was how they made people believe. Through fear.

'Try to think about Caitlin instead of yourself,' he said. 'Surely we have to give our baby any chance we can. *Any* chance.'

'I don't wish to discuss it. I *won't* discuss it.'

Chantorria refused to speak further on the matter. They finished their meal without saying another word, after which Chantorria changed Caitlin Happymeal's nappy and Trafford threw away the tea things. Then they went to bed. They were exhausted. Caitlin Happymeal kept them up most of the night and they had got into the habit of going to bed as early as her in order to snatch what sleep they could.

They didn't sleep, of course. Caitlin was whingeing in the heat just like every other infant in the building. Some were ill, of course, coughing and sneezing, and it seemed to Trafford as if all of them were in the same room as him and Chantorria.

After half a restless hour or so Chantorria turned up the sound on the video wall.

'Do you have to?' Trafford asked irritably.

'I can't bear listening to those poor kiddies any more. Not tonight.'

It wasn't just the children who were shouting and screaming. It seemed as if the whole city was awake and emoting at the top of its voice. Everybody was up, shouting and screaming as they fought, shouting and screaming as they had sex. And those like Chantorria who were not shouting and screaming were turning up the sound on their video walls to drown out the noise. But all there was on all the channels and on every MyTube podcast was more shouting and more screaming. And the night rang to the sound of sex, violence, reality cop shows, talent competitions and endless, endless karaoke – a cacophony of human excess from the slum suburbs of Reading in the west across the whole London archipelago to the shores of Kensington in the east.

13

The following day Trafford was tasked to work at home and Chantorria had booked a visit to the gym.

'I've left it a month. People will talk,' she said loudly for the benefit of the webcam as she sat on the edge of the lavatory, her knees resting against the opposite wall as she applied bikini wax.

'You go burn it, girl,' said Barbieheart through a mouthful of tortilla chips. 'Wish I could be with you but, as you know, I am a woman of size.'

'I'll do an extra K for you, Barbieheart,' Chantorria shouted, wincing as she ripped the wax from her inner thighs.

'You have fun, girl.'

'Will do, Barbieheart. I'm lovin' it.'

Trafford, who was listening in the kitchen, knew that Chantorria was lying. She was not lovin' it and she would not *be* lovin' it. Chantorria hated the gym; it was one of her secrets, and the fact that Trafford knew she hated it was one of his.

The vast majority of women looked forward to a trip to the gym as it involved almost no exercise at all. The vast Temple-funded facilities which all women were expected to attend after the birth of a child offered a series of massages, steam baths, inspirational seminars, mass holistic 'treatments' and extravagant communal declarations of faith, and clients consumed enormous quantities of 'health bars' and 'health drinks' while sitting about in towels. In fact, because the gym experience consisted principally of hours of sloth, personal indulgence and guilt-free eating, people tended to come out heavier than they went in. Most women would be pregnant again before they had had the chance to get their figures back anyway. Nonetheless it was important to be *seen* to be making a personal commitment to self-improvement. Pretending to exercise was an important part of the ritual of self-love and self-love was of course the love of God.

But Chantorria found the gym a torture. She did not have the kind of self-assertive personality that made social situations easy. Trafford knew that she would end up sitting miserably in her towel on the very edge of a group before eventually being driven to do some exercise. She would spend her day with the hard-bod brigade of confirmed bachelors and honest spinsters, pumping away on various machines, not even pausing, as most of them did, to inject steroids.

'Trafford!'

She was calling him from the bathroom.

'You're going to have to shave me. I can't see it while my tummy's all floppy like this.'

Trafford did as he was bidden. Chantorria would be using a communal shower at the gym and it was of course unthinkable that she should disport herself naked with hair upon her body. Female body hair was not illegal but it was recognized as having been visited upon the Daughters of Diana by the Love in order that their commitment to their femininity might be duly tested. The adolescent appearance of body hair was evidence of a loss of purity and what was a woman if she was not pure? A slag or, worse, a lesbian. Any woman who was so immodest and lacking in self-respect as to display her Love-given cooch with hair still upon it deserved the anger that she would no doubt bring upon herself.

Deep inside him, in the place where he kept his secrets, Trafford wondered why the Love had given women bodily hair at all, if he hated it so. Wasn't there a better way of testing a woman's purity and goodness than forcing her to spend so much time and effort depilating? And why, he wondered, if the most heinous crime on earth was paedophilia, did society wish grown women to return their sex organs to the appearance that they had had before puberty? Trafford had only seen full female pubic growths once, on a school trip to the Natural History Museum. The beautifully realized female figures who were depicted dancing among the dinosaurs at the dawn of creation were wild innocents, the first humans, who had not yet come to understand what the Lord and the Love expected of them. Trafford had been fascinated and had remained so ever since. This was what a naked woman actually looked like. If God had designed anything it had been this, and yet here he was scraping the stubble from his wife's cooch until it looked like the cooch of a ten-year-old. Secretly Trafford longed to see his wife as a woman and not as half a little girl, but that was out of the question. Only a heretic woman would let her vagina go covered like the chin of a bearded man. Therefore Trafford squeezed into the tiny bathroom, inched himself between the lavatory and the wall, ducked down underneath Chantorria's raised legs and bobbed up between them with the soap and a razor.

Chantorria gritted her teeth and gripped the edges of the lavatory seat with all her might. The stitches from Caitlin Happymeal's birth were still red and raw.

'Surely we can skip down here,' Trafford said. 'Just keep your legs together.'

'You know I can't risk it,' Chantorria gasped. 'You know what happens to immodest women, particularly if they're discovered by other women. Just get on with it.'

Trafford did his best and when Chantorria was satisfied that her appearance was suitably modest she pulled on her G-string, sports bra and trainers, hung a large plastic reproduction of her birthstone from the fold of flesh around her navel, gathered up Caitlin Happymeal, who was to go with her to the gym in order to be fed, and went on her way.

For a little while Trafford mooched around the apartment, throwing away the breakfast things and drinking a glass of Fanta before finally sitting down at his laptop. Even before he had focused on the screen there was an IM from Barbieheart.

Have a good day at work, Trafford.

Yes, thank you, I'm sure I will, Trafford wrote in reply before turning and waving at the wallscreen.

Barbieheart waved back and then typed, *Praise the Love.*

Praise the Love big time, Trafford wrote back, hoping that this might conclude their conversation. It didn't.

Caramel Magnum Moonbeam's giving Ice Blade oral sex at 14c, Barbieheart wrote, completing the sentence with a series of smiley face symbols. Trafford wondered whether Barbieheart had IM'd Caramel Magnum and Ice to inform them that he and Chantorria had not had any sex, oral or otherwise, for months. He imagined she probably had. Dutifully Trafford punched up 14c's web stream and watched as Caramel Magnum's head bobbed up and down at Ice Blade's waist.

'Great girl, eh?' Barbieheart's voice said through the speakers. 'She gives him plenty.'

'Yes,' Trafford replied. 'Good on them. But I really should be getting to work now, Barbieheart.'

It was a mistake, of course, and he knew it instantly.

'So-rry,' Barbieheart said angrily. 'I didn't realize I was

holding you up, Trafford. You looked in *such a hurry* to get going, after all!'

'No, it's only that . . . I just thought.'

'Some of us *like* a chat in the morning, Trafford. We are a *community*, you know. We do all have to live together, so it might be *nice* if some of us tried to mix a bit more,' Barbieheart's voice began to rise, 'instead of thinking ourselves a cut above. *Too good* for the rest of us.'

'No, really, Barbieheart, I didn't mean . . .'

'Whatever. It doesn't matter. It's your loss if you can't be pleasant, Trafford. Have a great day anyway.'

'Yes, thank you, Barbieheart. Drop in any time.'

Trafford turned once more to the screen and attempted a smile but Barbieheart had moved on.

'Go, girl, go!' the vast naked woman shouted.

Trafford heard Caramel Magnum Moonbeam's breathless reply that she adored the taste of Ice Blade's cum and that taking it made her feel like a natural woman.

'Praise the Love, girl,' said Barbieheart.

'Praise the Love,' Caramel Magnum Moonbeam replied and Trafford pressed his mute button.

He logged on to DegSep and for a moment managed to focus on his work. He was working on Location Information, part of a vast team attempting to construct a program which would establish the degree of *physical* separation that existed between people. Satellite positioning was of course as old as NatDat itself. As long as a person carried a communicator, their location on Earth was constantly tracked and recorded and had been for two

110

generations. Should the government, the police or television researchers wish to find out where any person had been at any point during the previous fifty years they had only to ask NatDat. What, however, had never been established were people's positions in relation to each other. NatDat knew where Mr A was, it knew where Mrs B was, and it kne ꞌ where each had been since the day of their birth. What it did not know was *the distance that had existed between them*. Currently that information could only be established by putting the two locations on to a map and working it out with a ruler.

DegSep had come to recognize this extraordinary information gap and had set about filling it. The job was enormous, involving as it did the construction of a program that would calculate and record the relative position of every single person in the country to every other person in the country on a continually updated basis, while also delving into the NatDat archive to establish the relative positions that everybody had had to everybody else since satellite positioning had first become a part of the National Data Bank. Once this information was recorded it would then be possible to search for patterns in the movements of complete strangers. Was a person destined to get closer to some people they had never met than others? If, for instance, one was to study two individuals (D and E) who at one point had been an identical distance from F, was there anything to be learned from the subsequent distances between D and F and E and F? Equally importantly, what would then be the locational story of D and E? Would their shared positional relationship with F in any way affect the relationship that existed between them?

It was hoped that data of this type would contribute enormously to the general understanding of the workings of fate, kismet, chance, the stars and numerology. Trafford knew that this was unlikely as it was pretty certain that no one would ever actually study the data.

His concentration did not last long. Within moments his mind wandered – which it was legally entitled to do under the Health, Safety and Respect legislation that protected all employees.

Suddenly, out of the blue, Trafford found himself Goog'ing Sandra Dee. He had not been planning to Goog' her, the impulse simply came upon him and there he was, Tubing her up and reading her blog.

What he read astonished him. After the spirited display of individuality that Sandra Dee had put up at work he had been expecting something different, something interesting, but what he found was simply drivel. The worst kind of nonsensical, meaningless rubbish.

Another beautiful morning, Praise the Love . . . Feeling very chilled but also sooo positive about everything . . . Work was really good and chilled, what a fantastic, magic crew. I'm sooo lucky . . . just Lovin' it . . . Had my star chart done and it's all good, very positive with lots of great stuff ahead but I have to be careful not to give too much, perhaps I'm too trusting but then that's Geminis for you . . . Tried the new limited edition barbecue brunch burger at Mac's! To die for. Seriously wicked

. . . Feeling very spiritual, sometimes I wonder if in a previous life I wasn't a handmaiden to the Queen of Sheba. I don't know, I just sort of feel it . . .

At first Trafford felt a deep disappointment, but reading on he soon began to realize that Sandra Dee and he had something in common.

Like him, she was a keeper of secrets.

Like her face, Sandra Dee's blog gave absolutely nothing away; it contained token entries self-evidently written to keep up appearances. Trafford knew that the girl who had bravely returned Princess Lovebud's stare was not the empty-headed imbecile revealed in these blogs. He pressed 'view all entries' and then, on an impulse, copied and pasted a few sentences on to the 'find' engine. Instantly his computer informed him that it had found hundreds of matches. Trafford realized with a chill of excitement that Sandra Dee did not even bother to write a blog at all: she just repeated a small selection of previous entries ad nauseam, changing only the dates.

Next Trafford pasted the same paragraph on to the general search engine and with mounting excitement discovered that Sandra Dee had not even written the entries in the first place. She had simply copied them from the Space page of a young woman called Cuddlehug.

Trafford was astonished at the audacity of it. What cool! What sangfroid! Everybody was expected to commit their thoughts and emotions to a blog at least once a day. It was an act of faith, a reaffirmation of pride in oneself and in one's significance as an individual (which was, of course, a reflection of the significance of the Creator). It was only through constant openness and sharing that the duty of man, which was to represent God on Earth, could be celebrated.

But Sandra Dee just didn't bother. She did not even pretend to celebrate her significance as an individual or her pride in herself. She did not want people to know what she had done that day, or, more importantly, *what she was thinking*.

Trafford was breathless with admiration. By playing the simplest of tricks, Sandra Dee had in one stroke relieved herself of the odious duty of the daily confessional and, above all, she had kept her secrets. Anyone could lie in a blog; Trafford himself did it all the time, but in making up a lie one must inevitably reveal something of oneself. No matter how hard a person might try to cover his tracks the lie must still be written, it must be imagined and hence something of its author must be displayed. The solution that Sandra Dee had found was so elegant, so armour-plated, that Trafford could not believe it had never occurred to him. But then clearly this woman had far more courage than he had. She had the confidence to trust that nobody ever actually read anybody else's blog, at least none but the most notorious or popular ones, the blogs written by stars or local bullies, faith leaders or close neighbours. If you kept your head down you would be ignored, and this was clearly the trick that Sandra Dee had perfected.

Having made his first discovery, Trafford turned his attention to Sandra Dee's Tube Space. Here she had clearly had to be more careful and was thus more exposed. As Trafford knew from recent personal experience, faith leaders scanned their congregation's video history and no individual, no matter how anonymous, could afford to deny the community access to significant digital documentation of their lives. Sandra Dee had therefore dutifully posted an acceptable selection of personal and intimate video diaries.

There were the obligatory early birthdays and adolescent parties. Gory footage of a teenage appendix operation. The Cherry Pop vid was there, of course. Trafford had half expected Sandra Dee to have found a way of avoiding this one, but she had not: no young woman could afford to defy convention by keeping private their sacred and celebratory, life-enhancing, God-respecting moment of 'losing it'.

There were numerous other sex videos, demonstrating, as custom required, Sandra Dee's energetic commitment to a series of sexual partners. And like every single other Tube page on the planet there was karaoke, endless karaoke.

As he punched up video after video Trafford felt let down. When he had read Sandra Dee's blog, he had, for a moment, imagined that he had lucked upon evidence of a genuine free spirit, a private revolutionary who had laid claim to her own existence and was aggressively defending it from appropriation by the community. But her blog was now revealed as a small protest when set against her video diaries, in which she had been forced to conform in every way. In reality she was no more liberated than he.

Then Trafford noticed the scars. And the absence of scars.

He was watching Sandra Dee make love, a poor, grainy video featuring the usual loud and dirty sex. The sort of sex that was expected in such diary pieces. The sort of sex that was just 'amazing'. The sort of sex in which the participants 'did everything' and just 'went for it'. Sandra Dee was astride some grunting one-night stand, her head bowed and her body moving like a piston as she pumped away on top of her lover. Up and down she went, her breasts bouncing in the opposite direction with each frenzied movement. They were not big breasts, of course, Sandra Dee having famously forsworn enlargements, but as Trafford watched them he thought them surprisingly dome-like for the naturals he knew them to be. He knew from personal experience that natural breasts moved in a different way to surgically implanted ones. But the ones he was watching did not move naturally at all; they moved in the jerky, solid sort of way that suggested enhancement.

He pressed the pause button. Nudging the image forward half a second at a time, he arrived at the moment when the two breasts were at the highest point of their yo-yo-like movement. Then he zoomed in. The recording was not of good quality and the light was dim, nonetheless Trafford thought he could see two small scars at the base of Sandra Dee's breasts, the unmistakable evidence of implants. Perhaps Sandra Dee had had her breasts enhanced after all? Perhaps that was her secret? If it was, Trafford thought it a poor one, nothing like so exciting an example of subversion as to actually refuse to do with one's body what the Temple expected. Except then a thought struck him and he zoomed out a little until Sandra Dee's waist came into view.

Something was missing. There was no appendix scar. The Sandra Dee having sex in the video diary was not the same person as the Sandra Dee shown having her appendix out. Trafford pulled out further to bring the girl's face into view. Except that it did not come into view: there were glimpses of it but the hair was in the way and the wild movement of the head made a clear view impossible. Trafford began to reverse through the videos that he had just watched. They were all of poor quality, a little blurred, dimly lit, and they all featured girls with hair partially obscuring their faces, often with their backs to the camera. But now that Trafford's suspicions had been alerted, it was obvious that these were *all different girls*. They even had different tattoos. What was more, Trafford was reasonably certain that not one of them was actually Sandra Dee. Trafford reloaded the Cherry Pop vid. It wasn't her either: it looked like her certainly, the teenage girl praising the Lord and the Love as she squealed in pain had the same pale colouring and similar features, when they could be observed, but she certainly was not Sandra Dee. With the childhood videos Sandra Dee had scarcely bothered to find lookalikes, and the little girls featured opening presents and bobbing for apples were clearly all different.

It was incredible, wonderful. This girl, whom he had scarcely even noticed at the office (which surely, he recognized now, was a part of her genius), had posted nothing but lies about herself. Or at least, and much more importantly, she had failed to reveal one single solitary truth. As with her blog, she had simply uploaded a few stolen moments of other people's self-obsession, making a passing effort to avoid obvious physical differences, and left it at that.

It was clear to Trafford that this extraordinary girl had come to the same conclusion as Cassius had, that a bold front was the best disguise. She had guessed that nobody was interested in her. They were all too interested in themselves; self-obsession was, after all, high piety. If anybody – her Confessor, for instance – did happen to Goog' her or Tube her up, a glance would be enough to see that she was doing what society expected of her, even if the footage was of rather poor quality.

As Trafford closed Sandra Dee's pages (or, more accurately, the pages full of nobodies behind whom Sandra Dee hid) he was certain of one thing: Sandra Dee was by an immeasurable distance the most exciting woman he had ever encountered. He would say nothing, of course; certainly nothing to her. She had made a secret of her life and he had no right to intrude on it. Besides which, he didn't want to, because that would spoil it.

He would keep her secret a secret.

It would be his secret.

Trafford typed 'birthing' on to his computer and Goog'ed it. Within a second there were millions and millions of hits. He added 'girl' and halved the number. Next he chose the ten thousandth Goog' page and began to punch up the hits. Within three tries he had found what he wanted, the agonized, screwed-up face of a woman of similar colouring to Chantorria giving birth to a girl. Trafford downloaded the tape and then copied it on to his own Face Space page. He titled the document 'Hello Caitlin Happymeal and welcome to the world! Trafford and Chantorria Sewell's birthing video.'

14

He told Chantorria what he had done when she came home from the gym. Wanting to get it out in the open, he risked muting their community podcast long before dusk had fallen when it would have been socially acceptable to do so.

He had expected her to be horrified and she was.

'You put up somebody else's birthing diary on to our vid blog? *A complete stranger's!* Why?'

'Because I wanted to keep ours private.'

'You can't keep things private, Trafford! You'll get us into the most terrible trouble. They might even charge us with abuse and take Caitlin away.'

'Abuse?'

'Caitlin has as much right to be bigged up as anybody else. To be loved and admired. You're denying her that right.'

'Nobody would have watched it anyway.'

'Why do you have to be so *weird*?' Chantorria wailed. 'You have to upload the real vid right now. Just do it.'

'I don't think that would be a good idea,' Trafford replied. 'Putting up a hoax tape is one thing but then swapping it around is quite another. Like returning to the scene of the crime. That's always what gives people away in the end.'

'So everybody is going to be staring at our baby and it won't be our baby at all! Or my cooch for that matter. I don't want people looking at some stranger's cooch and thinking it's mine. It's not natural.'

'I've told you, nobody's going to look at it. Don't you see? That's the point. We could put up any footage of any baby and it wouldn't matter because no one will look at it anyway. Confessor Bailey will check that it's been posted for the sake of orthodoxy but after that it'll never get a hit again. Who is interested in us? Nobody. Who could possibly want to see Caitlin being born apart from you and me? Nobody. We *are* nobodies. Isn't that good? Doesn't that make you feel just a little bit more free?More liberated?'

Chantorria clearly took no comfort from Trafford's bleak analysis of their social position. 'Nobodies?' she said, suddenly more sad than angry.

'Well, aren't we?'

'No! Nobody is a nobody. We're all special. Everybody is special.'

'Well, if everybody is special then special must be pretty ordinary.'

'And that's good! Ordinary people are special.'

'Which means being special is completely ordinary.'

'I don't know what you're talking about! I just know you've done a really stupid, pointless thing and you don't play stupid games with Confessor Bailey. Privacy is a perversion, Trafford, you know that and you know what the Inquisition does to perverts.'

'No one will—'

'What about Barbieheart!'

'Barbieheart does not want to share your joy, Chantorria. She is only interested in sharing people's pain. She might glance at it but I doubt it. Please, Chantorria, think about it. Half the people in our tenement are uploading their *entire lives* on to the web, fights, fucks, births, funerals. How can anybody watch any of it?'

'My mother will watch ours.'

'You sent her a file, she's seen it. Why would she Tube it?'

'She might.'

'She won't.'

'Her friends might.'

'Chantorria, nobody is interested in anybody but themselves. Besides which, who cares if your mother's friends look at a fake video?'

'I care!'

'Well, I don't.'

'It isn't your vagina!'

'Oh please.'

'Why do you have to be so *weird*?'

'Stop calling me weird. That's all you ever call me these days.'

'Well, you are weird.'

Trafford shrugged and turned away.

They did not have time to argue any more as they were going to a concert that evening. Their tickets had been texted to them the previous day, and although they were both horribly tired there was no option but to put on their ribbons and wristbands and make a banner. Failure to attend a Faith Festival mega gig when you were lucky enough to have drawn an e-ticket was unthinkable; it would without doubt result in denunciation from the pulpit at the next Community Confession.

The concert, as with numerous previous concerts, was to be called Big Love Live and it was a major event, awesome in its scope, its ambition and its line-up of A-list celebrities. This concert wasn't just for London either: it was to be global in its outreach and would mark a new beginning in the way people thought about themselves, about poverty, about the environment and about their relationship with God and with their fellow men. After this concert (plus its accompanying blanket media coverage) nothing would ever be the same again.

The evening crackled with excited anticipation. It was most inspiring to live in a world where 'people power' could mean so much, where a single concert could change the world irrevocably for the better, where things could be improved just because the people wanted them to improve. Simply by massing, cheering, listening to music and eating enormous amounts of takeaway food everyone knew they could make a real difference.

News was already filtering through that this concert was to be even bigger and even more globally life-changing than the one held the previous week. This was astonishing, stunning news – particularly in the light of the fact that the previous week's concert had, up until this point, been considered the biggest and most epoch-making Faith Festival of all time, having spectacularly surpassed the one before.

Crammed in among the mass of sweating humanity, Trafford wondered in his secret self whether the following week's Faith Festival might be even bigger and more significant than the one which he and Chantorria were attending, but of course he said nothing. The thought was just another little secret he would keep to himself and enjoy in private. Outwardly he joined his voice to those of the quarter million other people who poured forth from the boats in which they had crossed Lake London and began making their way up Wembley Hill.

The message which flashed from every street screen and every communitainer could not have been clearer.

You can make a difference!

If you want it, it will happen.

After endless shuffling and pushing, sweating and gasping in the dank, fetid, malaria-buzzing air, Trafford and Chantorria finally gained access to the stadium. The concert had begun already, of course; everything had always begun already. Trafford had scarcely ever in his life witnessed the beginning of any entertainment for which he had queued. Few people ever did. Only those whose faith was so fervent that it led them to push and shove to the front ever saw the start of anything, and as these people tended to be the largest and most aggressive it was often not possible to see anything beyond their massive frames even when you did find a position.

'We can do it!' a well-known pop star was shouting from the stage. 'It will happen because we want it to happen! It's up to us!'

The cheer was deafening.

'Here today,' the pop star said, 'right now at this time and place. We say NO to hunger. We say NO to poverty. We say to our leaders that it is time they listened to the *people*.'

'Yes! Yes! Yes!' the people replied, punching the air in massed unison, hamburgers held aloft, hot dogs and doughnuts crushed into every fist. 'Oi Oi Oi!' they cried, stamping the ground with feet shod in training shoes that had been made far, far from Wembley and, coincidentally, by people who lived in the very poverty which the crowd were calling upon their leaders to eradicate.

Between each exhortation that the world should be improved there was music. The biggest bands played the biggest hits and the people bobbed up and down. This was the part of the proceedings that Trafford dreaded most, the part when he was required briefly to carry Chantorria on his shoulders. It was an important element of the ritual of Faith Festivals that at some point the girls sat on the boys' shoulders, their arms spread, their banners held high and their breasts proudly displayed. Of course most of the women were far too large and the men far too unfit for this to be possible, so the Temple organizers provided aluminium frames like stepladders upon which the women would sit and inside which the men would stand. Inevitably there were never enough and of course Trafford had not been able to grab one and so, like many others, he was forced to do his best unaided. Chantorria was not particularly heavy but then Trafford was not particularly strong and he struggled to hold her aloft even for the entirety of one song, which was the minimum that strict piety allowed.

Between each song there were more speeches. Chat show hosts and reality stars of whom nobody had ever heard ran on to the stage and exhorted the crowd.

'Each individual can make a difference! Poverty, war, crime, drugs and intolerance can change! They *will* change if *we* want them to! Every one of us is important! Every journey starts with a single step.'

There were films showing people dying in the flood plains of the Other World, and heartbreaking mini-features in which major reality stars spoke of the drug hell they had experienced prior to learning how to love themselves.

Then came a surprise. It was a wonderful surprise, a surprise that sent the crowd into even greater ecstasies of frenzied anticipation than they had so far experienced. Tonight, if the people so ordained it, there was to be made a new Wembley Law.

A hush fell as the stage was cleared of the anonymous celebrities who had dominated it so far and filled instead with elders of the Temple. Each community that had been ticketed for the concert was now represented on stage by their Confessor, and Trafford recognized the big red face of Father Bailey as it appeared among all the other big red faces on the massive TV screens which framed the stage.

Slowly more senior figures of the Temple began to emerge – evangelists, healers, preachers and latter-day born-again sinners – and finally, to an ecstatic welcome from the crowd amid fanfares and fireworks, a member of the High Council appeared, Bishop Confessor Solomon Kentucky, High Prophet of the London diocese.

The law which Solomon Kentucky had come forth to proclaim (should the people so ordain it) was one that had been a long time coming; a law which was needed now more than ever before; a law from which the people could draw the strength they needed in order to go forth and do the work of the Lord and the Love on Earth; a law which would make them worthy of the sacrifices that Baby Jesus and Diana had made for them; a law which had long since been on the spiritual statutes of the beacon land across the Atlantic sea and which now finally was to be proclaimed here, in Great England, in Great Scotland, in Great Wales and across the water in the Emerald Country, that it might give strength and succour to the faithful.

Henceforth, from this time and place and across the

whole land, Solomon Kentucky wished it to be known (should the people so ordain it) that every single person would by law and by statute be famous.

'That's right!' Solomon Kentucky bellowed as the phlegm from his throat danced in the glare of the massive spotlights. 'As of today, should you wish it, every single one of you is famous! By law! By statute! By holy writ and by divine right you are famous! Full stop, no argument. No back-pedalling. No false witness and no Devil-born trickery. Famous. Short and sweet. Famous. Simple and to the point. Famous. Nothing more and nothing less. Do you want it?'

The response was so thunderous it hurt Trafford's ears.

'I said DO YOU WANT TO BE FAMOUS?' the Bishop Confessor roared back at them.

'Yes! Yes! Yes!' the answer came in solid walls of sound.

'It's a simple straightforward question, people! I want a simple straightforward answer. No half-truths. No wishy-washy demi-faith. Only the Devil procrastinates. Only Satan drags his feet. People of the Lord BELIEVE! Do *you* believe? Do you believe that you have enough love, enough beauty, enough FAITH to be famous?'

Once more two hundred and fifty thousand voices (including Trafford's) screamed the affirmative.

'Then you ARE famous!' the Bishop Confessor replied. 'It's the law and you can't argue with the law. You'd be a fool to try. Each one of you is famous. Every person of faith in this city, in this *country*, is famous! Does it feel good?'

128

It did feel good and the crowd let the Bishop Confessor know it.

'Let me hear you say Yeah!' Kentucky shouted.

'Yeah!' the crowd shouted back.

'A'let me hear you say Yeah yeah!' Kentucky demanded.

'Yeah yeah!' roared the people.

'A'let me hear you say Yeah yeah yeah!' Kentucky insisted.

'Yeah yeah yeah!' came the emphatic response.

'I'll bet it does,' Solomon Kentucky replied. 'I'll bet it feels good. Let me hear you say Love!'

'Love!' they screamed.

'Let me hear you say Everlasting Love!'

'Everlasting Love!' came the reply.

'Ev Love!'

'Ev Love!'

'Ev ev ev Love!'

'Ev ev ev Love!'

'All right!' said Solomon Kentucky by way of conclusion.

And then the great book of statutes was brought forward and this latest one was duly inscribed therein.

Everyone is famous. By law.

After this stunning and thrilling interlude the concert reached its emotionally draining conclusion. The only possible end to a vast gathering such as this one was a solemn tribute to the departed children, a mass keening for the born-again babies, those infants who had died here on Earth but who were most certainly living again in Heaven.

There was weeping, there was singing, people tore at

what few clothes they wore until they were entirely naked. They pulled at their hair, beat their chests and fell upon the ground. They hugged each other, kissed each other, rolled about together in great sweaty huddles; many made love and some began speaking in tongues.

They cried that they *would* make a difference. They committed their lives to love, to Jesus, to the kiddies and to themselves, that they might be worthy of the solemn responsibilities that fate had placed upon them.

The concert ended as it did each week, with the stars gathering on stage together with the political and spiritual leaders to sing 'We Are The World'. As they did this, the screens filled with the faces of dead babies and tens of thousands of people writhed on the ground, on the carpet of discarded food wrappings.

Trafford and Chantorria did not join the orgy. They hung back with those who, while voluble in their emotional support, could not quite summon enough ecstasy to have sex with strangers to prove their faith.

Finally, as the last bars of music faded and the last voice from the stage commanded the crowd to 'go home and make a difference', Trafford heard another voice calling out nearby.

'Repent your sins!' the voice shouted. 'You who worship pleasure in the name of God, repent your sins.'

People turned their faces towards a slight figure in a loincloth. The man had brought a box to stand on and from it he was haranguing those around him.

'Jesus cleansed the Temple!' the figure said, waving in

his hand a plain-covered book that looked like no self-help manual Trafford had ever seen. 'He turned out the greedy, the gluttonous, the fornicators and those who sought only bodily pleasure! He believed in modesty and fidelity . . .'

It was a Chris-lam, a man who purported to love Baby Jesus but who did so in the shameful, shame-ridden, life-denying manner adopted by those who worshipped the anti-God of Islam. Trafford had heard of such people but he marvelled that any had the courage to show themselves publicly, particularly among a crowd whose emotions were running at fever pitch.

'Oi!' screamed a voice at Trafford's ear. 'You fucking paedo! I find your point threatening! You are making me feel uncomfortable!'

In a moment the mob turned from a disparate rabble of angry voices into a single terrifyingly violent scream. The Chris-lam was torn from his box and if the police had not intervened there could be no doubt that he would have been at the very least severely beaten. Instead he was arrested for inciting religious hatred and disrespecting the will of the majority and the police led him away.

15

That night, after they had collected Caitlin Happymeal
from the tenement childminder, Trafford approached the
subject of the Vaccinator once more.

'Did you see the faces on the screen?' he asked
Chantorria as she was tucking Caitlin into her cot.

'Of course I saw them,' Chantorria replied.

'Do you want Caitlin Happymeal to be one of those faces?'

Chantorria looked up angrily. 'Don't you dare speak to
me like that! I gave birth to her; she's part of my body.'

'Then you should want to save her.'

'Only the Lord can save her. How can we possibly
change fate?'

'Well, if everything's preordained anyway what difference
does it make what we do?'

'Don't be a smart-arse, Trafford. That's what people
don't like about you. They know you think you're clever.'

Chantorria had finished with the baby and begun getting ready for bed herself. Their little fold-out shower cubicle had long since broken down and was now used as an extra cupboard. Instead she stood in a washing-up bowl and sponged her body at the tiny basin that was bolted to the wall in the corner of their bedroom. Chantorria usually played footage of splendid waterfalls on the wallscreen while she bathed but this evening she did not bother.

'I don't even know why you're so sure that this awful thing will work,' she said, dabbing at her body with the sponge.

'I'm not sure. Of course I'm not sure. How could I be?' Trafford replied testily. It was four in the morning by this time and his head ached. 'But when I think about it, it seems possible, very possible. I mean I can sort of *understand* it, the logic. I find that very compelling.'

'Compelling?'

'Yes. Intellectually.'

'Trafford,' Chantorria hissed, 'we are talking about our daughter. We are talking about heresy! What the fuck has your intellect got to do with it?'

Trafford took up his communitainer and flicked through the tenement podcasts. The streams from each apartment in their building appeared on the wall in turn. Most of the occupants were asleep. There were a few fights, one or two couples still having sex, a few others watching them having sex, or watching porn or reality TV. Barbieheart was at her post of course, but snoring loudly, slumped forward over a bucket of fried chicken which was still clasped between her vast arms.

'Let me ask you this, Chantorria,' Trafford said, sugaring the rims of two glasses and filling them with Bud corn-syrup beer. 'Don't you ever get tired of not knowing anything?'

'What do you mean? I know as much as anybody.'

'Which is nothing.'

'Trafford, please don't go off on one. We need to sleep. Caitlin will want feeding soon, she's only had formula all night.'

'Let me put it differently. Don't you ever want to *understand* something?'

'I'm going to sleep.'

'The Lord made Heaven and Earth. The Lord made us. The Lord does this, the Lord wants that. We don't know how or why, we don't need to know, it just happens. There's never any explanation, it's all a miracle. Children are born, some die, it's God's will, we can't change it. Don't you think that, in a way, that's sort of . . . sort of . . . ?'

'Sort of what?'

'Pathetic?'

Whatever else Chantorria had expected him to say, it clearly wasn't this.

'Pathetic?'

'Well, to just . . . give up . . . leave everything to God. I mean why did he bother making us in the first place if the only function we serve is to believe in him and then die. Isn't that a bit pointless?'

'I wish you wouldn't talk this way, Trafford. It's *weird*. Our job here on Earth is to have faith. Faith is an acknowledgement that there is something bigger and more important than us, which I certainly hope there is. What's pathetic about that?'

'Well, perhaps I want something else in my life, something *other* than faith.'

'What could there be other than faith?'

Trafford struggled to think of the word. He knew there was one, he had heard it used in different contexts, but this was the context for which the word had been coined.

'Reason,' he replied.

'A reason? Isn't Caitlin Happymeal a reason? Isn't your daughter a reason? Aren't *I* a reason?'

'No, not *a* reason. Reason itself. I want to work something out in my own mind. I want to arrive at a conclusion because I've thought it through, not because I've been told to believe it. I want to take part of my life back from God.'

'Trafford,' Chantorria replied, and there was fear in her eyes, 'you can't deny God! They'll burn you!'

'I'm not denying God!' Trafford said hurriedly. For all his brave words, he was a long way from wishing people to think him a heretic. 'Surely you can act independently without denying God? I would have thought that any God with half a brain would *expect* that of his children.'

'Trafford!'

'I mean wouldn't faith itself be more valuable if it was arrived at through question and doubt? What's the use of blind faith? Seriously, it's not difficult saying you have faith if the alternative is being burned alive. But does that mean you *really* have faith? That man this evening, that Chris-lam. *He* had faith.'

'Trafford, he very nearly got *beaten to death*. You want to get us both beaten to death? Is that it? That man was mad.'

'Of course he was mad to do what he did. To risk dying for his faith. You wouldn't do that. I wouldn't do that. Faith to us is anything we're told to believe. If Confessor Bailey told us that a cherry alcopop represented the blood of Diana we'd worship it without a thought. But that man tonight—'

'Who could have been *killed*—'

'That man had arrived at his faith *despite* what he has been told. His faith was personal. He'd *thought* about something and decided to act upon the conclusions he'd drawn. I'd like to do that.'

'You want to get beaten to death?'

'You're not listening to me! What I'm saying is, wouldn't it be an astonishing thing to act independently? To think something through? Decide upon a course of action and then follow it. Wouldn't that feel good?'

'How would I know? Who's ever done that?'

'This vaccination. Don't you see! I have looked at the evidence available to me and drawn a conclusion.'

'What evidence?'

'There was once a science that protected children from childhood diseases . . .'

'You don't *know* that!'

'That's my point. Of course I don't *know* it. It's not a

faith! It's not something in which I can believe absolutely. It's a conclusion, that's all, a supposition based on the evidence at hand, which is the mortality statistics for the year 15BTF. I have arrived at an *independent thought!* Doesn't that sound exciting to you?'

'I'm not poisoning my baby because you want to have exciting thoughts.'

'Chantorria,' Trafford said gently, speaking just loudly enough to be heard above the general noise of night. 'You're an intelligent woman. I know you are, we've lived together for almost two years and a marriage doesn't last that long without people really knowing and respecting each other.'

'Trafford, we have to *sleep.*'

'If Caitlin Happymeal dies, as statistically she has a fifty per cent chance of doing—'

'Shut up!'

'If she dies,' Trafford insisted, 'do you really believe that she will be instantly alive again in some sweeter and better place?'

Chantorria raised herself up on her elbow and looked Trafford hard in the eye.

'Yes,' she said firmly, 'I believe that absolutely.'

'Then why do you not wish her dead this instant?'

'That's a stupid, stupid question. Go to sleep.'

'Come on, Chantorria. It isn't a stupid question. It's an absolutely obvious one. What is our life? Nothing. How was your day? Shit. You spent it at the gym pretending to be something you're not for fear that people might discover what you actually are. We live a shit life in a shit city rammed up against millions of shitty people. Why would you wish a life like that on Caitlin Happymeal when she could be in Heaven?'

Chantorria's expression became half angry and half sad. She did not try to deny the truth of Trafford's words.

'Because I'd miss her,' she said, tears starting in her eyes.

Trafford shook his head. 'Of course you'd miss her but you're not a selfish person. You'd do anything if you thought it would make her happy, even let her go. The truth is that secretly in your heart of hearts you doubt that, were Caitlin to die, she actually *would* be transported into the arms of Diana. You know that all those pictures and paintings on the walls of the faith centre cannot truly be real. Kiddies die every day, they can't *all* be in Diana's arms, she wasn't an octopus. You know that Heaven cannot be full of beautiful angelic people, for most people who die are infants and the old. Heaven would actually be filled with screaming babies and fat old crones.'

'It isn't literal! The Confessor always says that.'

'Why isn't it? Everything else they teach us is literal. The story of creation, the day of judgement, astrology, speaking in tongues, the miracles, tarot, Hell, the angels. They're all real according to Confessor Bailey. Why not Heaven? And if it isn't real, what is it?'

'It's the Love.'

'What do you think will happen to Caitlin Happymeal when she dies, as statistically she—'

'Stop it! Stop saying that!'

'You don't know, do you! And that is why you fear her death! *Reason* forces you to dread her dying. If the only thing that moved you was faith, you'd celebrate the prospect of her death because Heaven is a better place. But *reason* makes you suspect that when she dies she might just be going nowhere and so she'd be better off alive. And we could save her! Damn it, I understand the process! The body has an immune system, we all know that. Even the Temple admits it. It was through the immune system, they tell us, that God sent a plague to punish the Sodomites. Vaccination educates the immune system. It's . . . it's logical.'

'But Trafford, sticking poisoned needles into helpless babies . . . It just feels wrong.'

'Exactly. It *feels* wrong. You have to decide, Chantorria. You have to decide between what you feel and what you *think*.'

Just then Caitlin Happymeal began crying for a feed.

'I don't want to talk about it,' Chantorria said with finality.

16

Trafford tried repeatedly over the following days to persuade Chantorria that they had a duty to have Caitlin Happymeal vaccinated. There had been some terrible quarrels but he had failed to move her, so by the time the next Fizzy Coff day came around he had decided to begin the process without her consent.

He felt empowered, almost elated, as he joined the appalling crush in the street outside the tube station. Even the news of a suicide bomb at the local pumping station, which would mean many hours of delay, could not entirely dampen his spirits. Nor could the enormous hairy belly crushed against his back or the enormous hairy arse crack against which he was crushed bring him down. Nor the fried chicken being gobbled inches to his right or the burger to his left. Nor the *duf duf – duf duf* from the innumerable headphones or the news loop playing on every plastic coffee bucket. None of the thousand people, none of the million things that normally made Trafford's skin crawl and his brow sweat and his heartbeat quicken with tense loathing, affected him that morning. Because this was the morning when, no matter what the danger, he would begin to ensure the future health and well-being of his daughter Caitlin Happymeal.

But there was a second reason for Trafford's uncustomary sense of anticipation and elation that morning and it had nothing to do with saving his daughter. He was in love.

He had been in love before, of course. He had loved his first crush, he had loved his first wife, and he had definitely loved Chantorria. He had loved her utterly, in the days when she had laughed, when she had owned her own spirit and when her dark eyes had flashed with private passion and inner merriment. He still did love her, in a dull, dutiful kind of way, as the mother of his daughter and for the woman she had been before fear corrupted her. But this new love was different. It was strange, exhilarating and exotic. It was unlike any love he had ever known; no stronger than the love he had felt for Chantorria but different, different in that he knew *absolutely nothing* about the woman upon whom his soul had become fixated.

Trafford did not know how old Sandra Dee was, if she had children or had ever been married. He didn't know her star sign or her birthstone, her ideal dinner party or what she would say to God when she met him. He didn't know what had been her most embarrassing moment, or what were her big likes or her major turn-offs. He didn't know what would be her perfect day, ideal evening's viewing or most exciting sexual position. He didn't know her favourite colour or her top soccer team. Nor did he know the reasons why she loved and respected herself or what it was for which, every day, she thanked the Love. All this information was available, listed clearly as was expected on Sandra Dee's Face Space. It was there but Trafford knew that it was all lies, copied and pasted from other people's inane waffling, constructed from the clichés of countless near-identical sites. And that, of course, was the one thing that he *did* know about Sandra Dee. She kept secrets. He knew that he *knew nothing*. That literally every single thing about her, be it minor or be it significant, Sandra Dee kept private. Trafford thrilled at the thought, for nothing could be more magnificent, more bold, more original or more deeply, truly, dangerously *erotic* than secrets.

Trafford did not even know what Sandra Dee's body looked like. It was incredible, in a world where near-nudity was ubiquitous, that this woman somehow managed to keep a significant amount of her skin covered all the time. Trafford knew more, much more, about Princess Lovebud's body or Kahlua's or that of any of the other women in the office, or in his tenement. Trafford knew more about the bodies of the people who were surrounding him in the dreadful crush outside the tube station. There were breasts, stomachs and backsides everywhere. Convention required that only a person's genitalia remain covered in public but that they should, for decency's sake, be properly and fully exposed on a person's website. Sandra Dee, however, had never once exposed her breasts at the office. Even her stomach was rarely shown. Trafford realized with a start that he had *never seen her navel*! She was almost certainly the only female he had ever met whose navel he had *not* seen. Even little girls' bodies were universally exposed, for it was one of the curious inconsistencies of society which Trafford noted but kept secret that while the community lived in dread of paedophiles, mothers chose to dress even the youngest of their daughters in the same highly sexualized clothing that they wore themselves.

But even on the hottest of days Sandra Dee never came to work wearing only a crop top and thong. Instead she chose light skirts, the hems of which sometimes fell as far as halfway to her knee. Such lack of pride in one's body was of course severely frowned upon, being seen as evidence of an absence of self-respect and proper piety. But Sandra Dee didn't care; she defied convention. Even when Princess Lovebud upbraided her for her lack of femininity and inappropriate dress sense, Sandra Dee simply stared her out. Trafford had once heard her remark that, as a pale-skinned woman who was prone to freckles, she had some excuse for wearing a greater expanse of clothing; the Sun was, after all, little more than a cancer delivery system. For Princess Lovebud, this had added insult to injury. Deep mud-brown tans were extremely fashionable among white women and cancer was surely a risk worth taking in order to look nice for the Lord.

However, despite peer group pressure, Sandra Dee kept her body a mystery and it seemed to Trafford that this was the most all-consumingly erotic thing he had ever experienced. He was secretly in love with a secret. What could be more seditious? More illicit? More perfect?

There was much excitement at the office when Trafford arrived. Bunting had been hung and sparklers and party poppers had been placed in the pen jars at every computer terminal. Princess Lovebud was fixing up her 'Praise the Love' LED blinking banner and the flags of all the Nations of the True Faith hung from the light fittings.

'What's the celebration?' Trafford asked innocently.

'What's the celebration?' Princess Lovebud replied, aghast. '*What's* the celebration? *Duh!* What do you *think* is the celebration?'

'Uhm . . . I don't know.'

'We're *famous*, that's the celebration! All our lives we've wanted to be famous and now we are! We're all famous and this is the first time we've all been together since it happened. Don't you think we should celebrate?'

It had been a week since the Faith Festival at which the new Wembley Law on fame had been announced and Trafford had almost forgotten about it. The new statute had been big news at the time; many spontaneous street parties had erupted, and the local pubs had been crammed to bursting with people celebrating their good fortune. There had been disturbances far into the night, with gangs of newly famous people hunting for perverts and conducting running battles with the police.

But that had been a week ago. The world had moved on; there had been more bombs, more riots, more nightmare engagements for the peacekeepers overseas. The novelty of being famous had long since worn off for most people, though no such evaporation of enthusiasm had affected Princess Lovebud. This was a very big cake moment indeed: as she explained, if even *one* member of their crew had become famous overnight it would be cause for celebration, so how much more mad for it should they be now that it had happened to all of them?

The music began and Princess Lovebud led the karaoke and then the dancing. At first she was content to allow the more timid souls to hang about on the edges, perched on desks, smiling with nervously feigned enthusiasm while she and her acolytes bumped and boogied and writhed about in the space that had been cleared around the social hub. Inevitably, though, Princess Lovebud soon became irritated at the lack of universal party spirit and began to harangue those who held back.

'Come ON! How boring are you?' she demanded threateningly as her vast near-naked silicon-stuffed bosoms swung from side to side to the rhythm of the song. 'This is supposed to be a *party*!'

One by one, each member of the office staff began to dance, self-consciously mirroring in miniature the extravagant faux-erotic gyrations of Princess Lovebud and her friends. Trafford noticed that Cassius joined in quite early, not so early as to excite Princess Lovebud's suspicions but not so late as to provoke her anger. He was giving,

Trafford thought, a pretty good impression of enjoying himself too; a man with as big a secret as his needed to be well practised in blending in. Trafford and Sandra Dee were the last to join the dancing. Sandra Dee never made any effort to court Princess Lovebud's approval, and in a way that was her defence for it undoubtedly provoked in Princess Lovebud a kind of grudging respect. Under normal circumstances Trafford would have joined in earlier but Sandra Dee's courage inspired him. Together but separately they defied the brutal social pressure until Princess Lovebud announced the formation of a conga line and further protest became impossible.

And so the twenty-five or so Senior Executive Analysts who occupied the north-west corner of Floor 71 of the National Data Bank's Degrees of Separation Building formed a conga chain and Princess Lovebud led them as they kicked and skipped between the desks and social hubs and celebrated their fame. Some danced with wild abandon. Others smiled but only through gritted teeth. A few, Sandra Dee in particular, did not even bother to smile.

Only Trafford conga'd in a dizzying cloud of joy. For he had managed to place himself behind Sandra Dee. Her thick, strawberry blond hair bobbed up and down in front of him and he could feel her waist through the thin material of her cotton dress. He wondered if anything had ever felt so exciting. This was the body that she kept secret, and yet here he was, almost touching it. Only a thin layer of hot, damp cotton lay between him and that which belonged only to her. He was holding a living, breathing secret in his hands; he was touching her private places because all of her was private. It was perfect, the exact level of intimacy required for absolute erotic fulfilment. Any closer would begin to unravel her mystery, the very thing which made her so truly beautiful.

When the dance was over Sandra Dee did not turn to speak to him or even smile, but walked away without a backward glance. Trafford did not mind. It was her mystery that he adored. He was in love with everything that he did not know about her. As he turned away to find a desk he honestly believed that if she had marched up to him there and then and offered to disappear with him into the stationery cupboard or a lavatory cubicle, as couples did at work from time to time, he would have denied her. No real sexual encounter could ever match the secret one that he could nurture in his imagination and of which she knew nothing. No living flesh could ever be the erotic equal of flesh kept private, untouchable and unknowable.

17

'Care to grab a bite of lunch?' Trafford said to Cassius.

Cassius looked up and Trafford smiled. He had been waiting for this moment all morning, looking forward to it eagerly despite the danger of what he knew they would discuss. For Trafford, the office had suddenly become a repository of secrets, a place of excitement in which only three people existed: himself, Cassius and Sandra Dee. The rest, as far as Trafford was concerned, were no more real than the pixilated avatars prancing about on their computer screens with which they endlessly amused themselves through their long, pointless days at work.

'I'd be delighted,' Cassius replied.

'Praise the Love,' said Trafford.

'Big time,' Cassius replied with enthusiasm.

It was Trafford's turn to choose the restaurant and he took Cassius to McDonald's.

'Are we celebrating something?' Cassius enquired.

McDonald's was the oldest and most venerable of all the numerous food-consumption chains that crowded every mall and retail hub. Established long Before The Flood, it was one of the very few institutions to have survived into the Age of Faith. It therefore had a certain cachet and was seen as a cut above the rest, classy and special. Full nudity was not allowed and it was the number-one choice for christenings, celebrations of the solstice and weddings.

'Yes. Yes, we are celebrating something,' Trafford replied as they wheeled their little food trolleys to a table that had just become vacant. 'We're celebrating the day I begin to defy the Temple.'

'How splendid,' Cassius remarked as he began to clear their table of the usual mess of food spills, empty cartons and snotty tissues. 'And how exactly do you intend to achieve this excellent ambition?' he asked. He always spoke like a guru figure in a kung fu video game but Trafford suspected that it was not from these that he had picked up his style.

'I want to go through with what we discussed,' Trafford replied.

He said it loudly, firmly, feeling inside himself a sense of liberation even as he did so. Another secret to keep, another act of defiance, and this time one which might even deprive the Temple of another soul.

Cassius's expression did not change. He continued to smile as he unwrapped some of his cartons of food and took a bite of burger. This caused the smile to disappear briefly from his face but he had it fixed once more as he replied, wiping the sticky sweet mayo from his chin.

'Is your wife in agreement with this?' he asked, before muttering irritably, 'They even put sugar in the damned mayonnaise.'

'No, Chantorria has forbidden it,' Trafford said defiantly. 'But I don't care.'

'If we're caught you'll be stoned, you know, or burned,' Cassius said.

'I lost a child. I can't imagine a greater pain than that.'

'Easy to say, but think of the flames licking about your feet. If at the point of punishment you could save yourself by sacrificing the thing you love, wouldn't you do it?'

'Perhaps I would – but fortunately that's not the order in which I have to make the choice. All I know is that right now I have the courage.'

The two of them chewed for a while in silence as all around them hundreds of voices shouted about the food, about celebrity gossip and about the latest diktats of the Temple.

'So, will you do it?' Trafford asked. 'Will you vaccinate my daughter?'

'Of course.'

'Even though my wife forbids it?'

'I would vaccinate a child against the wishes of both parents if I could, just as I would attempt to rescue a child from a father who held a knife to its throat. It is not about the parents, it is about the children. I have a duty to save them. I've told you, it's my faith.'

'Do Vaccinators believe in God?'

'Some do. Many don't. It is not required. Certainly none are followers of the God that the Temple imagines: a vengeful, murderous, insufferably quixotic and illogical God who apparently has the time and inclination to know each individual's heart and hear their prayers and yet kills and maims utterly indiscriminately.'

Their conversation was suddenly drowned out by loud music. A very large noisy birthday party was assembling at the next table and a number of the guests were broadcasting their personal choice of entertainment to the entire restaurant. Huge containers of whipped ice cream filled with crushed sweets were being placed before the guests and party sacks containing many more kilos of sweets were being distributed, to whoops and squeals of delight. Interactive balloons sang 'Happy 50th Birthday, Stargazer' when they were patted, and a large flat screen was playing a lengthy series of loud video tributes from those who could not attend the party. All this, added to the cacophony that had already filled the room, made the noise in the restaurant almost deafening.

'How will we do it?' Trafford shouted at Cassius, who was scarcely half a metre away from him.

'Well, it's a question of which vaccine I have available and when,' Cassius replied at the top of his voice. It seemed strange to Trafford to be conducting such a dangerous conversation at such a pitch but it was clear that there was little chance of anyone or any microphone overhearing them. 'Many things kill kiddies,' Cassius went on. 'One jab does not cover them all. We can only do our best.'

'Where do you get the vaccine?'

Just then the noise dipped suddenly. Trafford had been lucky. Had he begun his sentence a fraction later, he would have screamed the dread word 'vaccine' into the lull and who knew what the results might have been.

The relative lull had occurred because the duty manager had asked the fiftieth birthday party if they could tone things down a little as there was a funeral lunch being conducted at another table. At first the partygoers had refused, pointing out that they had paid for their food, that they were as good as anyone else and had as much right to do whatever they liked wherever they liked as anybody did. However, when the manager had pointed out that the funeral was for a kiddie they had grudgingly agreed to reduce the volume somewhat.

Inevitably the noise level began to grow again but for a little while Cassius and Trafford were able to converse in something below a scream.

'There is a network,' Cassius said, answering Trafford's question. 'Some is created in kitchen laboratories here in London or out in the country. Some is smuggled in from abroad. The North European members of the Alliance of Faith tend to be a little more liberal in their view of this sort of thing than we do. Vaccination was actually legal in Scandinavia until fifteen years ago but pressure from the Great Ally put paid to that. No faith means no military umbrella, you see, and with upwards of half the world's population flooded out and anxious to come and live with us you need a military umbrella, don't you? Or perhaps it would be more apt to say military wellington boots.'

At this point conversation was halted once more as a particularly large and heavily tattooed male reveller from the birthday party backed into their table. The table was bolted to the floor but it shuddered as the huge backside crunched down and the scarcely covered buttocks spread across the plastic surface like two vast hairy draught excluders and ended up touching the sides of Trafford and Cassius's milkshake cartons. The man was attempting to get sufficient depth of field to record the party on his communitainer, and each of the guests was videoing the scene on their phone. Apart from eating, it seemed to be the principal activity of the group. It was almost as if the party had been held simply in order that people might record themselves attending it.

Trafford and Cassius sat quietly. They did not admonish the man who had intruded on their space and who was now virtually sitting in their food. London was getting more crowded each day, everybody was on edge and society was divided firmly into two types of citizen, those who sought to provoke and those who did their utmost to avoid giving provocation. Trafford, and everyone who preferred a quiet life, had learned early on that those who were most vigorous in upholding their right to do what they chose were the first to consider themselves disrespected if anybody should seek to uphold their right not to be inconvenienced by them. It was as certain as the

Sun going round the Earth that any objection made to the man who was sitting in their food would provoke nothing but righteous anger, accusations of disrespect and probably violence. Trafford and Cassius, in unspoken communion, therefore resolved to wait until he went away.

But those who wish to provoke rarely take no for an answer and something in their silence seemed to alert the intruder to the ever-present possibility of disrespect.

'You got a problem with me sitting here?' he demanded, attempting to swivel the upper part of his huge torso so that he faced them.

'No. Not at all,' Cassius said quickly.

'Cos if you have, we can sort it out right now if that's what you want, if you know what I mean.'

'We don't have a problem, I assure you. You're at a party, go for it.'

'Cos I'm just taking a fucking vid, that's all,' the man stated, beginning to realize that he would find no fight here but still reluctant to give up.

'Absolutely. Go right ahead. Please, be our guest,' Cassius assured him. 'We'll move if it would make things easier.'

'Good. Glad that's settled,' said the man, turning back to continue recording his companions' revelry.

Cassius and Trafford sat self-consciously waiting him out. It was not possible to conduct a conversation of any kind while looking directly at a person's buttocks. They could only sit and watch the sweat flow down the great cleft and disappear into his bottom cleavage, then re-emerge on to the table (having soaked through his tiny satin shorts) and form a spreading puddle in which their food cartons stood.

Finally, with a tremendous creaking and bending of the table, the man raised himself to return to his companions. He farted hugely as he did so, to the enormous amusement of his friends.

'Oh, I *do* beg your pudding,' he said with heavy sarcasm.

Trafford and Cassius smiled through gritted teeth. If they left the restaurant or moved table, this might easily draw forth an accusation of disrespect. After all, the man's flatulence was as good as anybody's and there was no law against farting.

Eventually the unpleasantness dissipated and Cassius and Trafford were able to resume their life-and-death discussion, one that might mean life for Trafford's daughter and death for him and Cassius.

'Who makes the serum?' Trafford asked.

'Chemists. People who secretly study the forbidden science.'

'All science is forbidden, surely?' Trafford said.

'Don't be ridiculous, of course it isn't. Science runs what's left of the country. It pumps the flood water from the Underground lines; it drives the trains and buses. It packages and preserves the food, runs the microwaves and freezers.'

'Oh I see, you mean wisdom.'

'No, I do not mean wisdom,' Cassius replied testily. 'Wisdom reflects attitude and opinion. Science deals in facts. The Temple may call science "wisdom" when they teach those bits of it that they require for their own purposes. But what they are actually teaching is what remains of what was once called science.'

'Wisdom, science?' Trafford asked. 'Does it really matter? It's just words.'

'Yes, words with completely different meanings. Wisdom is subjective. Science is objective. Don't you see how important that is? Science has nothing to do with *faith* or *feelings*. Science is about what can be established through observation and deduction, what can be *proved*.'

'Yes, yes, of course, I see,' Trafford replied eagerly.

He was fascinated, thrilled even. Everything Cassius was saying was in accordance with his own secret thoughts, thoughts which he had never before had the opportunity to discuss.

'The problem for the Temple and its lackey the government,' Cassius went on, 'is that they *need* science. They may claim to despise all that was known and discovered in the time Before The Flood but in fact they rely on that learning absolutely. The surgery they force upon women; the physics that keeps the remaining aeroplanes aloft and guides the missiles that they fire at migrant infidels; the chemicals which grow and preserve this foul mess we're eating; above all, the microtechnology that delivers what they call information to everybody, everywhere, every second of every day. All this was the work of that very same intellectual community which they condemn and despise, that same community which once developed vaccines and put a man on the Moon—'

Trafford interrupted him, excited but also incredulous. 'Do you really believe that men once walked on the Moon?' he asked.

To the Temple, the so-called Moon landings were the most celebrated conceit of all the lies and myths of the time Before The Flood. They had been a trick rigged in a television studio, a complex plot to prove that man was cleverer than God.

'The Moon landings happened,' Cassius said firmly.

'It seems incredible,' Trafford replied, suddenly doubtful. 'I mean walking on the Moon? Flying through space?'

'Incredible? You really think so? That idiot over there, giggling about his flatulence, holds in his fist a device which can record sound and vision in perfect detail and broadcast it instantly via the internet to any corner of the planet. Do you find that incredible? I do. The cheapest child's communitainer contains technology many thousand times more complex than that which took men to the Moon. The Moon landings were a matter of simple ballistics and the harnessing of the force of gravity.'

Trafford's eyes were wide. Everything that Cassius said contradicted everything he knew. 'But surely gravity is the force which draws things to the Earth?' he protested weakly. 'How could it possibly help you to get to the Moon?'

'Gravity,' Cassius said with scarcely concealed impatience, 'is the force which draws everything to everything. The Earth does not have a monopoly on gravity, which is why it does not lie at the centre of the universe.'

'You really think it doesn't?'

'Of course it doesn't. There is no centre of the universe. The Earth, like everything else that exists, is suspended in time and space, held in its position by the gravity of the objects which surround it.'

Thrilled at the ease and confidence with which Cassius uttered such heresy, Trafford said quietly, 'I want to know what you know. I want you to make me understand.'

'You can't make someone understand, any more than you can *make* them truly believe. It is a rule of my calling that while the Temple knows no argument but force we recognize no force but argument. If I cannot convince you of what I know by rational exposition then what I know is of no value.'

'Is that a rule of the Vaccinators?'

'I belong to a broader collective. We are all dedicated . . . to reason.'

Despite the oppressive heat, Trafford felt a chill. Reason, the very means by which he had struggled to convince Chantorria that it would be right to vaccinate Caitlin Happymeal.

'I . . . I would like to dedicate myself to reason too,' he said.

'Trafford, a moment ago you thought it incredible that I believed that men landed on the Moon.'

'I don't! Not any more. I'll believe it. I believe it now!'

'We Humanists are not interested in what you believe. We are interested in what you *understand*.'

'Help me to understand. I want to understand. I want to be a . . . a . .'

'Humanist.'

'Yes. A Humanist. I don't know what it is but I want to be one.'

'Why?'

'Because there has to be more to life than this and I know that it can't be found on the outside, not in this terrible, sweating nest of half-drowned ants we call a city, so it has to be on the inside. I want to explore new worlds and I know that they can only be found inside my head.'

'Well then, perhaps we shall talk again. In the meantime we have the welfare of Caitlin Happymeal to consider.'

'What medicines do you currently have access to?' Trafford asked.

'I do not deal in medicines. This science is about prevention, not cure. I deal in vaccines. Do you understand the difference?'

'Yes. Yes, of course I do.'

'Good, because words are important, Trafford. Clear thinking. Logic. Precision. Above all, understanding. You can understand nothing if words can mean anything.'

'Yes. Yes, I see that. All right. What vaccines do you have?'

'You are fortunate. My chapter of the faith is currently well supplied. I can help protect your child against what is called the pustules, the hacking rip, the dead shivers, the running sores and the bone lock, or, as they were once known, measles, whooping cough, meningitis, smallpox and tetanus.'

'When can we do this?'

'Whenever you can bring me the child.'

18

Chantorria was grateful for Trafford's offer to take the baby off her hands for a few hours. She was *so* busy. Tinkerbell was to be married the following Saturday and the whole tenement was buzzing with the preparations.

Weddings were a very big deal, absolutely central to the life of the community. There was nothing upon which the Temple placed more importance than the sanctity of marriage.

'That solemn pronouncement,' Confessor Bailey thundered at every meeting, 'of unity between a man and a woman, that children might be created and family life perpetuated, lies at the very heart of a peaceful God-fearing society.'

Marriages were good. It therefore went without saying that the more of them a person had, the better, more holy and more filled with love that person was.

There had of course been a time when the nation's spiritual leaders, in their weakness and ignorance, had misunderstood that which the Lord and the Love desired from the great institution of marriage. Then it had been assumed that Jesus's supportive words delivered during the wedding at Cana indicated that the ideal spiritual course was to *stay* married. It was now understood that Jesus had in fact stressed the importance of *getting* married.

'Jesus did not celebrate a *marriage* at Cana,' Confessor Bailey assured his congregation, 'he celebrated a *wedding*.'

It was the wedding that counted: that special moment when a woman and a man committed themselves absolutely to each other in body and in soul and in the Love of the Lord. This was an event which (for the good of society) simply could not happen too often.

'Faith is no faith at all if it is mundane and workaday,' Confessor Bailey explained. 'What use has the Lord for a love which has grown so tired that it must be nurtured even to survive? That's not love! That's habit! Don't stumble through life accepting second best. Life is not a rehearsal. You get no second shot! Go for it! Grab it. Take what you want. You deserve more! More of everything! More fervour! More rapture! More ecstasy. More food, more drink! More worldly goods! More sex! Take them, they're yours! Grab them in the name of the Love. What could be better than a wedding? What could be better than food, wine and the pleasures of the flesh? These are gifts from God! At a wedding all three are in abundance, all consumed in solemn observance of our spiritual vows. What's not to like about that?'

For Trafford, society's obsession with weddings was just another frustrating contradiction which he must keep secret.

It was obvious to him that the emotional energy of the wedding was based on the absolute certainty that the marriage would last for ever. The day only worked if everybody connived in the fiction that this wedding was *the* one, the greatest love of all, a union quite literally made in Heaven. Every song, every speech, every tear and every vow was dedicated to the once-in-a-lifetime specialness of the day and the unequivocal, lifelong commitment that the bride and groom were making to each other – while every single person in the room, not least the bride and groom, knew that the union would almost certainly be over within two or three years. Every aspect of society, both legally and spiritually, was geared to the indulgence in serial marriages and yet each of these marriages had to be entered into as if it was to be the only one.

'I never truly loved Sabre,' Tinkerbell assured her numerous maids of honour. 'Not Supernova either, nor Love Man. All my other marriages have been shams. Lexus is the only man I ever truly loved.'

Everyone in the building was thrilled for Tinkerbell, filled with outspoken admiration for the way she had turned her life around. She had bigged herself up after her split from Sabre and refused to be a victim, and through the loss of Gucci KitKat she had learned and grown to be a better, stronger person.

'I've been talking to God a lot,' she assured the crowds of friends who dropped by her apartment and the many more who followed her blog, 'and he's been telling me how beautiful I am.'

Watching her on the wallscreen, Trafford could not help wondering how deep Tinkerbell's new-found happiness ran. She had lost her child only a few months previously and he simply did not believe it was possible to put such a thing behind one so quickly. Looking into her pixilated eyes as she sucked her alcopops and assured the webcam how happy she was, he saw nothing but sadness. Perhaps he was imagining it, transferring to Tinkerbell the emptiness he felt every day over the loss of Phoenix Rising, but he doubted it. Trafford suspected that Tinkerbell was acting in the manner she was because she believed that was how she ought to act.

'And the best thing of all,' Tinkerbell stated from the wall, 'is that I know, I just *know* that my little Gucci KitKat is watching and he just loves his new daddy. In fact I believe that somehow Gucci KitKat found Lexus and led him to me.'

Did she really believe that? On what possible evidence could she base this colossal assumption? Surely that would be the question Cassius would ask. Which he, Trafford, *should* ask, but he didn't of course. Like everyone else, he assured Tinkerbell that her dead baby's return to Earth to guide her to the pub where Lexus, a local vermin control agent, had pulled her was the most likely explanation for her sudden, overwhelming happiness.

'And the sex is just spectacular,' Tinkerbell told her little world for the thousandth time. 'Lex is just the best. He knows what to do for a woman all right. We do everything. I expect some of you will have seen. Wow! I am such a lucky girl.'

Chantorria was helping with the dress. She had volunteered to hand-staple the thousands of blinking, multicoloured lights required for the train. Tinkerbell, like every new bride, wanted her dress to be the most spectacular dress ever made and ten whole metres of white plastic sheeting were to be used in its construction.

'I was in cream when I married Sabre,' she explained, 'but I owe it to Lexus to go white this time since he's paying to have my hymen reconstructed so I'll be a virgin again. It means we'll have to go without for forty-eight hours before the wedding. Isn't it *romantic*?'

Chantorria was a maid of honour, as was every woman under fifty in the tenement. It was quite clear to Trafford that Chantorria had been invited to make up the numbers; Tinkerbell was a major face in their little community and it befitted her to have a massive wedding. There would be a carriage and matching thrones, of course – the traditional elements of any wedding – but the real status of such an event depended on the number of identically dressed women the bride could gather around her. For the purposes of the big day Chantorria had been enlisted in the ranks of Tinkerbell's closest friends and she was thrilled to have been asked. In Chantorria's mind, this was a level of public acceptance that gave her some security against bullying. Trafford did not agree with her; he knew that loyalties were paper-thin and that nobody was safe if the mob turned. After all, the one thing people liked even more than a wedding was a burning.

19

Trafford left Chantorria alone in their flat with her staple gun and thousands of flashing lights and carried Caitlin Happymeal towards the bus stop, where, after watching several full buses go by without stopping, they were finally able to get a ride to Heathrow Central. There was only one terminal at Heathrow now. At one time there had been seven but as the oil slowly ran out they had been closed down and redeveloped as housing estates. A museum of aviation had also been built and it was here that Cassius had instructed Trafford to meet him.

They were to spot each other as if by chance, work colleagues who happened to bump into one another. Trafford was to introduce his baby and engage in brief small talk, after which they would decide to join the queue for the cinema.

After nearly two hours of shuffling, during which

Trafford cuddled Caitlin Happymeal and she laughed and giggled constantly, as was her wont, they finally gained entrance to the darkened auditorium. At this point, as Cassius had instructed, Trafford gave Caitlin a bottle of infant formula laced with a dose of antihistamine. By the time they took their seats Caitlin was asleep so she missed the looped entertainment, a ten-minute film entitled *Global Warming: The Great Lie.* 'CO_2 didn't cause the planet to be flooded. God did,' said the narrator firmly.

The film told the story of how man in his vanity sought to claim credit for his own destruction, blaming God's righteous vengeance for man's wickedness on something called greenhouse gases.

'The simple explanation just wasn't good enough for us,' the stern voice of the narrator continued. 'What could be more clear? Man was wicked, God punished him. Hey, it's that simple. But no, the so-called scientists of this Godless age had a different idea. They said that the floods came from polar ice melted by the heat of the Sun, trapped upon the Earth by the exhaust from oil-fired engines. Yeah, right. That's exactly what happened, I don't think.'

While they watched this, Trafford was holding Caitlin Happymeal on his knee as Cassius had instructed, and now Trafford sensed the Vaccinator feeling for the infant's leg. Trafford shifted his position a little to allow Cassius to reach her more easily. Looking out of the corner of his eye, Trafford could see Cassius feel for the chubby part of Caitlin's thigh and slip a needle into it. 'Hold her!' Cassius whispered as the pain woke the infant up and she began to scream.

Trafford struggled to keep her still while Cassius gently depressed the syringe plunger.

'Poor thing, is she teething?' Cassius asked, withdrawing his hand.

'Yes, I think perhaps she is,' Trafford replied. 'I'll take her outside.'

As Trafford got up, Cassius offered him his hand.

'Good to see you,' the Vaccinator said.

As they shook hands, Trafford felt something being pressed into his palm.

'Let's meet up some time,' Cassius continued.

Later, on the tube home, when he felt safe to do so, Trafford glanced down at what he had been given. It was a slip of paper. On it, as well as an address and a time and date, was a message: *Do join us. Reason dictates it.*

20

When he got home, Trafford found Chantorria still swathed in metres of white plastic.

'Some of the other girls were supposed to help,' she explained, 'but Tinkerbell needs hugs. She's gone all emotional on us. So I'm doing this on my own while the other girls are there for Tinks.'

Trafford glanced at the multistream on the wall; he could see that Tinkerbell's apartment was crammed with at least a dozen of the young women from the tenement. They were all drinking alcopops and eating crisps and chocolates.

'She really really needs her mates right now.' Barbieheart spoke up from her corner of the wall. 'Mates and chocolate, a girl's best friends.'

'Yes, that's right, Barbieheart. She really needs her mates to be there for her,' said Chantorria, her fingers red and sore from stitching the thick plastic. 'We're all trying to do our bit for Tinkerbell.'

'Yes, you're all lovely girls, in different ways,' Barbieheart agreed. 'Tink is lucky to have such an ace crew.'

'Well, she's been such a great mate to me and all that . . . to all of us,' Chantorria replied, and Trafford felt wretched to see his wife so needy and so put upon. He understood that she was meekly accepting her lowly position in the social pecking order for fear of having no position at all. He leaned forward over the video table and kissed her.

Perhaps sensing his pity, Chantorria returned to her work on the bridal dress with renewed energy. She hardly spoke for the rest of the evening but focused grimly on stitching the flashing lights to the plastic sheet.

Occasionally the prospective bride deigned to drop in over the tenement podcast to see how the dress was progressing.

'Good on you, babes,' Tinkerbell slurred drunkenly. 'Don't know what I'd do without you. You are so amazing. Do you know that, babes? So amazing. The wind beneath my wings actually.'

Behind Tinkerbell, Trafford could see the other women laughing and screaming. Inevitably pizzas had arrived and the karaoke had begun.

'Gotta go, babes,' Tinkerbell said. 'My song's up next. Love you, babes.'

Having her crew be there for her was clearly working wonders for Tinkerbell's emotional well-being. She had cheered up enormously and, as Chantorria finally put down her stitching and began to prepare for bed, the party to which she had not been invited seemed to have only just begun.

Trafford had spent part of the evening doing what he had done every night for some weeks, which was to go to his computer and look at what lies Sandra Dee had chosen to upload that day. His secret obsession made him desperate for any connection with her, and although he knew that everything she posted was stolen he hoped that by studying the lies he might glean some truth about her and begin to unlock her secrets.

For instance, Sandra Dee often cut and pasted items into her blog which had been written by childless women, women writing about their deep desire to have kiddies. Clearly Sandra Dee must be childless herself; she was always careful not to copy blogs which blatantly contradicted the reality of her circumstances. But how did she feel about being childless? Trafford wondered whether her choice of stolen blog indicated that she really did want children or whether she posted it merely for the sake of convention. Could she in fact be *happy* being childless?

He had come to the conclusion that it was the latter. Based on no real evidence at all, he had decided that Sandra Dee did not want children. Was she therefore a user of contraception? Condoms and Dutch caps were illegal but readily available, as was the pill for those who were rich enough. The Temple tended to turn a blind eye to this particular vice, especially in the case of women who were already raising large families. But for a childless woman to habitually seek to avoid becoming pregnant was not acceptable, and if the woman was discovered she would certainly be whipped and then placed in the stocks. After that, although the official punishment would be over, she could also expect to become a target for rape.

If she was using contraceptives, it would have to be with a man who was prepared to go along with the deceit. Or a woman! The Temple of course regarded sapphic sex as the lust of the Devil's whores (except in sex games played out for the benefit of men) and if Sandra Dee was indulging in that sort of thing then it was no wonder that she chose to hide behind a tissue of cyber lies. Trafford knew that the video diaries she posted, purporting to be of her having 'great' and 'amazing' sex, were not recordings of her at all but those of strangers plucked from the net. Did her choice of recordings indicate what she actually wanted in bed? Or was it the opposite? Did she really crave two or sometimes three big men using a woman roughly as the videos she posted often showed? Or was this a double bluff to further protect her privacy? Did she really crave gentleness, sensitivity, perhaps even the touch of another woman?

There was always the possibility that Sandra Dee was celibate. This would be a position acceptable to the Temple as long as it was genuine and consistent. The Temple rather approved of totally non-sexed-up women as long as they practised self-denial for reasons of faith, although it did prefer such women to follow their calling in properly ordered covens.

'What are you looking at?' Chantorria's voice penetrated Trafford's reverie.

'Oh, you know, just surfing,' he replied hastily. 'Checking a few blogs and diaries, trying to commune with my community. Isn't that what you want? What the Confessor says we should do?'

'Sandra Dee,' said Chantorria, leaning over Trafford's shoulder and reading the name on the page banner, 'looks like one hell of a raunchy chick.'

The video on screen was indeed a raunchy one, in which the head of a girl with similar colour hair to Sandra Dee's could be seen bobbing violently up and down.

'Yes. A girl from work. She asked me to check out her site. Everybody always wants you to check out their sites. Extraordinary, the pride some people take in them.'

'So you decided to check out hers,' Chantorria replied.

'That's right.'

'Every night.'

There was a pause, during which Trafford exited from the video Sandra Dee had posted.

'You've been looking at my history?' he said casually.

'Any reason why I shouldn't?'

'No.'

'So why do you always look at this Sandra Dee girl? Do you fancy her arse or something? It certainly looks like she knows how to work it. I didn't realize you were into those obvious types of girls. Nice bod, too. Of course, kiddieless bitches usually have nice bods, don't they?'

Clearly Chantorria had been reading some of Sandra Dee's blogs too.

'I'm just trying to log up some screen time, Chantorria,' Trafford said, trying not to sound too defensive, 'so I don't look so weird. You told me not to look so weird; you told me to spend more time perving.'

'Yes, but not just on one chick. You're supposed to perv on loads of chicks.'

'That would be better, would it?'

'Of course it would!'

'Well, I'll certainly remember next time!' said Trafford, feigning righteous anger and slamming down the lid of his computer.

They remained for a little while in silence, he still hunched over the closed laptop, she behind him.

'Well, look at me, for God's sake, why don't you?' Chantorria demanded suddenly.

Turning round, Trafford saw that she had dressed herself in what was known as 'the full linge'. This was a phrase derived from the old word 'lingerie' and it meant dressing specifically to sexually excite one's partner. It was applied to women only. There was no male equivalent of the full linge because men were not required to attempt to excite their partners, although they were under considerable pressure to become excited once they had been linged. Any woman who donned the full linge for her partner, particularly in a sexually moribund relationship, held a strong moral position. Healers and counsellors would deem her to be making the effort to put fire and spice back into their sex lives, and the man was expected to react with unalloyed delight.

Chantorria was wearing the classic Temple-approved linge ensemble for women of faith: five-inch black stiletto heels, a chocolate-flavoured edible G-string and a leather cupless bra.

'I went to Dirty Sexy Filthy Bitch,' she said.

Dirty Sexy Filthy Bitch was one of the ubiquitous chains of shops that sold lingerie and sex toys, which were the only serious rivals to fast food outlets for domination of the shopping malls.

'We haven't had great sex big time since before Caitlin Happymeal was born,' she said.

'I know that,' Trafford replied.

'People will talk.'

'People always talk. They'll talk whatever we do.'

'Aren't you going to sort me out then?' Chantorria asked in a small voice.

Trafford looked at his wife. He was still fond of her. It was not her fault that she was scared and put upon. He felt scared and put upon himself most of the time. On the other hand, he found the things she was wearing quite ridiculous. If he did not wish to have oral sex with her, why would he feel any more inclined to do so because her vagina was covered in chocolate? There was chocolate in the fridge, a kilo of it, and none of it was vagina-flavoured. What was even more excruciating was that he knew Chantorria herself was feeling ridiculous. Even in their thrilling, early days together she had never been the sort of girl who favoured 'erotic' toys and costumes. Then, of course, it hadn't mattered; their sex life had been so full and active that it had gone unnoticed in the tenement that Chantorria was in fact quite shy about her body. Then they had made love naked but beneath the sheets, and the nurse's uniforms and pink fluffy handcuffs she had been given as engagement presents had lain unused in a drawer. Now it was clear that Chantorria was feeling the need to make an effort and it was equally obvious to Trafford that she hated it. Her expression as she stared down at him was challenging and defiant rather than sensual, and although she trembled Trafford knew it was with embarrassment, not passion. His heart went out to her but at the same time he felt angry to see her neediness so cruelly exposed.

'Do you want me to sort you out because you feel like great sex big time or because you're worried that people will talk?' he asked.

'Both, of course,' she replied.

But Trafford suspected he knew which reason was greater. A vigorous and hearty sexual appetite with a natural desire to 'do anything' was considered the proper thing for a respectable woman of faith to exude. A woman was expected to 'want it' and want it 'big time'. She was also expected to provoke an insatiable lust in her partner, otherwise it was understood that her man, being a man, would 'get it' elsewhere. Any woman characterized as 'frigid' might find it difficult to gain a new husband when her current partner moved on, as inevitably he would. The pressure on young women to be highly sexualized at all times was enormous and Trafford knew that if ever the community noted that he had not been sorting out Chantorria on an appropriately regular basis she was the one most likely to be stigmatized. Hence her decision to linge him up, a tactic that publicly put the ball back in his court.

As if to prove the point, suddenly Barbieheart's voice broke in on Trafford's thoughts.

'Oh my God! Doesn't she look *fabulous*! Oh my God, girl, you look *so hot*!'

Trafford turned to the wall. Barbieheart, a chicken drumstick in each hand and a big smile spread across her greasy mouth, was nodding her approval.

'Hey, girls!' Barbieheart shouted. 'Check out Chantorria. What a *babe*!'

On the part of the wallscreen which was tuned to Tinkerbell's apartment, the girls halted in their drunken partying to turn and stare.

'Way to go!' they whooped. 'You *own* that look, girl. What are you waiting for, Trafford? That girl is *hot*. She is to die for. *Sort her out!*'

Chantorria smiled shyly at the attention although she must have known that it was nothing more than common manners for women to loudly big up any of their number who had gone the full linge.

Suddenly Trafford was furious. He wanted to scream at the wall. He wanted to tear those faces from it and stamp on every one. How dare they burst in like that! How dare they presume to intrude upon his wife's efforts to excite him!

He said nothing, of course. Why would any man object to the world seeing his wife in her sexiest attire? Wasn't he proud? Wasn't he proud that she was proud? Wasn't she beautiful? What was wrong with him? Had either of them anything to hide?

Trafford clenched his fists and struggled to master his anger.

'Wow,' he said finally. 'Yes, my babe certainly looks hot.'

'If you don't sort her out now, Tiger,' Barbieheart said through a mouthful of fried chicken, 'you never will.'

'Oh, I'll sort her out all right!' Trafford said. 'Just you try and stop me.'

There were more whoops and shouts from Tinkerbell and her friends.

'I'll leave you two to it then,' said Barbieheart.

But as he muted the sound on their community podcast Trafford knew that Barbieheart would not be leaving them to it. Barbieheart would be watching. Itching to tell the whole building that Trafford had failed to sort out Chantorria even after she had linged him up. That they were 'having problems'. That she was frigid. That he was impotent. That their relationship was a pathetic lie in which there was no great sex, either big time or any time.

'I'll have to fake it,' he whispered to Chantorria as they crossed into the bedroom. 'Too much pressure.'

'I don't care. Just make it convincing,' his wife whispered, desperate not to be publicly humiliated as a woman who could not arouse her man even while wearing heels, a G-string and a cupless bra.

And so, for the benefit of the neighbours, Trafford and Chantorria performed a pantomime of lovemaking in which, having briefly and perfunctorily consumed her chocolate G-string, Trafford lay between her legs, grinding his flaccid penis against her while she whimpered in mock ecstasy.

When they had finished their performance they wished Barbieheart good night.

'Way to go, kids,' Barbieheart replied, opening a bottle of fizzy drink. 'I am *so* jealous. Back in the day you should have seen me go. I was *mad* for it!'

As a woman dealing with size issues, Barbieheart was exempt from the social pressure to have a fantastic sex life. Trafford could not help wondering in his secret self how mad for it she had ever been. How mad for it was anybody in the stinking-hot rabbit warrens in which they lived? Did other people fake it for the cameras too? How much of the sex that was streamed on the community webcast was actually a pantomime? The social pressure to be an obsessively sexual being was all-encompassing. Every advert, every song, every reality show seemed to be about almost nothing but sex. Sometimes it seemed to Trafford as if, with the exception of some of the news, nothing was broadcast at all that was not about sex. All comment, all discussion, all marketing appeared to be based on the assumption that there were only two proper states for a person to be in, either 'up for it' or 'at it', and if they weren't one of those two things then something was very wrong. Trafford knew that this was rubbish. He liked sex as much as anyone but people had children to raise, money to earn, vermin to kill, problems to deal with; it was impractical for sex to be the number-one priority *every* minute of the day. How would the washing get done?

Was everybody lying? Did they all have secret lives? If they did then they were all heretics, Tinkerbell, Barbieheart, Sabre and Lexus, all of them. Enemies of the Temple. It occurred to Trafford that if only all these people could be brought to Confession together and made to speak the truth, there would be a revolution. For a moment he indulged in the fantasy of appealing to the camera for common sense. 'COME ON!' he cried out in his mind. 'Are you *really* all so ecstatically fucking happy? Don't you occasionally long for a bit of calm? A bit of quiet? A bit of *privacy*?!'

Unable to speak, Trafford got up and went into the kitchen. For a few moments he stood over Caitlin Happymeal's cot, watching her as she slept. Her lashes were long and dark, just like her mother's. Trafford wondered if one day his tiny, happy baby would grow up to have the joy crushed out of her as Chantorria had – or would Caitlin find the strength to keep her secrets and make of them a shield? After a little while he went to the table and sat down at his computer. Sandra Dee had updated her lies since he had last looked; she was very conscientious about maintaining her cover. There were new sex videos, a badly focused tape of a woman singing karaoke in a pub and a new blog discussing the latest entrant into a popular reality show. *She looks like a total bitch to me*, it said. *But fair play to her, she's a strong woman and I love her big time.* Trafford copied and pasted the sentences on to his search engine and soon discovered that the blog had actually been written by a woman named Vosene who lived on one of the islands of the South Downs.

Caitlin Happymeal began crying. Chantorria got up to feed her.

'How's your girlfriend?' she enquired sarcastically as she emerged through the beaded curtain that stood in for a door between their sleeping and dining area.

'She's not my girlfriend,' Trafford replied, 'she's a colleague who gets bullied. I feel sorry for her, that's all.'

'Whatever,' Chantorria replied, and putting Caitlin on her breast she returned to bed.

Thinking about his baby, Trafford felt a surge of pride. He had had her vaccinated. He had acted independently in defiance of the Temple. He had begun his own private revolution.

21

The address that Cassius had given Trafford was for a small communications shop in Finchley. It was not an easy place for Trafford to get to, as it involved crossing Lake London with his bicycle and disembarking at the Paddington jetty, then cycling for miles along the rickety stilt paths and stinking, muddy, half-submerged streets of what was left of Kensal Green and Kilburn. As he half pedalled, half waded his way towards his destination, Trafford's emotions veered between intense excitement and intense fear.

If he had guessed Cassius's intentions correctly, he was about to enter the secret company of Humanists, people with whom he hoped to experience an intellectual liberation that weeks before he would not have imagined possible. On the other hand he was also putting himself among heretics, on a collision course with the Inquisition. What was more, to do so he was having to journey into a particularly desperate area of town. It was a grim, fearful place where fresh water was currency and teenage street gangs ran illegal tolls on every bridge; where ferrymen rowed with guns held ready between their knees and even the police and the Inquisition travelled only in packs, rarely leaving their boats. A brutalized and embittered local population lived in a state of continuous war with the incoming immigrant underclass, both communities struggling to scratch a living from the rubbish that floated on the canals.

As Trafford hurried along, the grim environment and the knowledge of his secret mission preyed on his nerves. Every passer-by suddenly looked like a Temple spy and every leaky punt a police launch. Beggars demanded money in menacing tones that seemed to say, 'I know where you're going, boy. Pay up or I shall denounce you.'

Trafford inwardly chastised himself for being weak and fearful. If Sandra Dee were with him, he thought, she would not be starting at shadows and scared of weak and pitiable beggars. She'd face them with the same steady assurance that she faced that bitch Princess Lovebud. Trafford felt emboldened. Sandra Dee showed no fear and nor would he. He would be worthy of the secret love he harboured for a secret person.

Finally, after wading up and down a seemingly endless series of mostly deserted back streets just south of the Nag's Head market, Trafford found the address he was looking for. The building, which bore the legend *Books and Pamphlets Bought and Sold*, stood in a grubby terraced street very slightly more prosperous-looking than the ones through which he had been forced to pass. He mounted the scaffolding stairs to the first-floor window and entered a small, dimly lit emporium.

Communications shops had enjoyed something of a renaissance in recent years. The manuals and pamphlets they sold had traditionally been ordered from the net, but with the deterioration of the courier services and the continuing rise in the water level there had been a revival in what was known as 'direct commerce'. Shops had become viable as businesses once more. This one was stuffed to bursting point with the usual religious, faith-based and self-help manuals which for some reason people still seemed to prefer to consume in hard copy rather than view on the net. Everywhere Trafford looked, celebrity hypnotists, healers, pop singers, astrologers and spiritualists promised step-by-step programmes that guaranteed personal improvement. Thousands and thousands of books all offered to make the reader a strong, rich, powerful and successful person. Trafford had seen many such books; people read them all the time. There was clearly an enormous desire to be strong, rich, powerful and successful. The interesting thing was that despite all these books and their vast following of readers, Trafford had never met anybody outside the Temple hierarchy who actually *was* strong, rich, powerful and successful. It was just one more of the many contradictions that Trafford noted but never discussed.

He picked up a book at random, a slim volume which

promised to show him how he could recognize the God within himself and use it to attract a better class of sexual partner. As he was glancing through the contents, the manager of the shop approached him. A small man with the thickest glasses Trafford had ever seen, he looked a bit like an owl.

'Was there anything in particular you were looking for?' the manager enquired.

'Well, actually I was hoping to meet somebody,' Trafford replied.

'Any particular *reason* why you were to meet this person here?' the man asked.

Trafford recognized his cue. 'Oh yes, of course. *Reason* dictated it.'

'In that case I think you'll find your friend just through here.'

Trafford allowed himself to be led into the back room and from there down two flights of stairs to the cellar of the building, which by rights should have been flooded but was not. It was extremely dark and before Trafford's eyes had time to grow accustomed to the dimness he heard the familiar voice of Cassius.

'Trafford,' he said.

'Is that you, Cassius? Where are you?'

Cassius stepped out of the shadows.

'Greetings,' he said. 'Are you ready to cross the Rubicon?'

'What is the Rubicon?'

'A river.'

'What about it?'

'In Ancient Roman times Caesar defied law, convention and superstition by crossing it with his army. For him it was a point of no return. You have arrived at such a point. Will you cross your Rubicon?'

Trafford had heard of Caesar; he knew that he was an emperor from the distant past.

'I don't know anything about rivers,' he said, 'but when it comes to defying the law, convention and superstition, I'll cross any river you like.'

'I hope so,' Cassius said. 'We have to be most careful whom we approach.'

'Don't worry about me. I'm sure I believe what you believe.'

Cassius frowned. 'You earn the right to come here, Trafford, not by *believing* but by *understanding*.'

'Understanding what?'

'Understanding that in time everything can be understood. You have no doubt heard your Confessor speak of the Love that passes all understanding?'

'Of course.'

'Well, I reject that thesis. I do not believe that there is anything in the universe that passes all understanding. It is merely that there is much that we do not understand *yet*. Some people, most people, fill that gap with God. I and my friends wish to fill it with knowledge.'

'The other Vaccinators?'

'Not everyone who comes here is a Vaccinator, although most Vaccinators are Humanists. You told me that you wished to join us.'

'I do, I do.'

'You realize that if you are caught you will be killed, and if you betray us we will kill you? This is the Rubicon.'

Trafford needed no persuasion; he had been waiting for a moment like this all his life.

'I understand the risks and I would never betray you.'

'Do you know what a Humanist is?'

'Not really. Perhaps a little.'

'Then how can you know that you wish to be one?'

'Because you have spoken of knowledge and understanding and those are two things that I desire more than anything else on Earth.'

'Do you *know* what knowledge is? Do you *understand* what understanding is?'

'I know only one thing and I understand only one thing: that everything I have ever been told by the Temple and everything I pretend to believe is a lie. Beyond that I am utterly ignorant. Whoever you are, I want to join you. I am lost. I am alone. Every thought I have I must keep secret. Everything I claim to believe I actively despise. I would rather be a dog than a man: animals know nothing but they don't *know* they know nothing. I do. I am aware of my ignorance. I am aware of the pointless banality of my existence. It's a curse to have a mind if it is illegal to use it. It's a curse to have intelligence if you are forced to cloak it in a lifetime of wilful stupidity. If you and your friends can bring light into the miserable darkness of my life then I will be a Humanist and die a Humanist.'

'You may well have to,' Cassius replied. 'Follow me.'

He turned towards the wall, which was now revealed as

containing a secret door. The smell hit Trafford the moment the door opened, although it was not so much a smell as a texture to the air. It was *dry*. He had never before breathed completely dry air. The humidity in the city was pretty constant and every breath one took was laden with moisture. This air was different though: it wasn't fresh, far from it – in fact it smelt dusty and in a strange way *old*. But it was dry.

The room itself was as unique as the air in it. It was clearly carefully sealed because as the false wall closed behind him Trafford was aware that the noise of the city had disappeared. He was in a large room made up of the cellars of the next three houses in the street knocked through into one space. Even ground floors were normally ankle-deep in water and home to rats and mosquitoes, so it was most unusual to find a basement occupied. Somehow or other this space had been waterproofed and Trafford could now see that the quality of the air was the result of a large dehumidifier attached to the ceiling.

There were half a dozen men and women in the room besides Trafford and Cassius. They were sitting together around a small table on which stood a pot of tea, a bottle of wine and some plain-looking biscuits of a variety that Trafford did not recognize. The rest of the room was packed to bursting point with books. Old, old books. The people at the table scarcely looked up when Cassius entered, they were so engrossed. Each of them sat hunched over a book, taking an occasional sip of tea or wine.

'This is one of our reading rooms,' Cassius explained in a whisper.

For a moment Trafford wondered why Cassius was whispering. It was strange to hear anybody speaking at anything other than the top of their voice and he had already noted that the room was sealed from the outside world. Then he realized that Cassius did not wish to disturb the people around the table, who were *concentrating*.

Trafford felt a thrill. Nobody concentrated, ever.

No video screen stayed on the same image for more than a few seconds and no conversation remained focused on a topic for any longer. After all, an important aspect of being a person of faith was always to say the first thing that came into your head and to say it as loudly as possible. There was never any need to concentrate: God knew everything and you did what the Temple told you to do. What was to concentrate on?

And yet here, in this strange room, there was nothing but concentration. Quiet, focused concentration. Trafford wanted nothing more on Earth than to join those figures sitting round that table.

There was even an empty chair waiting for him.

'These are books that we have collected and continue to collect,' Cassius explained. 'After the flood, when the darkness of ignorance began to creep across the land, the first of the New Humanists began to store them. Most books were lost, of course. Many rotted in the deluge and then, as faith replaced reason, others were pulped for pamphlets or burned as fuel or used as lavatory paper. But we saved some and still do. Even now they can be found, stuffed into wall cavities or washed up on ledges in sewers. I once found Plato, Aeschylus and Aristotle lining a hen coop.'

Trafford had never heard of Plato, Aeschylus or Aristotle.

'We grab them when we can,' Cassius went on, 'clean them, dry them, repair them and above all *read* them. That is our bounden duty, to inwardly digest and understand the knowledge and the literature of the past.'

'Have you scanned them? Digitized them?'

'No. Only paper is safe. The authorities are ever vigilant for sedition on the net. As we have learned to our cost, they scan constantly for the key words and phrases. Oh, a story or a poem might survive undetected for a while; I doubt that the average policeman or Temple elder would recognize a Shakespeare sonnet if it were to beat them with a rubber truncheon. But there are key names and areas of knowledge which they pursue relentlessly. Not surprisingly, these are the same names and areas which every Humanist is pledged to study and to understand. Darwin and evolution above all, for the theory of evolution is the creed at the very core of the resistance, but there are many thousands of others – Galileo, Copernicus, greenhouse gas, Tom Paine and his *Rights of Man*, the Big Bang, George Bernard Shaw, Isaac Newton . . .'

Cassius was interrupted by a loud clearing of the throat. Trafford turned to see that one of the readers sitting at the table had looked up from his book and was glaring at them fiercely. In the excitement of listing his favourite inspirational names and topics (none of which, apart from Darwin, Trafford had heard of) Cassius had allowed his voice to rise a little and he was disturbing the peace.

'Sorry,' he whispered. 'Almost anything that we might wish to read could be located on the net instantly and traced straight back to us. The internet was supposed to liberate knowledge but in fact it buried it, first under a vast sewer of ignorance, laziness, bigotry, superstition and filth and then beneath the cloak of police surveillance. Now, as you know, cyberspace exists exclusively to promote commerce, gossip and pornography. And, of course, to hunt down sedition. Only paper is safe. Books are the key. A book cannot be accessed from afar, you have to hold it, you have to read it.'

'And that is what you do? You read books?'

'We study. We also organize secret seminars and lectures. Each one of us is an intellectual revolutionary. By our very existence we defy the forces of blind faith and ignorance. Doggedly we piece together the science of the past, the history of the past, and the imagination of the past.'

'The imagination of the past?'

'That which people in the past imagined. Literature, fiction, glorious stories written in an age when a person's mind could wander free . . .'

Trafford struggled to contain his mounting excitement. He was among genuine heretics, freedom fighters of the mind. He felt as if his whole life until this moment had been on 'pause' and only now could he press 'play'.

'May I read something?' he asked.

The empty chair was beckoning him. The great piles of books were calling.

'But of course. That's why we're here,' Cassius said cheerfully. 'You must start by acquainting yourself with the fundamentals of human understanding. Then, when you are ready, it will be your duty as a Humanist to go out and attempt to spread this knowledge even at the risk of your life.'

Cassius handed Trafford a copy of an old and battered book.

'This is where we all begin,' Cassius explained. 'You see the title? *A Child's Guide to the Wonderful World of Science and Nature*. It was published considerably over a hundred years ago and it was intended for quite young children. You will find almost everything in it complex and completely new to you. Much of the natural world that it describes has of course long since disappeared beneath the waters of the flood, but the analysis of how our planet works and its place within our galaxy remains entirely relevant. When you have mastered the contents of this book and explained them to me to my satisfaction, we will progress to more adult texts.'

Trafford took his place and began to read. It was extremely difficult at first. The text was so very dense and Trafford found himself wondering how anything could be so long-winded. Perhaps sensing his difficulty, Cassius came over and poured Trafford a glass of wine.

'Stick with it,' he whispered. 'You'll soon get your eye in.' And quite quickly, to Trafford's surprise he did.

Suddenly his eye was racing over the pages, absorbing every word, luxuriating in the pleasure of looking through a window of understanding, shining a light into the darkness of his ignorance.

After two hours during which Trafford scarcely raised his eyes from the pages, Cassius commented that he had a long journey home and suggested it was time to leave. Before Trafford could register his disappointment Cassius produced the empty jacket of a self-help tome entitled *New You: Twelve Steps to Inner Fulfilment and Material Success*. Taking the copy of the book Trafford was reading from his grasp, Cassius slipped it inside the pamphlet jacket.

'A simple subterfuge but effective,' he said. 'Be brazen. I told you before, the fastest way to draw attention to yourself is to look like you want to avoid it.'

Then Cassius took another book from the shelves. It had a picture of a man smoking a pipe on the front and was called *The Adventures of Sherlock Holmes*.

'For fun,' he said, putting it inside a manual that promised better sex and a trimmer tummy through the power of positive thinking. 'Bring them back in a week and tell me how you get on.'

22

A week proved far too long. Trafford had devoured both the science book and the stories Cassius had given him by the following evening. He had even tried to read as he cycled down from the library towards the Lake London ferry, which nearly resulted in his being dunked in the murky waters of the Kilburn High Road. Trafford loved *Sherlock Holmes*; he had never experienced proper narrative before, stories that grew and developed instead of simply repeating themselves like the computer fantasy games with their endless cyclical destruction of digital enemies. His education progressed quickly and within a few visits to the library Cassius pronounced that it was time for him to tackle Darwin's *Origin of Species*.

'This,' Cassius explained, 'is the core Humanist text. Nothing is more important to us; nothing is more hateful to the Temple.'

'Because it denies God?' Trafford asked.

'No. It doesn't do that at all, although it certainly denies that strange deity known as the Lord and the Love who is supposedly represented here on Earth by your Confessor. This book does not *disprove* the existence of a Divine Creator, that was not Darwin's purpose. What this book does do is prove beyond any reasonable doubt that, however man was created, he did not emerge fully formed in a single morning along with every other creature on Earth a few thousand years ago.'

Cassius also gave Trafford a copy of a book called *Pride and Prejudice*.

'This is by a once-celebrated female author,' he explained. 'Read it and ask yourself how the fascinatingly complex rituals of human courtship could have been reduced to the brief preamble to sex that passes for a relationship today.'

Cassius wrapped both books inside the cover of a gossip magazine that promised to expose the acne and cellulite that celebrities wished to hide.

'Remember,' Cassius said as Trafford mounted his bicycle outside the shop, 'Darwin is the key. Evolution is our only hope.'

The weeks went by and, as Trafford spent more and more of his time reading, not surprisingly he and Chantorria drifted further and further apart. They conversed little and aside from the pantomime sex that had to be endured occasionally for the benefit of neighbours there was no longer any intimacy between them at all.

It was not just Trafford's never-ending reading and the fact that his mind was clearly always elsewhere which caused the tension. Trafford also knew that ever since Chantorria had confronted him about reading Sandra Dee's blog she had suspected him of having an affair. Which, in a cerebral sort of way, he was doing, for the only thing capable of supplanting his rapidly expanding knowledge of history, science and literature was his obsession with the secrets of Sandra Dee.

Gradually Trafford and Chantorria came to accept that their marriage was drawing to its natural end. They had nothing to be ashamed of: they had had an appropriate run, two years was neither particularly long nor particularly short for a marriage to last and the Temple would view their divorce without censure. First, however, the necessary public emoting and testification must be gone through, for no partnership could end in private. Every detail of the marriage, every reason for the separation, must be announced at the Community Confession and be duly cheered or booed by the congregation. The proceedings must also be broadcast on the web, for the benefit of those like Barbieheart who could not attend the Confessions in person. After that the public would be invited to log on with their comments about the success or failure of the marriage, which could also be given a star rating of one to five.

One day, therefore, Trafford and Chantorria went by mutual agreement to see Confessor Bailey in order to ask that the break-up banns be posted and that they be allotted time at the following week's Confession to begin the public parading of the dysfunctional nature of their relationship. After this they could humbly request that in due course, if the Confessor was satisfied that every option for healing, growing and learning had been exhausted, he might grant them a divorce.

Confessor Bailey received them in the airy splendour of his Spirit House, a large converted pub which he and his wives and servants had all to themselves. The Confessor expressed (as convention required) great sadness to see such a fine marriage come to an end and made no secret of taking Chantorria's side. Nor did he make any effort to disguise his attraction to her, pronouncing himself amazed that Trafford could have grown tired of having sex with such a fine-looking woman who had been blessed with such impressive natural breasts.

'You must be dead from the waist down, Trafford,' the clergyman sneered. 'Barbieheart, your chat room moderator, had of course informed me that you good people were having trouble and she also Tubed me an edit of Chantorria lingeing you up, Trafford.'

The Confessor touched a button and there on his wallscreen appeared Chantorria standing behind Trafford in her heels, cupless bra and chocolate G-string.

'Very nice. Very beautiful and pure,' Confessor Bailey said, licking his big glossy lips. 'You're a credit to your sex, Chantorria, and I'd be prepared to wager you won't stay long on the shelf.'

'Thank you, Confessor Bailey,' Chantorria said, blushing, 'that's very kind.'

'I mean it. You mark my words. There'll be any number of decent red-blooded boys of faith and good family trying to get a piece of your big holy arse. In fact I should like to see your breasts right now in the name of the Love.'

Without a word Chantorria undid her bikini top and stood topless before her Confessor.

'You're crazy, Trafford,' Bailey said, having feasted his eyes. 'Still, we always knew you were a little touched.'

The Confessor then noted down the forthcoming testification, entering the title of the dysfunction that Trafford and Chantorria had agreed into the Order of Service:

He won't sort me out and prefers to perv on other girls' Tube diaries.

Trafford had been happy for Chantorria to be the injured party. Indeed, he could think of nothing for which to blame her and no good reason why the marriage should be over. Nor could he confess to being in love with someone else since his love was secret and therefore a sin. It didn't matter: only one partner was required to be injured and nobody would take much notice of an insignificant couple like them anyway. Confessor Bailey completed his paperwork and dismissed them.

The following Sunday Trafford and Chantorria went as usual to the local youth centre where the Community Confession was held. Both were a little sad, conscious that this would be one of the last times they would attend Confession together as a married couple.

Glancing through the itinerary as they took their seats, Trafford could see that it was going to be a very busy evening. The Confessor would have his work cut out to fit everything in. Trafford was relieved that there was no shortage of entertainment and so nobody would mind very much if he and Chantorria simply went through the motions.

Three couples were scheduled to confront their issues before Trafford and Chantorria had their turn. None of them were asking for divorce but instead for community counselling in the hope that they might learn and grow through their difficulties and in due course heal. Trafford knew all three couples: they were local celebrities, people who loved to confess, who gloried in the drama of it and the parish notoriety that it brought them. He read the three proclamations:

He hates my mum which I can't forgive but then he sorted her out and also my sister although I blame her for that, the bitch.

My tarot reader says he's the wrong man but I love him. Should I leave him? Who should I trust? My husband or my healer?

She won't let me give it to her from behind and I have to lie when my mates talk about how much anal they get. Is she frigid?

The congregation screamed and stamped their feet as Confessor Bailey took the stage to lead them in the opening testification of faith before inviting the first warring family to join him on stage.

'OK, we have a lot to get through,' he said. 'First up, listen to this. How would you feel, girls, if your husband had sex with your mum and also your sister? That's right! Would you blame him? Would you blame them? Or would you blame yourself? Would you fight to keep your precious man in your loving home or would you let the scheming love rat go? Let's find out how one family is dealing with just these issues. Madonnatella, Angel Delight, Heavenly Braveheart and Ninja, please join me on stage and face your community!'

The cheering, whooping and shouting rose to fever pitch as the four parties of dysfunctional testification strutted arrogantly on to the stage, sneering and grimacing at each other and at the congregation before taking their seats.

'All right!' Confessor Bailey shouted above the din. 'Madonnatella, what's your beef? What's going on here? Let's see if we can't sort this out right here, right now.'

Madonnatella rose and turned to look at the man sitting on the furthest chair from her. Her big face, which had been made lumpy and strange from too many cheap injections and implants, was wound up into a grimace of fury.

'We live in a small flat, right?' Madonnatella said in tones of righteous outrage. 'And ever since my mum got dumped by my last stepdad she's lived with us, right? Which I don't mind because I love her to bits and at the end of the day she's my best mate, right, even if she is a bitch. Well, one day I come home from shopping, right? And him, right! Yeah, you, Ninja! You know who I'm talking about.'

Ninja and the other two women on stage were already vigorously shaking their heads in a furious pantomime of denial and disbelief, even though as yet Madonnatella had accused them of nothing.

'Yeah, you, Ninja, don't you shake your head cos you know you done it. He was sorting out my sister on the couch, right? And when I told him he was out of order and that I felt uncomfortable and threatened by his behaviour he told me he'd already done my mum!'

The chorus of boos that met this testimony was deafening. Throughout it, Ninja, Angel Delight, who was the sister concerned, and Heavenly Braveheart, the mother, continued to shake their heads and make gestures of defiance at the crowd.

Confessor Bailey turned to Ninja.

'Well, Ninja?' he asked. 'Is it true? Did you have sex with your wife's mother and sister on the family couch while she was at the shops?'

'She's always out at the shops,' Ninja protested, shaking his big tattooed arm at Madonnatella.

'I am *so* not always out at the shops,' Madonnatella replied, shaking her fist back.

'Answer the question, Ninja,' Confessor Bailey insisted sternly. 'Did you sort out your own mother-in-law and sister-in-law on your family sofa?'

'Well, maybe I did. I ain't perfect, I know that,' Ninja

said, 'but so what, big deal, move on. Madonnatella should get over herself and find closure.'

Angel Delight and Heavenly Braveheart nodded vigorously at this.

'Angel Delight,' Confessor Bailey said, turning to the sister, struggling once more to force his voice above the chorus of boos and cheers with which the crowd reacted to Ninja's excuse. 'You gave a piece of your big arse to your sister's husband. Doesn't that make you a wicked, cheating, conniving, disgusting bitch?'

Angel Delight rose to her feet, her tattooed breasts heaving as she stared down the baying crowd.

'Yes, yes, I am! I'm a bitch, all right? I know I'm a bitch . . . but I am one *sexy* bitch, right!'

There were many whoops of appreciation for this defiant stance, which Angel Delight acknowledged by turning round, wiggling her bottom at the crowd and then doing a little dance.

'And if my sister can't keep her husband interested,' she went on, 'then I've got every right to get in there and sort him out. He's fantastic and I love him and we have amazing sex and he really understands the needs of a woman and he's dead sensitive and caring and that and we do everything together and he says I'm the best he's ever had and he's never had nothing like it.'

This vigorous defence won Angel Delight a great deal of support among the crowd and the mood of the room began to shift against Madonnatella.

'OK. That worked. The people like that,' Confessor

Bailey shouted. 'The people like your pride, Angel Delight, they like your sassy style. But what about Mum? We haven't heard from Mum yet. OK, Heavenly Braveheart, bottom line. Isn't sexing your own son-in-law the greatest betrayal any mother could visit upon the daughter of her womb?'

'I kept the family home together,' Heavenly Braveheart protested. 'If me and Angel hadn't given Ninja what he needed he would have gone and got it elsewhere. We kept him in the family. I reckon we done Madonnatella a good turn.'

This argument produced loud applause, not least from Ninja himself. He sat clapping and nodding earnestly, giving every impression that, if anything, he felt he was the injured party.

'I hear you, Heavenly Braveheart. I hear you!' Confessor Bailey shouted. 'Family matters! Family is important! Nothing is more sacred in the eyes of the Lord than family. And while the Temple cannot *condone* a man enjoying the conjugal favours of his sister-in-law and his mother-in-law, I say there are worse things in the eyes of the Lord and the Love. Therefore I say to you, Madonnatella, the mote lies in your eye, for were Ninja satisfied in the communion of your loins he would not be seeking loinful communion elsewhere in the loins of your sister and mother. Therefore I say hug, make up, move on, find closure, get over yourself and put your house in order.'

This invitation led to Madonnatella assuring the Confessor that she would not only put her house in order but that she would do it immediately. Pulling off her brassiere, she strode across to Ninja and shook her enormous breasts in his face.

'These good enough for you?' she screamed. 'I'll show you amazing sex. I'll make Angel Delight look frigid! I'll make that cow look like a stick of wood!'

The crowd's mood shifted once more and this gesture of self-confidence won the day. They cheered and stamped their feet and Ninja, having punched the air a number of times in celebration, fell upon his wife, declaring that he loved her so much that he would never look at another female member of her family again.

The following two testifications progressed along similarly hysterical lines. The congregation showed enormous interest in the conflict between a distraught woman's personal inclinations and the insistence of her tarot reader that she must leave the man she loved. After considerable agonizing, Confessor Bailey ruled that the woman must take her spiritual guru's advice. It was, after all, impossible to ignore the workings of fate and clearly the planets and the stars (which were the creation of the Love) were pulling the woman towards new horizons that did not include her current love. Confessor Bailey expressed his confidence that new love was just around the corner.

Next up, Confessor Bailey summoned to the stage a couple for whom the wife's reluctance to allow her husband anal sex was causing issues in their marriage. Not only was the husband becoming frustrated but it was also putting him at a social disadvantage down the pub, where he was the laughing stock of his mates, whose partners, he claimed, were up for anything. There were numerous interjections from the floor on this subject, both for and against the husband's position. A number of women and some men stated that if the wife had issues with taking it from behind then she should not feel pressurized to do so. Many people pointed out that, as there was no possibility of begetting children from such a practice, it should be a matter of personal taste whether one indulged in it. The husband was loudly booed for claiming that a lack of interest in sodomy indicated frigidity. On the other hand a large body of opinion in the room felt that the woman should simply grit her teeth, stop moaning and get on with it. After all, it was well known that what a man could not get at home he would get elsewhere and there were plenty of bitches out there who would think nothing of stealing a woman's husband. Eventually the Confessor announced that, having taken into consideration the feelings of the assembly, he would rule in favour of the wife.

'A woman's big arse is a gift that she may bestow or withhold,' he intoned solemnly. 'It is not given to this congregation to suggest otherwise.'

Trafford's head was splitting. The heat and the stench of sweat in the room were overpowering and the frenzied emotions and hysterical shouting of the congregation battered his eardrums like an artillery assault. He was asking himself how much more he could take when finally Confessor Bailey summoned him and Chantorria to the stage.

'Trafford has stopped giving Chantorria that which any respectable woman has a right to expect from her husband,' the Confessor announced to a smattering of boos, 'and what's more, it appears that he gets his kicks perving on the blogs and video diaries of other women!'

Confessor Bailey tried to make it sound exciting but the crowd knew a bog standard break-up when they saw one. Trafford and Chantorria were no star couple. They were unknown outside the tenement in which they lived and pretty much ignored within it. Conservatively dressed and clearly uncomfortable to be the focus of so many eyes, they were not glamorous either. The crowd liked their testifiers to strut, to big themselves up and to play to the gallery and Trafford and Chantorria were a major disappointment.

'Hey! Be proud!' Confessor Bailey admonished as they shuffled to their places. 'Don't you want to emote to the congregation of which you are a member?'

'Yes, yes, of course we do,' Trafford said as he took his seat.

'Well then, let's get to it! Chantorria,' Bailey asked, 'tell us why your marriage is on the rocks.'

'We've grown apart,' Chantorria replied. 'It just feels like it's over, that's all.'

This was not a testification likely to provoke much excitement in the crowd.

'What about his perving on blogs and other girls' vid diaries?' Confessor Bailey demanded, clearly hoping to add a little spice to the proceedings. 'Doesn't it make you uncomfortable that he finds other girls more attractive than you? Don't you have issues with that situation? Don't you feel threatened by it?'

'Not girls, Confessor,' Chantorria explained. 'He's always looking up this one girl, her name's . . .'

And as Chantorria said those words, Trafford saw her. Sandra Dee.

She was a member of his own congregation! He knew instantly why he had never spotted her before. This was the first time in years that he had testified, the first time in as long as he could remember that he had viewed the whole room from the stage. Normally he never saw the faces of his fellow worshippers, only the backs of their heads. He saw their faces now though – and there she was, sitting crushed in at the rear of the tiered seating. Crushed in but clearly alone. That was why she had caught his eye among the crowd: she was so very different. She wasn't shouting or shaking her fist. She had not leaped to her feet and her face was not contorted with rage; she was just sitting there, alone. A still figure in a frenzied crowd, her face calm, blank even. Giving nothing away.

'Sandra Dee,' said Chantorria, completing her sentence.

Now Sandra Dee's expression changed as it dawned on her that a colleague had been cyberstalking her. She looked shocked of course but also, Trafford felt, scared.

'Who is this Sandra Dee, Trafford?' Confessor Bailey thundered. 'Is she the reason you are no longer interested in your wife?'

Sandra Dee was staring at him, her face glowing red. Now their eyes met and instead of looking away as he had expected her to do, she continued to stare. Her gaze burned into him, a silent, furious accusation. Here was a woman who had gone to extraordinary lengths to remain private and he had caused her name to be cited publicly from the stage of a Community Confession; what was more, cited as the only tangible evidence in a divorce case. In the end it was Trafford who looked away, unable to meet her eyes any longer for the guilt and remorse that they provoked in him.

'No!' Trafford shouted. 'Absolutely not! I don't know her at all. It was just a random blog, a hit that . . . a hit that intrigued me.'

Trafford and Sandra Dee might have been finding this exchange intense but for the crowd it was a very dull business. They wanted passion, sex, blood even. They weren't interested in some nonentity net-perving on a girl he had not even had sex with. Confessor Bailey could see that the congregation was getting restive and decided to move on, granting them their notice of intended separation and dismissing them from the stage.

As Trafford crossed the room to resume his seat he did not look up towards where Sandra Dee was sitting but he was certain that she was still staring at him. He could almost feel the heat of her eyes burning holes in him.

'Well, that's over with,' Chantorria said as they sat down. But Trafford knew that she was wrong.

23

The measles-plus epidemic, when it came, was shocking in its suddenness and severity. These epidemics always were. The Lord and the Love, as Confessor Bailey often said, had no time to mess around.

'Oh, he's got a temper,' the Confessor assured his congregation, 'and when he smites, he smites hard. Some people call it vengeance, which of course it is, but I like to call it tough love.'

There were those who believed that other factors were causing the ever-increasing severity of the epidemics. The reckless overuse of antibiotics had played a part, they felt, as had appalling diet, sinking standards of public hygiene and deteriorating water quality in what was now a subtropical climate. These issues were discussed on the more serious chat shows and various health-orientated websites. Never for a moment was it suggested that these factors were anything other than God's work; people merely hinted that man in his sin might like to consider eating more fruit and vegetables, and completing the courses of those antibiotics that were still being prescribed.

The truth was that the deadly potential of all the major diseases grew with each new plague and measles, or measles-plus as it was now known, was no exception. The virus was constantly evolving so that each time it returned it was more violent and more deadly than before.

It was the same with mumps-plus, whooping cough-plus, meningitis-plus and all the other diseases of childhood. For it was in pre-faith-school illnesses that the deterioration in public health was most alarming. Infant afflictions that had once been survivable had steadily become more and more lethal. Conversely, those who survived the first few years of their lives seemed better placed to fight off the plagues of adulthood. As Confessor Bailey said, those who were chosen to survive were clearly righteous and strong and favoured in the sight of the Lord. Or, according to the health websites, they had developed viral immunity due to some fortunate minor exposure (which had of course been arranged, in his wisdom, by the Lord). But infants, in their innocence, had developed neither righteousness nor viral immunity and therefore a great winnowing regularly took place in the cot and the nursery.

Trafford and Chantorria became aware that there was measles-plus in their building one morning as they sat down to breakfast. Just as the news was being broadcast to the wallscreens in their kitchen, Trafford and Chantorria heard the first mother sobbing through the thin fabric of Inspiration Towers. A new strain of measles-plus had been identified and it was ripping through their little community like a hurricane, borne upon every cough, every sneeze and every breath. The authorities were already setting up a quarantine zone around the half-dozen tower blocks that made up the estate.

Chantorria looked at Trafford, her face a picture of alarm and misery. This was the moment every parent dreaded, to be trapped on the wrong side of a quarantine fence, imprisoned in a hotbed of infection. The authorities would not lift the barriers until the disease had run its course.

'Caitlin looks fine!' she wailed. 'They have to let us out before she gets it!'

'You know they won't,' Trafford replied. 'They never do.'

It was true: everyone had heard stories of distraught parents trying to storm quarantine fences with their children in their arms. It never worked. The police were prepared to shoot rather than risk infection escaping.

'But she looks well!' Chantorria lamented once more.

'That's right, she does.'

'They have to let us out!'

'Chantorria.' Trafford spoke quietly. 'They are not going to let us out. We're quarantined. But all the same, I think she will be OK.'

Chantorria was hardly listening. Already she had placed a mask sprayed with air freshener over Caitlin Happymeal's face and she was now stuffing wet rags into the crack at the foot of the front door in an effort to keep out the germ-laden air.

'Chantorria,' Trafford repeated, 'I said I think she may be OK.'

His wife looked up at him angrily.

'Think! *Think!*' she shouted. 'What's fucking *thinking* got to do with anything? We need to *pray!*'

'Don't you think they're all praying, Chantorria?' Trafford asked. 'In every room in this building they're praying to the very same God who they claim sent the damn plague in the first place.'

Chantorria was crying now, tears of impotent panic.

'Well, we have to do *something*,' she wailed. 'Help me seal the windows . . . or go and buy some lavender . . . or just shut up and read one of your stupid manuals! Anything. We have to do something. We can't just let her die.'

'I don't think she is going to die,' Trafford replied. 'You see, Chantorria, I already did do something.'

Chantorria looked at him, hope starting in her eyes.

'You mean . . . ?'

'Yes. I had Caitlin inoculated.'

Within hours the tenement was filled with the sound of weeping, as baby after baby succumbed to the fever and mother after mother succumbed to despair. Toddlers and little children had more strength to sweat it out but the smallest all quickly became very sick. All, that is, except Caitlin Happymeal.

In and out of the streets and corridors of the estate and all through every building mothers watched helplessly as their infants' eyes grew redder and throats grew more painful. As long as the symptoms were similar to those of a cold or flu there was still hope, slim hope but hope nonetheless. Each parent tried to believe that their child had only caught a chill and would prove miraculously resistant to the carnage enveloping the community. But once the spots arrived people knew in their hearts that hope was lost and all that remained was prayer. The spots began around the ears and spread to the body, growing in size and number until they formed a solid rash, a rash that sucked the life out of the infected babies as their temperatures rose and rose. With the rashes the weeping of the mothers decreased, to be replaced by the deep sadness of silence as parents sat over cots awaiting the inevitable. Such was the suddenness and ferocity of the epidemic that almost every child suffered simultaneously, and thus the numbing pain of the mothers was synchronized also. On the Dying Day, as such days had come to be called, a terrible hush descended across the whole estate as in the space between two sunsets a tiny generation succumbed.

When the local health department finally lifted the quarantine, one month after the fevers had begun, in Inspiration Towers no child under one survived.

No child, that is, except Caitlin Happymeal.

Caitlin had remained unaffected and oblivious to the tragedy going on around her, and as the tiny coffins were carried from the building she played happily in her cot.

With Caitlin's miraculous survival came a change in Chantorria. The month that the family had spent cooped up in their apartment while the air rang with the agony of dying babies had affected her deeply. The long nights of watching Caitlin, scarcely daring to hope that Trafford's act of heresy might save her, had also left their mark. Chantorria became rather distracted and, to Trafford's astonishment, bearing in mind the nature of Caitlin's deliverance, more spiritual.

Their divorce had been only days away from finalization when the plague struck. But the couple had put everything on hold during the quarantine period and now it seemed that Chantorria had changed her mind. She wanted reconciliation.

'You made a miracle,' she said on the evening when the authorities officially declared the plague to have run its course, 'and I love you.'

'I didn't make a miracle,' Trafford replied. 'Miracles can't be explained. You know exactly why Caitlin survived. Her immune system had been primed to withstand the epidemic.'

'I don't care how it was achieved, it's still a miracle,' Chantorria said, 'and I think it's a sign.'

'A sign?'

'Caitlin's survival means she wants us to stay together.'

Trafford was astonished. 'Please tell me you're not serious,' was all he could think of to say.

'Of course I'm serious. She's here because she wants to help mend our marriage.'

'Chantorria, Caitlin is less than one year old. She doesn't "want" anything apart from more booby.'

Trafford was horrified at the direction Chantorria's mind had taken. How could it be that the very thing which should have turned her away from bogus self-serving spirituality seemed to be drawing her towards it?

'Our daughter,' he said firmly, 'is alive today because of the intervention of man-made science. Her survival has nothing to do with her wanting us to stay together.'

'I still don't want a divorce. Not now. Not after what we've been through.'

But Trafford did want a divorce. He wanted his freedom: freedom to read and to learn. That was his passion now. Every moment spent in the real world, working through the mundane detail of day-to-day life, was a moment lost in his search for knowledge, understanding and experiences of the imagination.

He wanted privacy and time to concentrate. If he and Chantorria split up he would get it. She would keep their flat because of the child and he would have to find a roof elsewhere. Most men would have viewed this prospect with horror; the housing shortage was permanently acute and single men usually ended up in a hostel or at best a bed-and-breakfast. In terms of physical comfort this would be a huge step down for Trafford: family apartments were cramped certainly and damp, rat-infested and insanitary, but compared to the tiny plasterboard cupboards offered in bed-and-breakfasts or the sardine-can dormitories of the hostels they were palatial. But it was not comfort for the body that Trafford needed, it was comfort for the mind and the soul. He wanted simply to be left alone. A cockroach-infested bunk in a crowded dorm would be fine by him as long as he could shut out the world by tuning his communitainer to some bland, forgettable New Age chillout and disappear into the vast unmapped universe of history, science and literature.

Besides, he was in love with Sandra Dee.

After the night at the Community Confession when Chantorria had named her in the divorce testification, Trafford had restrained himself from visiting Sandra Dee's site. Even so, she remained at the forefront of his mind and the fact that at the last Fizzy Coff she had furiously avoided his eye had only served to increase his fascination. In his mind all the heroines in the stories that Cassius gave him to read looked like her. Elizabeth Bennet was Sandra Dee, Heathcliff's Cathy was Sandra Dee, Anna Karenina, Juliet and Ophelia were Sandra Dee. Even the women in the history he was reading took on her likeness: Marie Curie developing radium, Emily Pankhurst ensuring female suffrage, Elizabeth I, all had the face of Sandra Dee.

'I just think we should continue as we planned,' Trafford said to Chantorria. 'After all, we've made the public announcement and everything.'

'That doesn't make any difference,' Chantorria said. 'Some couples break up and make up once a fortnight.'

'We're not them. We should see through what we've started.'

'Don't you love me any more?' Chantorria asked, tears welling in her eyes.

'Chantorria, we both agreed to divorce. You don't love me either.'

'But in these last weeks, we've been so close again.'

'Because we thought our daughter might die.'

'I thought . . . I thought . . . there was more to it than that.'

And the tears came. Chantorria wept and wept and of course Trafford went to comfort her.

'Don't cry,' he said, hugging her. 'Let's leave it a day or two and see what happens.'

'Caitlin needs us,' Chantorria sobbed. 'She wants us to be together.'

24

Life at Inspiration Towers now changed dramatically for Trafford and Chantorria. Trafford had half feared that their good fortune over the measles epidemic would provoke resentment among the other parents in their community and he was at first extremely relieved to discover that the opposite was the case. He and Chantorria suddenly found themselves being admired as people who had been especially favoured by the Lord.

Confessor Bailey set the tone by mentioning Caitlin Happymeal's miraculous survival from the pulpit at the first weekly Confession after the lifting of the quarantine.

'As you all know,' he said, 'the Inspiration Towers estate recently suffered a terrible reckoning. But in his wisdom the Lord favoured one baby girl to survive. I want to tell you that all the lost children live on in her. I say to the bereaved mummies and daddies of Inspiration Towers, when you see Caitlin Happymeal, see in her the spark of what is gone but which you will find again. Who knows the Love's purpose in preserving Caitlin Happymeal, but it is my belief that he has preserved her for some higher duty which is a mystery to us.'

Bailey pointed his finger to where Chantorria and Trafford sat.

'Nurture her, Chantorria, protect her, Trafford, for she is truly blessed and you are blessed to be the parents of such a child. So let us hear no more talk of divorce!' he added. 'The Lord and the Love has saved your baby. He has saved her for a purpose. He loves your family. He believes in your family. Go home in peace. Dance like there's nobody watching, sing like there's nobody listening and tonight make love like it's the first time.'

Out of the blue, Trafford and Chantorria became celebrities in their tenement. The gang of which Chantorria had previously been the most peripheral member now came knocking on her door. Any person whom Confessor Bailey saw fit to acknowledge from the pulpit was a big figure in the community and must be courted. Tinkerbell visited all the time now, having announced on her video blog that Chantorria was her new best friend.

'Would you like Lexus to pop down and look at that shower for you? I know Trafford's not much of a handyman, bless him, and I'm sure Lexus could get it working for you.' Tinkerbell always made a big point of holding and hugging Caitlin Happymeal and saying over and over again that being so close to Caitlin made up in some small way for the loss of KitKat.

'I just know that Gucci KitKat and Caitlin Happymeal would have been the bestest bestest mates,' she said, wiping away her tears. Then she added, with heavy emphasis, 'Does Caitlin have a godmother?'

'Only Barbieheart,' Chantorria admitted with some embarrassment. Barbieheart was godmother to all the children in the tenement so having her was nothing special. Chantorria could probably have assembled a better show if she had tried; most women were happy to take on the role of godmother because apart from getting drunk at the christening the post carried no special duties or responsibilities. When Caitlin was born, however, Chantorria had not been brave enough to ask anyone for fear of rejection. Even now she could not quite summon up the courage to ask directly.

'I mean, perhaps you . . . would you . . . ?' she stuttered.

'Oh my God!' Tinkerbell shrieked. 'Oh – my – God, I'd be honoured! We'll have to have her christened!'

'Well, she's been christened of course . . .'

'We'll do it again! But properly this time! A really big party! We'll get all the girls and just fucking go for it.'

Tinkerbell was as good as her word and a large celebration was organized in which all the women in the tenement queued up to offer their services as godmothers and to hug the last surviving baby in their building, no doubt in the hope that somehow Caitlin's luck or divine favour would rub off on them and that their future babies might also be protected by the Love.

Chantorria did her best not to appear too exultant at her new status – after all, it was only weeks since the plague had ended and the building was still in mourning – but with so many visits and gifts of cake and chocolate it was difficult for her to hide her delight. Barbieheart took to organizing her social diary, acting as an indulgent mother to a wild effervescent daughter.

'You've got Velvet Secret for coffee at eleven but you must get rid of her by twelve because Tinks and Flaming Ruby are taking you to lunch at McDonald's, no less, so Caitlin can have her first McFlurry.'

Chantorria's days passed in a whirlwind of visits. There was always chocolate and cake and usually plenty of fizzy wine, and always the golden daughter must be hugged for the Lord and the Love had selected her to survive.

All this suited Trafford very well. Chantorria had previously been rather a needy person, clinging on to Trafford and demanding his attention. Now she had so much to occupy her time that Trafford was able to find many hours a day in which he could sit and read. It was of course remarked upon that he seemed to have developed an extraordinary interest in self-improvement, but this was seen as a positive thing and evidence of the special plans that God had for him and his family.

'He's getting himself ready,' Barbieheart remarked, 'preparing himself for whatever task the Love has waiting for him.'

25

As Trafford emerged from the office lifts on the morning of his next Fizzy Coff, his mind as usual dwelling on Sandra Dee, he saw that he was not the only person to be focused on her that day. Princess Lovebud was standing before her desk. The simmering dislike which the office bully felt for Sandra Dee was always in danger of coming to a head and now it looked as if Princess Lovebud had found an excuse to engineer a major confrontation.

'Sandra Dee,' Princess Lovebud said, standing uncomfortably close to her proposed victim, 'I notice that you have stopped paying into the cake and doughnuts fund.'

'Yes, that's right,' Sandra Dee replied without looking up from her computer.

'Oi! I'm talking to you,' Princess Lovebud barked.

'Yes, I know. And I've replied. We are at work. We're paid to process information, not to discuss doughnuts.'

'Are you disrespecting me?'

'I am trying to get on with my work.'

Trafford glanced around the office. As usual it was divided between those in Princess Lovebud's camp who were all ears, relishing the mayhem to come, and those who kept their heads down, trying hard not to draw focus, hating the scene but grateful that it was not they who were the objects of the departmental bully's disapproval.

'Why ain't you paying into the cake and doughnut jar?'

'Because I don't eat any of the cake and doughnuts. I never have done and yet for quite a long time, out of politeness, I still put money in. I've paid for lots of the cake and doughnuts you've eaten but now I've decided to stop.'

'Don't you want to muck in? Don't you want to be a part of the team?'

'I don't think that forcing everybody to pay for the things that you and your mates want to eat means that we're a team, Princess Lovebud.'

Trafford was astonished. Nobody had ever challenged Princess Lovebud's authority before. It was utterly unprecedented and for a moment the team loudmouth was at a loss, clearly not knowing what to say next. Briefly there was silence, during which Sandra Dee continued to tap away at her computer. Then Princess Lovebud rallied.

'You think you're better than me, don't you?' she demanded.

'No, I don't.'

'Yes, you do. You think you're better than me.'

'Actually, I don't think about you at all.'

'Are you a racist?'

Trafford was surprised. This was a very serious allegation and took the confrontation to a whole different level.

'Of course not.'

'Because, as you know, I am a person of mixed race.'

'That is entirely irrelevant to this discussion, which is about a cake and doughnut fund that you set up and to which I do not wish to contribute.'

'Are you calling my race irrelevant?'

'Irrelevant in this case.'

'Which is the case we happen to be discussing!' Princess Lovebud said triumphantly, as if she had scored a major point.

Trafford knew it was useless for Sandra Dee to attempt to reason with Princess Lovebud. The quarrel had taken on a life of its own and anything that Sandra Dee said would be wilfully misinterpreted by Princess Lovebud in support of her own argument.

'Have you got a problem with the fact that I'm a quarter Irish, a quarter Croatian, part Cornish and one-sixteenth Afro-Caribbean British?' Princess Lovebud continued. 'Because I'm proud of who I am.'

'Actually, I don't care what you are.'

There was an audible gasp from the bully mob at this. Princess Lovebud had listed her antecedents and the only socially acceptable response to that was to gush with ecstasy and exclaim at full volume how much one loved all the racial and national groups that had been mentioned. Sandra Dee should have assured Princess Lovebud that she loved Irish people, she loved Croatian people, she loved the Cornish and she loved Afro-Caribbean British people. Her indifference to Princess Lovebud's pride in her racial mix was truly shocking.

'That is totally and utterly RACIST!' Princess Lovebud screamed. 'I can't believe you said that! I cannot BELIEVE you said that.'

'Said what?'

'You said you didn't care about Irish and Croatian, Cornish and Afro-Caribbean British people. You did! You said it! You need counselling, you need re-educating! You need to start growing, woman, because you are out of order.'

'I said I didn't care about you.'

'Yes, well, I am all them things and if you don't care about something then you don't have any respect for it and that is being disrespectful and disrespecting someone because of their race is racism and I am going to blog you up! I am going to complain to the tribunal.'

This was a very heavy threat indeed. Ostensibly workplace tribunals existed to provide 'arbitration' and 'reconciliation' services to employees who felt uncomfortable or threatened by the behaviour of a colleague. In reality they were kangaroo courts transparently manipulated by office bullies to settle scores and secure advancement, mini show trials in which Temple favourites could destroy anybody they wished to, simply by accusing them of socially unacceptable thinking. Any person at any time could find themselves accused suddenly of racism or sexism and be forced to appear before these tribunals, usually without understanding what it was they were supposed to have done. The charges were impossible to deny because over the years the words had come to be so widely and loosely interpreted as to be almost meaningless. In fact blatant racial discrimination and sexual harassment continued unchallenged, entirely separately to these trials, and often perpetrated by the very people who were claiming to be their victims.

Trafford decided that he must intervene. If Princess Lovebud were to take her complaint to a tribunal there was every chance that she would destroy Sandra Dee. She could with ease assemble many witnesses to support her grievance and if Sandra Dee was deemed to have made a racist remark the minimum punishment would be a course of re-education. She might easily lose her job.

'Princess Lovebud,' said Trafford, rising to his feet, 'I totally respect you big time and sincerely applaud the pride you take in who you are and where you came from. As a strong woman of Irish, Croatian, Cornish and Afro-Caribbean British heritage you are totally beautiful. However, I suggest that no way was Sandra Dee being racist and that you are well out of order, missus, so deal with it.'

Princess Lovebud swung round on Trafford in full attack mode. But then, just as the verbal assault was about to begin, she paused. Even a few weeks earlier she would have destroyed him. She was queen bee in their workspace and nobody told her she was out of order or to deal with it. She would have unleashed an expletive-ridden stream of invective that would have resulted in Trafford's total ostracism, and he might even have found himself being bundled into some dark stationery cupboard and physically attacked. However, things were different now. Trafford was no longer an irritating nonentity, a saddo and a weirdo who could, if the mob chose, be bullied at will. He was a Temple favourite. He had been mentioned from the pulpit by his Confessor and singled out for the Lord and the Love's special purpose. His child had survived a holy plague when all others in his building had succumbed. If Princess Lovebud were to disrespect him she would be disrespecting the will of the Temple, the will of the Lord even, and in that moment all her authority would evaporate. Suddenly it was she who would be the victim, naked and defenceless against all those who had previously feared her. And there were many.

'Yeah, well . . . all right,' Princess Lovebud said. 'If she wasn't being racist then that's fine, isn't it? I was only saying about the cake fund.'

'It is a voluntary fund though, isn't it?' Trafford asked.

'Of course it is. There ain't no rule, is there?'

'Then surely those who want to be a part of it should pay in and eat the things you buy and those who don't should simply opt out.'

'They can if they want.'

'Then I think I will,' Trafford said, 'if that's all right with you.'

'Whatever,' Princess Lovebud said and, taking up her money tin, she returned with it to the social hub where with exaggerated indifference she ate a doughnut. Nobody else took up the opportunity to withdraw from the fund; the power in the office might have shifted somewhat, but only for Trafford. For most people the idea of confronting Princess Lovebud remained unthinkable.

Slowly the office returned to normal. Trafford looked towards Sandra Dee many times during that day to see if he could catch her eye but she never once looked in his direction. He saw Cassius smile at him, though, and once more Trafford was struck by the thought that there were only three real, fully rounded human beings in the office. Himself, Cassius and Sandra Dee. There must be others, of course; he knew that. Kahlua he imagined was real and there were one or two more whom he suspected of hiding elements of individuality, but he could not be sure. In Trafford's mind, evidence of humanity was the keeping of secrets and he had no knowledge of theirs.

It was then that he had a huge and exciting thought. He smiled, remembering how Barbieheart had suggested that the Love had a task waiting for him. All of a sudden Trafford knew what that task was.

26

'It's out of the question,' Cassius said angrily. 'We can't possibly expand our recruitment programme. It simply isn't our way.'

'You said it was the duty of every Humanist to be a missionary, to spread the knowledge.'

'It's also our duty not to get caught and risk handing the whole damn network to the Inquisition!'

'Network! It's not a *network*. It's a cosy little club! You've said yourself there's barely a few hundred of you in the whole damn country of faith. Do you want the children you saved as a Vaccinator to grow up in the same shitty world we did? And what about their children's children? And the children after that?'

'Trafford, we can't start a revolution.'

'Why not? Why can't we start a revolution? We *need* a revolution.'

The two men were facing each other in the anteroom of the Finchley library.

'No, Trafford, we need *evolution*! Sober thinkers, not impetuous hotheads. What's your hurry?' Cassius asked. 'When you called me you said it was urgent. Why did you have to drag me across the lake to ask me this now?'

'It *is* urgent,' Trafford pleaded. 'Every second counts. I had to wait thirty bloody years to find you. To find this library. That's almost half a lifetime wasted! Wasted in ignorance and, more to the point, in utter stupefying *boredom*. The boredom of living in a world where the only idea is faith and the only diversions are sex and gossip. You know very well that before I met you, the best I could manage to maintain some sense of individuality was keeping a few paltry secrets! How fucking pointless is that? Hoarding feelings like a rat hoards rubbish. Always looking inwards, when I could have been expanding my mind. The day I became a Humanist was the day I was born. Until then, my mind was *in utero*, an embryonic consciousness. If I deserved this chance,' Trafford exclaimed, 'so do millions of other people.'

'They may very well deserve their chance,' Cassius replied and despite his anger he could not help smiling at Trafford's passion. 'But we have rules, Trafford. Serious rules. Each new follower is required to wait at least a year before approaching a new prospect of their own—'

'A year!' Trafford blurted.

'. . . and even then only with the utmost patience and caution. If you share your secret with the wrong person you will be denounced and almost certainly tortured into denouncing the rest of us.'

' "Patience"! "Caution"!' Trafford echoed derisively. 'The way you're going it'll take a thousand years to spread the light.'

'Better that than have it snuffed out for ever.'

'You brought me in. How could you be sure I wouldn't denounce you then?'

'You had allowed me to vaccinate your baby, Trafford. You were entirely compromised and in no position to denounce anyone.'

'Is that the best you can do to spread the word? Wait until you find someone with a baby that they'll allow you to vaccinate?'

'Well, you say you have a better way. Let's hear it then.'

'It's bloody obvious. I can't believe I didn't think of it immediately. That's why it's urgent: too much time has been wasted already!'

'Yes but what *is* it? What is your better way?'

'By *finding the people who keep secrets,*' Trafford exclaimed, his eyes bright with excitement. 'That was how you found me. You guessed that I kept secrets.'

'We work together in the same office. I had the opportunity to observe you.'

'But don't you see? That's the point. We at DegSep have the opportunity to observe everybody! We have access to a profiling tool of incredible sophistication which should, if we ask it the right questions, be able to find *people like us.*'

Cassius's eyes narrowed with interest. 'Carry on,' he said.

'We need to study ourselves,' Trafford continued, 'and our fellow Humanists. We need to identify common movements, characteristics and choices. Are we the sort of people who do such a thing in a certain way, at certain times and in certain places? When we have built up some sort of pattern which we feel is common to us all, or at least indicates a commonality, then I can put it through DegSep and look for matches. All we have to do is profile who we are, then we can find out who is like us.'

Cassius considered this idea for a moment.

'It *is* ingenious, I'll admit that,' he said finally. 'Do you really think you could manipulate DegSep undetected?'

'Why not, if I follow your rules and do it boldly? My job is to come up with nonsense to ask the computer, and this would just be more nonsense. I wouldn't even try to hide it.'

'Very well then,' said Cassius, and despite his efforts to maintain a cool, objective air it was clear he was excited. 'I'll think about it and speak to some of the others. You may have hit on something here, Trafford.'

'Of course I've hit on something. But I'll only do it on one condition.'

Cassius's face hardened. 'If you are a loyal Humanist,' he said tersely, 'then you will make no conditions!'

'I am a loyal Humanist but I don't care. I want to bring in a girl. I know I'm supposed to wait a year but I want to bring her in now.'

Cassius looked at Trafford long and hard. 'Is it the one at work? Sandra Dee?'

Trafford tried to hide his surprise.

'What . . . what makes you think that?'

'I observe people. You know that, Trafford, and I hardly think you would stand up to our charming Princess Lovebud for just *any* girl. I'm right, aren't I?'

'Yes. She's the one I want to bring in.'

'What makes you think you can trust her?'

'Because she's like me, she keeps secrets.'

'If you discovered that, then she can't be very good at keeping them, can she?'

'No, that's not fair. I discovered them because I went looking . . . I Goog'ed her up.'

'Why did you Goog' her?'

'Because . . . she fascinated me. I found her attractive. But when I read her blog and looked at her videos I realized that they weren't hers at all. They were all downloads scavenged from other people's postings. She's actually much, much better at keeping secrets than me, than any of us. We're forced to cover up what we do and who we are but she's developed a method whereby she gives absolutely nothing of herself away, so in effect there's nothing to cover up.'

Cassius thought for a moment.

'All right,' he said, 'you may approach this girl.'

'Thank you.'

'Just a book or two to begin with,' Cassius added, 'and you must claim that you found them yourself, by chance, in a dump or a gutter. Give no hint about us or our libraries. If the girl responds favourably to what you give her then "find" another book and then another until such time as you are sure that her imagination is sufficiently stimulated for there to be no turning back. Then come to us and, if we agree, then and only then can you tell her of our movement and bring her to the library to choose books for herself. Do you understand?'

Trafford assured Cassius that he did.

'Do you promise to abide by these conditions?'

'Yes. Absolutely.'

'Good. I would advise you to choose very carefully which books you give her to start with. As you know from your own experience, to begin to read anything of any value is a great challenge. We are no longer educated for such concentration and so you must grasp your reader's attention instantly. Believe me, you will not get a second chance. Anyone who reads one of the old texts is taking an enormous risk and you must make sure that it is sufficiently absorbing for them to be unable to resist continuing with it once they have begun.'

'Thank you. I'll think about that.'

27

Trafford had expressed great confidence to Cassius that Sandra Dee would prove a willing convert to Humanism. But in fact he approached the next Fizzy Coff with considerable trepidation. After all, he had scarcely ever spoken to her before and now he intended to introduce himself by suggesting that she become a heretic. It was true that at the previous Fizzy Coff he had defended her over the doughnut fund confrontation but she had given no sign of gratitude or appreciation. She would also no doubt still be furious with him because her name had been cited at a Community Confession.

All day long Trafford searched for a moment in which to catch Sandra Dee's eye, a moment when he might initiate a conversation, but no such opportunity arose. He hoped to catch her at the lifts at the end of the day but she left early and he missed that chance too. In the end it was Sandra Dee who approached him. He was walking from the office to the tube station, pushing his way along the crowded street, when he heard a voice behind him.

'Am I supposed to thank you?' Sandra Dee said. 'Is that the idea?'

She spoke loudly in order to be heard above the noise of the thousands of personal communitainers that were thudding and banging all around them. Some people used earphones, some didn't, clearly believing that as many people as possible should be given the opportunity to appreciate their musical taste. That, combined with the mass leakage from the headsets, created a terrible din and even discreet private conversations had to be conducted at a yell.

'For standing up for me against Lovebud? New Temple favourite comes to the aid of office misfit? Is that it?' Sandra Dee continued. 'Because I can look after myself, you know.' She was beside him now but although he turned to her, she continued to face forward as if she was not talking to him at all but to herself.

'Yes, yes. I'm sure you can look after yourself,' he said apologetically, although he knew that her confidence was pure bravado. She could not look after herself. No one could, not if they got caught up in an office witch hunt, not once the pack had formed and chosen its prey. Those things took on a life of their own and once started they were virtually unstoppable. Whatever nonsense it was that had been concocted in order to incense them, the attackers came quickly to believe in their righteousness and would not stop until their victim lay broken at their feet.

'I just got sick of Princess bloody Lovebud. That's all,' Trafford went on. 'I would stick up for anyone to irritate her.'

'Why did your wife name me at the Confession?' Sandra Dee asked abruptly, finally bringing into the open the elephant that had squatted between them, unacknowledged, since the night that Trafford and Chantorria had begun their divorce proceedings.

'Because . . .' Trafford began, realizing that there was no answer that would cover the facts except the truth, 'like she said, I'd been Tubing you up and reading your blog. She caught me at it.'

'So what? Don't all men perv on the net? Isn't that what you're all supposed to do?'

'Yes but . . . well, I . . . I was only Tubing you. Nobody else.'

They were deep in the crowd now, shuffling towards the opening and closing station gates. One great mass of humanity, hot, sticky and angry. Half a fried chicken was being consumed noisily not ten inches to the left of Trafford's face: he could see it out of the corner of his eye, the gaudy red and white bucket held up with two hands while its owner buried his face in it and consumed the contents as he shuffled, like a horse with a nosebag.

Chicken to the left of him, a huge sweating red neck in front of him, a belly pressing on his spine behind him, but to his right Trafford thought he felt lovely coolness. He knew it could only be an illusion, for Sandra Dee was human and hence not immune to the stifling, oppressive, bug-laden heat that wrapped itself around every individual like a thick woolly blanket. She must sweat and burn like the rest of them and yet somehow he perceived a kind of freshness emanating from her. And whenever her arm touched his, which despite her best efforts it continually did as the crowd moved this way and that, her skin cooled him.

'You only perv on my vids?' he heard her say.

'Yes,' he admitted. 'But I stopped . . . after, after what my wife said at the Confession.'

'I know you stopped. I started tracking my hits and you weren't there. Why did you stop?'

'Well . . . you looked so angry.'

'Angry? Why would a girl be angry because a guy pervs her up? I'm made up of course, totally flattered big time,' she said, toeing the socially correct line but in a voice that dripped with angry sarcasm. 'So a man likes watching me have sex. What's not to like? Isn't that what the Temple expects of me? Isn't that what every girl wants? To be watched, all the time? To be lusted after and thought *hot*?'

'Because . . .'

Trafford hesitated. He knew the answer. She knew the answer. But did *she* know that *he* knew the answer? 'Because the girls having sex in your vid diary aren't you.'

238

There, he had done it. He had spoiled her secret, the last thing he had ever wanted to do.

'Ah,' she said, trying to sound calm and matter-of-fact, 'I was wondering if you'd worked it out. I supposed you must have done. The lie wasn't built to withstand intense scrutiny.'

Trafford said nothing. The man to the left, having finished his chicken, paused in his shuffling to create a gap between himself and the person crushed in front, then dropped the box with its filthy, rat-magnet contents on the ground.

'Are you a cop?' Sandra Dee asked.

'God, no!' Trafford exclaimed.

'A Temple spy?'

'As if.'

'Then why are you interested in a girl who prefers to break the law rather than risk uploading an honest blog?'

'I was . . . fascinated. You see, I too value . . . privacy.'

'Then why did you draw attention to yourself by defending me from Princess Lovebud? She's a bad enemy to make even if you are currently a favoured one.'

Trafford's reply was almost as unexpected to him as it must have been to Sandra Dee. 'Because . . . I think I might be falling in love with you.'

He really did not know he was going to say it. He had not, up until that moment, truly admitted the fact to himself. Certainly he knew that he was fascinated by her, even obsessed, but this was the first time he had voiced the word 'love' in his own mind. And now in that same moment he had acknowledged it to the very object of his passion. The strangeness of the situation made him dizzy.

'Don't be bloody stupid,' she replied. 'You don't know a single thing about me.'

'Yes. You've made sure of that. Nobody knows anything about you. I think that's the reason I'm ... attracted to you.'

This seemed to make her think and for a number of minutes they shuffled on without speaking. The great gates opened and closed ahead of them as they drew closer. There were stern announcements instructing people at the back to stop pushing.

'Shall we find somewhere better to talk?' she asked finally.

'That would be great,' he replied. 'Where?'

'Stick with me.'

There was no question of retreating from the tube crowd now; it would have taken an hour to fight their way back out of the queue. Therefore they descended together into the appalling, breath-denying crush of the station.

'We'll just go one stop,' Sandra Dee gasped as they struggled on to the platform.

When the train arrived, the crush was so great that he nearly lost her. As usual, the mass of people surged forward to battle for places, hindering those who were attempting to leave the train.

After a few minutes of breathing the treacle-thick fug of the carriage, the train arrived at the next station and battle commenced once more. They fought to get off the train against the human tide that was attempting to board and then struggled to ascend the litter-strewn, long since broken-down escalator until finally, mercifully, they reached the surface and spilled out into what for one glorious moment seemed like fresh air.

'Where are we going?' Trafford panted.

'Down to the lake,' Sandra Dee replied. 'I have a little boat.'

'Wow!' Trafford was surprised and impressed. 'Pretty cool. How did you manage that?'

In the semi-flooded city, ownership of a boat was a great luxury. This was a world in which twenty square feet of folding plasma screen could be bought for almost nothing but a rowing boat was a rich person's plaything.

'There are ways and means,' Sandra Dee replied mysteriously.

Together they walked down to the shore at Notting Hill, where many thousands of private pleasure boats were kept moored to the tops of rusting lamp posts in a vast marina which had once been the Borough of Hammersmith.

'How do you afford to pay mooring fees, let alone own a boat?' Trafford asked as they made their way out along a floating jetty that threaded its way among the long lines of chimney pots.

'I have no children to support,' she said, 'no leeching lover. My money's my own. Besides, it's only a little skiff.'

Trafford did not enquire further although he knew there must be more to it. Whatever Sandra Dee's circumstances, paying for a mooring on a NatDat Senior Executive

Analyst's salary would not be easy. Perhaps, he thought, she had inherited money.

'Here it is,' Sandra Dee said.

They had arrived at one of many near-identical little aluminium-shelled open boats with a single short mast. They climbed aboard and within moments Sandra Dee had cast off and was navigating her way expertly among the derelict rooftops of Maida Vale.

'If I could spend the rest of my life on this boat I would,' said Sandra Dee. 'I hate people. Well, I hate most of them anyway. And I hate all of them when they're in a crowd.'

Trafford did not say anything for a little while. He felt suddenly so happy that he did not want the moment to end and he worried that if he said something it might be the wrong thing and so cause this unique woman to return the boat to its mooring and order him out of her little paradise.

'It's lovely,' he said eventually.

And it was. Perhaps, Trafford thought, as lovely as or lovelier than anything he had previously experienced. To be alone in such company, to be *away from the crowd*. Looking about him, he realized that the nearest boat was more than twenty metres away. He wondered if he had ever in his whole life been as much as twenty metres from another human being. It felt wonderful to be so alone. Except he wasn't alone, of course: Sandra Dee was with him, sharing the isolation, and that was wonderful too. She looked so beautiful and strong;

the warm breeze which gently filled the sail as she adjusted it filled also her dress, revealing her lovely legs to the thigh.

'So,' Sandra Dee said finally, 'how did you discover my secret?'

'By chance really,' Trafford replied. 'That day in the office when Princess Lovebud denounced you for not having breast implants – I Tubed you up that night and saw almost immediately that nothing you posted was real.'

'Why did you Tube me?'

'Because I found you compelling. And I felt . . . connected. I believed from just looking at you that you kept a part of yourself private in defiance of the Temple orthodoxy. It turned out I was right, although I had no idea of the lengths to which you went.'

'Privacy is illegal.'

'Of course.'

'You discovered me committing a crime.'

'Yes.'

'And you kept on looking at my crime until your wife got angry and then she went to Confession and drew my blog to the attention of the entire community, any one of whom might have decided to check it out.'

'I know. I put you in danger, I'm sorry.'

From beneath a reel of rope Sandra Dee suddenly produced a boat knife. It was a vicious-looking tool, the blade well polished and flashing wickedly in the sunlight.

'I could kill you now,' she said. 'Just thrust myself

forward, plunge the knife into you and it would be done. No one would notice, no one would care. One more corpse floating on the lake and all my secrets would be safe.'

'Your secrets are safe,' Trafford assured her with alarm. 'All I know is that you *keep* secrets. Everything else is a mystery.'

'So what? The Inquisition doesn't care what your secrets are, it only cares that you keep them,' she said, still fingering her knife, testing its edge with her thumb. '*Keeping* secrets is the crime. *Privacy* is the crime. I've been lucky, your stupid curiosity has done me no harm, but who knows? One day you might betray me.'

'I won't.'

'Why should I risk it?'

'I would never ever betray you. I'm in love with you. I'm in love with your secrets. I would rather die than betray you for keeping them.'

'Why are you in love with my secrets? What interest can they possibly have for you?'

She still played with the knife but she smiled too and something in that smile emboldened Trafford. Something in the way she crossed and recrossed her legs as she looked at him, something, even, in the way she held the knife gave him the confidence to reveal his own secret, silent passion.

'Because I've discovered through you that there is nothing more exciting than mystery. Nothing more erotic. Your body is a mystery to me. Your sexual soul is completely hidden and that's why I want it. I want nothing else. I'm breathless with desire for it.'

For a moment she seemed less confident, less in control. She even reddened a little; he could see it even beneath the sun block. Then slowly a wry smile spread across her lips. She put down her knife and leaned back in the boat, stretching, seeming to enjoy the heat of the sun as it shone upon the bare skin of her arms and legs.

'That's a very attractive observation, Trafford. "Hidden sexual soul"? "Breathless with desire"? A girl might get quite dizzy with it all.'

Trafford said nothing, preferring instead to drink in the sight of her. Languid and easy, lovely and lazy as she reclined in the sun. Her legs stretched out, the breeze folding her dress around her body, revealing its slim, toned shape.

'Do you want me now?' she asked, almost matter-of-factly. 'Do you want me to reveal my secrets?'

Trafford could only gulp, his throat suddenly dry.

'Would you like me to take off my dress, like a girl's supposed to do?' she continued, a bare foot creeping across the floor of the boat towards him. 'Do you want me to tell you how I like to "do it"? What turns me on, tunes my motor and melts my ice cream?'

'More than anything I have ever wanted,' he answered, but then added, 'except no.'

'No?'

'No, I don't want you to.'

'Why?'

'Because if you did, the anticipation would be over, the secret would be out, the mystery revealed and I couldn't bear it. I've discovered, through you, the thrill of denial. Ours is such a dull world, with everything revealed, everything "shared" and "proudly" on display. I know now that nothing is more erotic than almost knowing. Nothing can equal the agonizing intensity of *wanting* to see you naked, the pain, the *need* . . . I have never felt more alive than I do now and I want this moment to last for ever.'

'Are you imagining me naked now?'

'Yes, of course, and I'm imagining being naked with you.'

Sandra Dee smiled and for once her air of cool detachment seemed to desert her.

'What's it like?' she asked.

'It's perfect. Nothing could be more beautiful. Imagine that! Perfection. Beauty. When did you last experience either in this miserable world? And yet I can *imagine* them any time I like! It's incredible. To be transported by mere thought! By a *fiction* of the mind's eye! I never dreamed of such exhilaration.'

'Come on, Trafford,' she replied and to his surprise he saw that she was blushing. 'I *said* what's it *like?*'

'What's it like?'

Her cheeks were definitely red now and for a moment she looked away, seemingly afraid to meet his eye.

'I want to know what you're actually thinking,' she said quietly, almost in a whisper. 'I want you to tell me now.'

'You're sitting up,' Trafford replied, and to his surprise the words came easily. 'I've already undone the top buttons of your dress, kissed it from your shoulders and now it's falling down past your breasts. You look at me and you smile, then your mouth drops open a little and I can see your white teeth.'

'Really?' said Sandra Dee, her mouth dropping open just as Trafford had described. 'What happens next?'

'Together we undo the rest of the buttons.'

'Together?' she asked with a giggle. 'How do we manage that?'

She was looking directly at him once more but there was a softness in her gaze that Trafford had never seen before.

'You undo the first two or three,' he said, 'then you guide my hands into your lap and allow me to unbutton the rest.'

'And then?'

'Then I open your dress out completely and it slips from your arms and falls about you on the bench like the petals of a flower. You're sitting on it, your pale skin shining bright in the sun. Your underwear is quite plain – you chose it for your own comfort, not to fit some net-inspired pornographic template.'

'I see, so I'm a sensible girl, am I? That's nice. I like that.'

'You are your own woman. You dress to please yourself, not men.'

'Flatterer,' she said. 'I bet you say that to all the girls. All right, so here I am, sitting on the bench in my plain and simple bra and knickers. What happens now?'

'I put my hand on your belly, just above the waistband

of your panties. Your navel is beneath the palm of my hand. I feel you breathe. You lean towards me and as you do so I can see the fall of your breasts inside your bra, I can see the separation between them, and you reach out and pull my shirt up over my head.'

Sandra Dee shifted on her cushion and leaned forward a little, her hands between her legs.

'How do you look?' she asked.

'Well, how do you think I look?' Trafford replied.

'You look . . . very nice,' said Sandra Dee. 'What now?'

'I place my hands behind your back, I gently run my fingers up your spine to find your bra strap, effortlessly I unhook it and it falls away. Your breasts are revealed, firm and *real*, the nipples pale pink against the white skin, like half-ripened strawberries in cream. You lean back, your dress spread out around you, and you hook your thumbs into the top of your knickers. Your legs are very slightly apart. I can see a wisp of sandy hair protruding either side of the thin cotton gusset.'

Sandra Dee reddened once more. She covered her embarrassment with a laugh.

'An unkempt bikini line? That's not very proper, is it?'

'Your legs come up and you glide the panties down over them. Another secret revealed! Your bush is full and natural, no stupid shaven bristle or brutal reddened waxing, just the soft natural hair of a woman . . .'

Sandra Dee's mouth opened to speak but Trafford stopped her.

'Don't tell me if I'm right or wrong! I don't want to

know. Besides which, I *am* right because the Sandra Dee I'm describing is mine, the creation of my imagination.'

'I like her,' she said quietly.

'I'm on my knees before you, kneeling between your legs, staring. Staring at every detail of you. I raise my head to look into your eyes and you stare back. You stare at me almost ferociously, hardly even blinking, and then you smile, a sweet, sweet smile. Once more you lean forward; I see your breasts swing out from your body, hanging, perfectly formed and separate. I see the tiny creases in your stomach as you lean towards me; your navel half disappears into one of them; you reach out and undo my shorts, I stand up as you pull them down, I step out of them, and now you take hold of me and—'

'Stop!' she said and her voice was shaking.

'Stop?'

'Yes. Let's not do it today.' She looked at him intensely and briefly it seemed to Trafford as if there was sadness it her clear grey eyes. But then she laughed and added, 'After all, a girl doesn't want to imagine going all the way on her first date.'

Trafford laughed too. It had been a funny thing to say. That phrase about going all the way on a first date hailed from a distant past. People only used it ironically these days. These days everybody went all the way on every date. Why not? If a thing was desirable surely it was desirable to have it as soon and as often as possible. Trafford loved the idea that once more they were defying convention. Even in this imagined consummation they would not follow the crowd. Besides, he thought hopefully, if she was speaking of 'first dates' then perhaps there was to be a second.

'You mean . . .' he asked hesitatingly, 'that we can meet again?'

'Yes,' she said. 'I'd like that, it's been fun and I don't often have fun. You were right. It *is* exciting to . . . imagine.'

They sat together as the boat drifted. Sandra Dee had bought some beer from the marina shop and although it had long since lost its chill they drank it gratefully and listened to the water lapping against the boat and watched the sun setting behind the chimneys.

'Won't that wife you're supposed to be divorcing be wondering where you are?' Sandra Dee enquired. 'Shouldn't you call her?'

'I'm often out. She doesn't mind. She has plenty to fill her time these days, now that she's a queen bee in our tenement. Women come round just to hold our baby in the hope that the luck of the Love will rub off.'

'That must be nice for her.'

'She loves it. I think it's pathetic. They're such superstitious fools.'

Sandra Dee looked about nervously; this was reckless talk, even between two people who had confessed to a mutual love of privacy.

'Be careful, Trafford,' she said. 'You shouldn't talk like that.'

'I don't care. I mean it. They're stupid, superstitious fools.'

'You don't believe that your child was protected by divine intervention?'

'There are millions and millions of babies on Earth. Abroad, in the Other World, more die even than in the countries of faith. How could any God consider the fate of single individuals? And why would he bother? Kill most but save that one, for a *purpose*? It defies logic.'

'So how do you explain her surviving a measles plague?'

Trafford thought about the question before answering.

'I don't want to tell you,' he said finally.

'Another secret?'

'Yes.'

'I see,' she said, then added without missing a beat, 'so you had her vaccinated.'

Trafford was taken aback. Now it was his turn to look around nervously.

'I . . . I don't want to incriminate you by discussing such things,' he said quickly.

'Don't worry,' she said, 'your secret's safe with me.'

Once more there was silence between them, but now it was the silence that exists between friends. Sharing such dangerous confidences had created a bond.

'Tell me another,' Sandra Dee said finally.

'Another secret?'

'Yes, an exciting one.'

Trafford realized that he would never get a better opportunity than this.

'All right, I will.'

'Is it a good one?'

'It's a very good one.'

Sandra Dee waited while Trafford considered how best

to say what it was that he wanted to say, what he had been waiting to say ever since he had walked into the office to find her being bullied by Princess Lovebud.

'I hold the key to a door,' he said slowly, 'a door to another world. Another universe. In fact to a thousand universes.'

'Wow,' she said. 'Big secret.'

'I can step through that door and leave this terrible, terrible town we live in any time I like. In a single moment I can make Princess Lovebud disappear; I can make my chat room moderator disappear; I can make all the crowds of sweating, eating, belching bullies disappear. I can block out the infotainment loops, I can tune out the bullshit celebrities and the reality cop shows and the naked bodies fucking on every screen on every wall. I can forget the bombs and the wars that keep the peace and the Temple and all its stupid, illogical Wembley Laws. I can escape from it all. That's my secret. That's what I can do, Sandra Dee. I can make them all *disappear*.'

'Tell me how,' she replied eagerly. 'I want to know.'

'Well,' said Trafford, 'you said a minute ago that it was exciting to imagine.'

'Yes?'

'That's the key. The key to escaping this man-made thing that we call "reality" is through the mind, through reason and *imagination*. I have discovered . . . books.'

'Books?' Sandra Dee could not conceal her disappointment. 'Books are shit.'

'Wrong books,' Trafford replied.

Then he reached into a plastic bag and brought out what appeared to be a copy of *Feng Foodie*, a popular pamphlet which claimed that inner health and spirituality could be achieved by the proper alignment of one's food prior to eating it. Be it in the carton or on the plate, the way your fries interacted spatially with your burger could help or hinder your spiritual growth.

'You are joking, I presume,' Sandra Dee said, looking at the book with contempt.

Then Trafford removed the book's cover and inside was a battered paperback copy of *Wuthering Heights*.

'This,' he said, 'is a wonderful story written many years ago. I chose it for you, to read if you want. While you are reading it, the world we live in will go away. Instead you'll find yourself in the one described in the book: a world of genuine passion, eternal love, complex emotions and *space*, so much space. You will walk on windswept moors, the cold rain driving in your face. A soul adrift. A soul *alone*. Lost on the moorlands of secret, doomed love.'

Sandra Dee took the book from Trafford.

'If I was caught with this, the least I could hope for would be to be put in the stocks. They'd beat my feet.'

'It's worth the risk, believe me.'

'Where did you get it?'

'I . . . found it. I can find more if you like it. Would you like to borrow it?'

'Yes, I'd love to.'

The sun had nearly gone and with it the breeze. Sandra

Dee took down the sail and between them they rowed back to her mooring.

'I've had a wonderful time, Trafford,' she said as they took their leave of each other. 'I can't remember when I last spoke with someone the way we spoke today.'

'No, nor me,' said Trafford.

'And of course,' Sandra Dee added, giving him a kiss on the cheek, 'the sex was great.'

28

Trafford and Cassius walked up Hampstead Hill towards Jack Straw's Castle. Trafford had never visited this particular island of the London archipelago before; it was a place where rich men lived, Temple elders, civil administrators and prominent businessmen, a gated sanctuary protected by armed guards.

'We're visiting the house of Connor Newbury,' Cassius informed Trafford as they turned into a street of semi-detached houses each with its own private garden, which indicated occupants of enormous wealth. Trafford knew all about Connor Newbury: a popular TV and web chat-show host with a slightly foppish air, he was known for being boldly irreverent towards Temple elders, although in truth this never amounted to anything more than teasing them over their choice of jewellery and the breadth of their stomachs.

'He's one of us, you know,' Cassius explained as they approached the house.

Once inside, they were shown into a large sitting room. The room was unique in Trafford's experience in that, instead of being hung with plasma screens, it had static pictures on the walls which appeared to have been executed with nothing more than paint. The carpet was thick and luxurious and the furniture looked very old: deep leather armchairs, a huge, cushion-covered couch and elegant little coffee tables. Two of the armchairs were occupied. Connor Newbury himself was instantly recognizable in a characteristically flamboyant crimson man bra and silver hot pants. He was cooling his backside before a cheerfully roaring air conditioner and smoking an enormous cigar.

'Aha,' the famous personality boomed. 'Hail, Cassius, and hail, our new computer whiz. I'm Newbury but you know that of course, don't you, Trafford! These two are Professor Blossom Taylor' – a pleasant-looking elderly woman in a voluminous kaftan nodded absent-mindedly towards Trafford, 'and Billy Macallan.'

'All right, geezer,' said Macallan, a big shaven-headed man with hairy tattooed arms who looked more like an all-in wrestler than a literary type.

'We four make up the Humanist Senate,' Newbury continued, 'and I'm Chair because I've got the nicest house to meet in!'

Trafford shook hands with Taylor and Macallan. He didn't approach Newbury, who merely gave him a patronizing wave.

'Right,' Newbury continued, 'let us proceed to kick some intellectual butt! Cassius here tells us you don't think we humble revolutionaries are thinking big enough.'

Trafford was then given a drink and invited to explain once more the idea on which he had been working since he had first revealed it in embryonic form to Cassius.

'You may know that I am a systems programmer for DegSep, a division of the National Data Bank,' Trafford began.

'For which my sympathy,' said Newbury. 'What a *drag*.'

'DegSep stands for Degrees of Separation,' Trafford continued, ignoring the interruption. 'Our job is to route the connections between people, to record everything which is common between them in every possible way and from every possible angle. The program is massive beyond imagination, the proverbial grains of wheat doubling on every square of the chessboard, except that our chessboard is the size of a soccer pitch. We take each single characterizing item, from hair colour and choice of breakfast cereal to the number of times a person rides on a bus or a tube train, and then cross-reference each one against all other information stored.'

'And that's what our taxes pay for,' Connor Newbury interjected, unable to resist playing the role he performed each night on TV. 'Go figure, people.'

'My suggestion to Cassius,' Trafford went on, 'is that we Humanists pinpoint a series of characteristics which we share and which, when fed into the DegSep computer,

257

will start to lead us towards similar types of people. Once we've found them we can reach out to them.'

'By which you mean?' Professor Taylor enquired.

'We create a secure viral email which will first intrigue our targets, then begin to educate them and eventually organize them.'

'Biggish job, mate,' Billy Macallan observed.

'The Temple is a biggish enemy,' Trafford replied.

'Good point! Well said,' Newbury agreed. 'OK. Let's start with these personal coordinates. As it happens I think I'm unique ... Completely different to you, Trafford, obviously, but also to everybody in this room. What do you think I might have in common with the rest of you?'

'Well,' Trafford replied, 'as Cassius here may have told you, I think the key is secrets. My view is that anyone who has identified in themselves a desire for privacy is likely to prove a fertile prospect for conversion to Humanism.'

'That sounds reasonable,' Professor Taylor interjected.

'I don't think so,' Newbury replied. 'We're not all introverted little mice like you, Blossom! I'm a public figure and I love it. I'm a natural extrovert and showing off is how I get through my day.'

'But I notice that you have no plasmas in this room,' said Trafford.

'Well, yes, that's true,' Newbury replied. 'But I'm a celebrity, it's harder for us. Everybody looks at me all the time. I've got to turn off sometimes, haven't I?'

'With respect,' Trafford argued, 'I think a lot of people feel that way. Everybody looks at everybody all the time and you don't need to be a celebrity to feel the need for privacy. I myself was recently in big trouble with my Confessor for being slow to post a birthing video. I'm not talking about being either an extrovert or an introvert: I'm talking about people who don't believe privacy is a perversion, people who think it might even be a virtue.'

'All right then,' Newbury said, 'if we accept that idea, how do you propose to find these people?'

'I would imagine that our guest was coming to that, Connor,' Cassius interjected somewhat irritably.

'It seems to me,' Trafford hurried on, 'that one of the things we should be looking for is people who don't stream their lives 24/7. I need to write a search program that looks for people who try to establish gaps in their lives, periods when they are not being watched. Then, taking the flip side of that coin, our program should also be considering the amount of time people spend *watching other people*. We should look for those who scan the socially acceptable minimum of their neighbours' webcasts.'

'Why?' Newbury asked.

'Because I'm guessing that showing an interest in something other than voyeurism and gossip would indicate a potentially fertile mind.'

'That makes sense,' said Billy Macallan.

'Showing an interest in what?' Newbury asked.

'Anything,' said Trafford. 'Growing a pot plant. Trying to bake your own cakes. Building models out of matches and bottle tops . . .'

'Gardening? Baking?' Connor Newbury laughed. *'Building models? Sounds fucking awful to me.'*

'I build models,' Macallan said firmly.

Cassius was getting angry.

'I don't think it's fair to ask Trafford to produce a fail-safe template here, Connor,' he said. 'Every rule is inevitably going to throw up a thousand exceptions. What Trafford is trying to do is establish characteristics which, while innocent enough not to bring a person to the attention of the Temple, might identify in them an inner sense of self. And speaking of which, personally I think a reluctance to join Group Hugs would be a good indicator.'

Everybody, including Newbury, nodded at this.

'That's right,' said Trafford. 'I hate Gr'ugs too and when I can, I get out of them. Now most offices have a communal message board and usually the moderator's daily blog records the Gr'ugs, including, if my own office moderator is anything to go by, the absences. It should be possible to scan those blogs for names of people who are frequently absent.'

'Wow,' said Newbury, clearly impressed. 'I think it's lucky you don't work for the Inquisition.'

'Another thing I think we should be looking at is spiritual fervour.' Trafford was warming to his theme. 'For instance, it seems to me pretty obvious that the more evidence of blind faith a person publicly exudes, the less likely they are to want to question the Temple status quo. So if we bundle up a number of faith and superstition words like "tarot", "star chart", "psychic" and "reincarnation", we can then identify people who habitually include those words in their blogs and webcasts and then veto them from our search profile.'

'That'll get rid of most of my viewers,' said Newbury.

'Serial confessors should go too,' Professor Taylor suggested. 'Those awful people who never shut up at testification. And this might seem a small point, but I think perhaps frequent use of the words "please" and "thank you" might indicate a revolutionary spirit.'

'Sounds to me, Taylor,' Newbury argued, 'that we're in danger of advertising for bores.'

'I do not find manners boring,' the professor sniffed back.

'If I might recap on Trafford's behalf,' Cassius said firmly, 'he is to construct a search program which locates individuals who seek privacy, avoid tittle-tattle, pursue special interests, approach Group Hugs with distaste, evidence low-level use of faith words, testify minimally and mind their manners.'

'OK,' said Newbury, 'it's a start. And once our young friend has produced his list of people who fit this slightly depressing profile, what then?'

'We contact them, of course,' said Trafford, 'let them know that they are not alone. We begin to build a secret community. A network of people who want to *think for themselves*.'

'What do we say to them? No point just emailing to say, "Hi, we hate the Temple too."'

'The first thing we should do,' said Cassius, 'is send them a succinct summation of the theory of evolution.

Evolution is the key; it is the idea that the Temple fears most.'

'Exactly,' Taylor said. 'Isn't that the problem? If we start chucking evolutionary propaganda on to the net willy-nilly, we'll get picked up by an Inquisition search engine in no time.'

'We won't *be* "chucking it out",' Trafford explained. 'We'll be sending secure emails to specific addresses and I shall set up a secure address from which to send them. None of us will be traceable even if the messages are uncovered. But I don't think they will be uncovered. After all, nobody's looking for us. The police monitor the web for seditious sites and chat rooms but they don't read emails unless they have a person under surveillance. As we all know, most emails are spam anyway.'

'And that's another thing,' said Billy Macallan. 'How do you expect to get this lot we're after to open these unsolicited emails, let alone read them? I personally junk 95 per cent of all the crap I get.'

'I've been thinking about that a lot,' Trafford replied. 'It's all in the title box, isn't it? We need a line that will grab them, something to draw them in. How about: *Can you keep a secret?'*

29

About two months after the measles-plus epidemic had devastated the Inspiration Towers estate, a second plague struck. The local authorities had been expecting it, of course: the circumstances that favoured the incubation of one virus tended to favour many. Heat, damp, problems with waste disposal and water pumping, all these things contributed to the likelihood of a second dose of 'divine retribution'. Mumps-plus followed on the tail of the measles, borne once more on coughs and sneezes, and again the strain that took root among the children was of a previously unheard-of severity. Even within living memory mumps had been entirely survivable, a childhood rite of passage, unpleasant but not too serious. But with each fresh attack the virus had mutated until it had become deadly. Suddenly the fevers were back, along with the headaches, sore throats and telltale swelling of the parotid gland, and once more the little white coffins began emerging from the buildings of Trafford and Chantorria's little community. Most of the babies had been lost in the measles epidemic, so this time it was the turn of the toddlers and youngsters.

But yet again, as one by one they died Caitlin Happymeal seemed only to gather strength. She did not cough or run a fever and her glands did not swell. It therefore seemed more certain than ever that the miracle of the Love was upon the child, and so Chantorria basked in the undisputed position of one who was truly blessed.

Mothers would bring their sick children to Trafford and Chantorria's apartment in the hope that if he or she played with Caitlin Happymeal somehow their child might be saved too. Trafford had at first been surprised that Chantorria allowed these desperate, pathetic playmates into her home; after all, it was one thing to survive a plague and quite another to tempt fate so boldly by courting infection. He had been pleased and impressed by Chantorria's attitude, taking it as evidence that she had come to view the vaccination as a scientific fact, a process which could be relied upon. He was therefore most disappointed to discover that the opposite was the case. Chantorria had begun to distance herself from the steely truth of the vaccination. So devastating had been the plagues and so extraordinary did Caitlin Happymeal's survival seem that Chantorria simply could not bring herself to accept that such a miraculous thing could be the result of a mere pinprick. It was just too big a miracle to have been produced by the mind of man. Seduced by the jealous admiration that now surrounded her, dizzy with the attentions of Confessor Bailey and, above all, humbled with gratitude for the survival of her child, Chantorria was fast coming to believe that it had all been the work of the Lord and the Love.

Trafford was horrified and disgusted. The success of the vaccination had perversely driven Chantorria into the arms of the faithful.

'Our baby has survived because of a scientific process,' he exclaimed angrily on one of the few occasions when he was able to persuade his wife to mute the broadcast sound on their apartment webcast. 'The result of the intellectual activity of man. There's no mystery, no miracle, just cold hard facts.'

'No,' Chantorria insisted, 'I don't believe it. Have you seen what has happened to the children? The pain, the rashes, the fever, the swelling? They're all *dying*, Trafford. How could one little needle prick defend our child from that? Only the Lord and the Love could deliver her, just like Confessor Bailey says.'

'Confessor Bailey does not know that Caitlin has been vaccinated! You do! What's more, and speaking of little pricks, it seems to me that Confessor Bailey is rather more interested in you than he is in Caitlin Happymeal.'

'Oh, don't be ridiculous, Trafford!' Chantorria said, red with embarrassment. '*As if*. As if an important man like the Confessor would show an interest in *me*!'

But in fact there could be no doubt that Confessor

Bailey was taking an interest in Chantorria, although his attentions were always couched in references to the miracle of Caitlin Happymeal. Each week at Confession, as more and more mothers gave vent to their grief, the Confessor would summon Chantorria and Caitlin on to the stage. Ignoring Trafford, he would kiss Chantorria and hold up Caitlin Happymeal as evidence of the Love's deeper plan.

'He leaves us this one child,' the Confessor thundered, 'to show us that there is hope! He has not forsaken us. He has not washed his holy hands of his children, as we deserve that he should. He's still there for us! Caitlin Happymeal is here today to show us that the love that the Creator holds for all his children still lives! Just as all the children live! They still live! They live in Heaven and they live here in this child!'

The congregation would moan and wail and throw out their arms in worship, and as Chantorria took Caitlin back to her seat mothers would reach out to touch them.

Within her small community, as the second epidemic ran its course Chantorria came more and more to be seen as a living icon, even a saint. Stories began to circulate of minor miracles that could be attributed to her. Everyone outdid each other to speak of Chantorria's goodness and the goodness that flowed from it, anxious to show that they too stood in the reflected glory of the Love.

'It's like there's an aura,' Tinkerbell told people breathlessly, 'a sort of glow. Like a really spiritual vibe, you know what I'm saying? I'm not being funny, right? I had a terrible headache and I went and had a cup of tea with Chantorria, not because she's a saint or nothing, but because she's a mate . . . and my headache just went! It's true. She cured it! Honest, just by sitting there! I'm not being funny nor nothing, but she cured my headache.'

Stories abounded of similar extraordinary events. Food tasted better when eaten in Chantorria's presence, wounds healed faster, skin seemed smoother, softer and less prone to wrinkling. Breasts got bigger.

'I swear I was a C cup and now I'm a double D! Go figure. That is *weird*!'

The whole community beat a path to Trafford and Chantorria's door to witness the miracle child and be in the presence of her holy mother. Confessor Bailey himself took to calling regularly and often laid his hands on Chantorria's breasts in order to feel the Love.

Trafford stood apart, happy to be ignored. He was sad that his wife had allowed vanity to turn her head so ridiculously but delighted to be so comprehensively out of her loop. Chantorria did not need him any more. More than that; she actually did not want him around. She wanted to stay married, of course, because they were the chosen couple, but she was more than happy for Trafford to make himself scarce and for her to bask in the light of the Love alone. She had so many friends now and Confessor Bailey was being so attentive. Besides, Trafford's presence seemed to irritate her. He suspected it was because he was a constant reminder of the dirty secret about which she was now in total denial.

Trafford therefore had plenty of time to himself, which was fortunate because he had a very great deal to do. The more he thought about the plan he had presented to Cassius and the Senate, the more exciting it seemed to become. And the government would actually be *paying* him to do the work! That was the thrilling, subversive beauty of the idea. In its first stage it involved doing nothing more than Trafford did every day for DegSep anyway: making connections, constructing perfectly legitimate DegSep search programs exactly as he had been doing for years. The only difference was that, whereas before his activities had been soul-crushingly pointless, now they meant everything. He was a soldier doing battle against the Temple, a revolutionary seeking to foment a spiritual uprising.

Each day, therefore, leaving Chantorria with her friends and her alcopops, cake and chocolate, Trafford took his computer out into the stairwell of the building and logged on to work.

Propensity to doodle, he entered into his machine and was surprised to discover that doodling had so far not been considered at DegSep at all. A Temple banner appeared on his screen followed by a hologram of a fist punching the air in triumph. This was the computer's way of letting Trafford know that he had come up with an original search idea and that he would be receiving a cash bonus in his pay packet and a bottle of fizzy wine.

Trafford knew that the massive mainframe at NatDat would already be whirring. First of all, it would attempt to compute a series of visual triggers to fit its dictionary definition of doodling. It would consult the police body-language program on which psychologists worked, trying to formalize the visual characteristics that evidenced a propensity for anti-social behaviour. Then, having constructed a profile to search the trillions and trillions of hours of webcam and CCTV footage of the entire population, it would look for images of people scribbling with a distracted air.

Words not pictures, patterns or shapes, Trafford typed into his laptop and then added, *Whole sentences.*

Then Trafford thought of Chantorria and her little kitchen palmtop on which she had, in the days before her religious awakening, written rhyming verses. *Word processing without uploading*, he wrote, and then, *Pressing 'save' but not 'send'.*

Again he was rewarded with a flag and an air-punching fist. No one had ever thought to ask DegSep to look for people who wrote things down but did not then post what they had written on the net. That was two bonuses and two bottles of fizzy wine. Trafford's mind wandered for a moment as he imagined sharing the wine with Sandra Dee on their next outing together.

Since he had started to lend her books, Trafford had begun to see Sandra Dee quite regularly. She had turned out to have every bit as enquiring a mind as he had expected and every few days, when they could arrange it, they would go together to the Notting Hill marina and drift away in her little boat. There they would discuss history and physics, geography and astronomy, journeying billions of light years away from the dirty water of Lake London to the very edge of time.

On one occasion they went to the great Museum of Creation, where the fossils were kept that proved the reality of the first flood. Sandra Dee loved fossils. They would dutifully read the information displays which explained how these ancient images of fish, set in stone, had been discovered by early archaeologists at the tops of mountains, thus proving that the waters on which Noah sailed had once covered the Earth. Trafford and Sandra Dee smiled together as they read, sharing the secret knowledge that in fact those mountains on which the fossils were found had once been at the bottom of the sea. Of course it did not take Sandra Dee long to see through the lie that Trafford was 'finding' the books that he lent her and demand to know how he came by them.

'I finished these two days ago,' she complained, handing back *Jane Eyre* and *Sons and Lovers*, 'and I've had nothing to read since. Why do I always have to meet you to get my stories?'

'Don't you like meeting me?'

'Of course I do, you know that,' she said, adding with a laugh, 'I don't imagine sex with every lad I meet, you know.'

Sandra Dee had indeed seemed happy for them to continue to explore their fantasy world together and they talked about sex as much as they discussed the books they had read. She always appeared to enjoy Trafford's erotic flights of the imagination and even occasionally contributed something of her own. Nonetheless, Trafford sensed that his was the greater commitment and suspected her of humouring him.

Inevitably the excitement of mystery, about which Trafford had at first waxed so lyrical, had begun to wear thin for him. Despite everything he had said, he was tiring of sexual fantasy and more and more craved the reality of Sandra Dee's body. Unfortunately for him, though, whenever he hinted that perhaps they should move their sexual relationship beyond the realm of the imagination, Sandra Dee declined.

'Don't spoil it,' she said. 'It was such a lovely idea. No man ever asked me to imagine sex with him before.'

'Couldn't we imagine it sometimes and actualize it other times?'

'"Actualize" doesn't sound half as nice a word as "imagine",' she replied. 'Besides, I'm expanding my mind. I don't need physical complications.'

'So I'm just a source of books to you then?' he said, sulkily.

'Of course not. You know very well how much I like you and how much I love our talks. Things are good between us the way they are, and things change between people once they start having sex.'

'They wouldn't with us.'

'Trafford,' she said, wagging a finger, 'things *always* change. Amazing, all that reading and it seems you don't know anything about people at all.'

'I know enough to worry that if I tell you where I get the books from you won't want to see me any more.'

'That's a risk you'll have to take because I want to know and I insist that you tell me.'

Trafford knew that he would have to give in. Fuck Cassius. And fuck his precious friends. They didn't own the books; knowledge was universal. He was in love with Sandra Dee and he wasn't going to lie to her any longer.

'It began when I had Caitlin Happymeal vaccinated,' he said, and then he told her how he had become a Humanist.

'My God,' Sandra Dee exclaimed, 'they have an actual *library*!'

'Well, it's an atmospherically controlled room full of books.'

'Which I *think* constitutes a library. I can hardly believe these people are so organized.'

'On a small scale they are. I don't think there are very many of them.'

'You actually take classes in subversion?'

'Well, tutorials really. Discussions round a table. And not in subversion, in reason.'

'Which is about as subversive as you can get in a country where faith lies at the heart of the constitution.'

'In that case I do take classes in subversion, I suppose,' Trafford admitted.

'I want to come,' Sandra Dee said decisively.

'You can. You will.'

'No, you don't understand. I want to come now.'

'It's not possible. There are rules. I'm not even supposed to have told you that we exist. I'm supposed to keep claiming I find these books in attics and cellars or whatever. Introducing someone takes time. They have to make checks, establish fail-safes. They need to know that a new person can be trusted.'

'I can be trusted.'

'I know that. Of course I know that.'

'Then speak to them. Insist.'

'I already did that just to get you the books.'

'Well, do it again. I'm twenty-eight already and I've never been to school. Not a school where they teach anything worth learning. They *have* to let me in. I want to sit around the table in that library. I want to choose a book for myself.'

'You just have to wait a while, that's all.'

'I don't *want* to wait. I want to learn. I only have the rest of my life left and I need to make a start.'

Still Trafford hesitated, avoiding her stare.

'Supposing I slept with you?' Sandra Dee asked.

It was everything that Trafford wanted and she knew it.

'No,' he replied, after a very long pause. 'I love you. I couldn't blackmail you into trading sex for knowledge.'

'I'm glad you said that, Trafford, because I wouldn't have done it anyway,' she replied. 'I've spent a lifetime avoiding being pressurized into having sex and I certainly don't intend to change my habits now. If you won't introduce me to your friends I'll follow you till I find out where your library is and barge straight in.'

'They'd kill you. They may be Humanists but they are also a resistance movement.'

'I don't think I'd be very easy to kill, Trafford.'

He didn't doubt it. It was clear to Trafford that Sandra Dee was a survivor, far tougher, he imagined, than he was.

'All right,' he said, 'I'll talk to them.'

'Today?'

'No. We can only ever meet at appointed times, they're very strict about that. I can speak to them next week.'

'Good.'

Then Sandra Dee leaned back on the plastic cushions once more and smiled. She was wearing the same cotton dress that she had worn the first time they had sailed together and, as then, the gentle breeze moulded the light material to her body.

'Well,' she said, 'we've finished our books and now we have the rest of the afternoon to kill. What shall we do?'

Trafford said nothing but every nerve in his body hoped and prayed that she meant what he thought she might mean.

'You're a funny boy,' she said.

She had never called him a boy before and although he was older than her he loved it.

'You're a beautiful girl,' he said, and his voice was unsteady.

Then, slowly, Sandra Dee began to unbutton her dress.

30

A week later Trafford did as he had promised.

He had attended the library in order to report on the
progress of his DegSep program. When he was finished he
asked if he could make a special plea that Sandra Dee be
allowed to join them.

'You know you can trust her,' he argued. 'She keeps more
secrets than any of us.'

'That may be so,' Cassius replied, 'but she worries me. I
think she's impulsive. She stands out.'

'Because she has integrity.'

'There have been scenes.'

'Yes, because she refuses to have breast implants and she
doesn't want to buy Princess Lovebud's doughnuts. Is that
something to penalize her for?'

'We are wary of people who stand out.'

'She doesn't stand out. Princess Lovebud picks on her,

that's all. If she hadn't singled her out you would never even have noticed her.'

'But she *did* single her out.'

'Which is not her fault.'

'It's quite obvious that you're in love with this girl, Trafford,' Cassius said.

'I . . . I don't see how that's relevant.'

'Of course it's relevant, you fool. If you love her then you'd put her before the loyalty you owe to us.'

'Why would I need to? She feels as I do, she wants nothing more than to join us.'

'Don't you think that love might have clouded your judgement about her? Do you think it would be wise of me to accept the recommendation on so serious a matter of someone whose eyes may be blinded by their emotions?'

'No, because what I love about her are the very qualities that make her perfect to join us. Her strength, her passion, her character, her . . . secrets.'

For a moment Cassius was lost in thought, then he seemed to make up his mind.

'Very well then,' he said, 'since you have already told her so much. And since, as you say, she has threatened to follow you and discover us anyway. You may bring your friend to the library.'

'May she come today?'

'Today?'

'She's waiting for me to call her,' Trafford said, producing his communitainer. 'She really can't wait. It's almost as if she's desperate. I think she's been very alone all her life and very frustrated too. She talks about joining us as if it were the beginning of life, which in many ways it is.'

Cassius smiled. 'Well, I suppose there's no time like the present,' he said. 'You may call her.'

Trafford dialled the number and began to tell Sandra Dee that she had been given permission to visit the library. He was about to offer her directions when he was cut off.

'Damn, lost her,' he said, beginning to dial again but as he did so the man with the thick glasses whom he thought of as the Owl came into the room. He looked extremely angry.

'There's a young woman in the shop who says she's a friend of Trafford,' he said. 'She claims she's expected.'

'She is,' Cassius replied. 'Please let her in.'

The Owl gave Cassius a look of withering disapproval but did as he was told.

A few moments later Sandra Dee was standing in the library.

'I followed you anyway,' she said. 'May I choose a book?'

31

When Trafford arrived home he found his apartment crowded, as usual, with Chantorria's new friends.

'Here he is at last!' said Barbieheart from her place on the wall. 'Inspiration Towers' very own superstar.'

'What the Hell are you talking about, Barbieheart?' Trafford enquired. One of the advantages of his new position as father of an angel was that he no longer had to pretend to be nice to Barbieheart. It was she who had to make an effort to be nice to him.

'It's wicked. Amazing, so fierce,' Barbieheart replied, ignoring his aggressive tone and speaking as if all was sweetness between them, as if they were best mates, soul-mates, co-members of a magic crew. 'Tell him, Chantorria.'

Chantorria, holding Caitlin Happymeal in one hand and a large glass of wine in the other, could scarcely contain her excitement.

'We're only on the news, lover! Can you believe it? Us! We are on the news!'

'Isn't it so cool?' Tinkerbell exclaimed. 'We're all going to be stars . . . Well, you and Chantorria are, but people are bound to start hitting up your webstream now and then whenever we come round people will see us too!'

Tinkerbell turned to the webcam and began waving and shrieking excitedly. Soon all the girls were waving alongside her.

'Of course people will see you, Tinks, and you're so telegenic I bet you end up with your own perfume,' Chantorria gushed. 'And I hope you come round and visit me all the time, babes.'

'Course I will, babes,' Tinkerbell replied. 'We are sisters.'

'Why have they put us on the news?' Trafford demanded angrily.

'Why do you think?' Chantorria replied.

'They heard about Caitlin Happymeal,' said Tinkerbell, pouring wine, 'and they liked the story. And they liked Chantorria, of course. She looks hot!'

'Oh stop it!' Chantorria protested.

'Girl, you know it's true. That shot of you lingeing Trafford up is *hot*!'

'They've used stuff from our stream?' Trafford asked. 'They've put Chantorria lingeing me *on the news*?'

'Of course they have! They trawled your history. What else do you think they're going to use? Wish they'd put some of *my* stream on the news!'

All the girls agreed with this sentiment wholeheartedly.

'It's incredible, Trafford,' Tinkerbell continued. 'Don't you understand, you're on the news, everybody is looking at you!'

'But . . .'

Trafford stopped himself. He had been about to say that he did not want to be on the news, that he did not want people looking at him. But he could not say that, that would be weird. Who would not want to be looked at? What was not to want? Trafford knew that he must grin and bear it. His social position was stronger than it had once been but not strong enough to protect him if he revealed himself as preferring privacy over self-exposure. Nothing was more insulting to the creed of the Temple.

'But what?' Chantorria demanded angrily, clearly not prepared to allow her husband's perversity to spoil her day.

'But . . . it's a bit of a shock, that's all. A wonderful shock, of course,' Trafford replied, forcing a smile.

'Check it out, babes,' said Tinkerbell. 'It's on the news infotainment loop.'

She touched a button and an image of Inspiration Towers appeared on the wallscreen accompanied by a syrupy voiceover.

'Every now and then,' the voice said, 'something wonderful happens to remind us all why we believe, why we have faith . . .'

There followed a three-minute 'human interest' item about the miracle baby of Inspiration Towers who had survived both a measles-plus and a mumps-plus epidemic to become the only child under two still alive on the estate. The story was illustrated with numerous shots taken from Trafford and Chantorria's webcast, including a clip of Chantorria in her chocolate G-string and cupless bra bought from Dirty Sexy Filthy Bitch. This of course was greeted by whoops and cheers from the girls in the room.

'You see, Trafford,' Chantorria said drily, '*some* people think it looks sexy.'

Trafford laughed woodenly, as if she was joking.

'Little Caitlin Happymeal,' the voiceover continued, 'has become a mascot for the whole local community. In her is manifest the love of the Love for all his lost children.'

Just as the loop finished and the girls were insisting that they must all watch it once again, the face of Confessor Bailey appeared on the screen.

Chantorria immediately jumped up to turn off the news and mute the other streams on the wall. When a spiritual guide dropped in for a web chat he must of course be given immediate attention.

'Chantorria,' Confessor Bailey said, and notwithstanding his usual pompous superiority he looked pleased, excited almost, 'and you, Trafford, I suppose,' he said as a rather sour afterthought, 'I should appreciate it very much if you would come pay me a visit this evening at the Spirit House.'

The room had fallen silent, as was appropriate in the cyber presence of a Confessor, but this caused murmurs and intakes of breath among the girls. A private invitation to a spiritual guide's personal residence was quite an honour.

'But of course, Confessor Bailey,' Trafford stammered. 'What time would you like us?'

'You are summoned for eight, Trafford, and will present yourself at that time,' Confessor Bailey snapped before turning to stare from the screen directly at Chantorria. 'You, Chantorria, might perhaps like to come a little earlier. I find your presence . . . soothing. We can read the words of the prophets together, speak of faith and consider the divine mysteries of the Love.'

The murmuring ceased. Trafford stared at the screen while Chantorria reddened and looked away. Tinkerbell and one or two of the other girls looked away also, as if fearful that their faces might reveal what they were thinking. It would not do to disrespect a Confessor.

'Shall we say six, Chantorria?' Confessor Bailey said with an oily smile.

'Yes, of course, Confessor. Whenever you wish,' Chantorria replied.

'And eight for you, Trafford. I'd advise you not to be late because . . .' Confessor Bailey paused for dramatic effect before delivering his coup de grâce, 'I am entertaining Solomon Kentucky, High Prophet of the Love and Bishop Confessor of the Lake London Diocese.'

Having made this truly dramatic statement, Confessor Bailey ended his web chat and disappeared from the screen.

After a moment's pause the screaming began. Barbieheart screamed. Tinkerbell and the girls screamed. Chantorria screamed, which of course caused Caitlin Happymeal to scream. They had been preparing to scream anyway, for the fact that their Confessor was now quite openly requesting spiritual comfort from Chantorria was reason enough. For a woman to be privileged to bring succour and calm to her spiritual leader was exciting but that a High Prophet of the Love, a *Bishop Confessor*, was to visit their parish, to sit in the house of their Confessor, and that Chantorria and Trafford were to meet him was simply astounding. No Temple elder of that rank had ever come to their community before.

After a while, when the jumping and the screaming and the hugging had died down a little, Tinkerbell issued her orders. There was no time to lose. If Chantorria was to read the holy words with her Confessor and discuss the nature of faith with him prior to sharing an audience with a High Prophet of the Love, then she must have an immaculate pedicure and a perfect bikini wax.

'You come with me right now, young lady,' Tinkerbell commanded sternly. 'This is the first time ever that a girl from our tenement has been invited to spiritual communion with our Confessor and we are not having your shaggy follicles letting down the whole building.' Tinkerbell was well known locally for her skills as a beautician. A few months previously she would not have dreamed of wasting her talents on so insignificant a figure as Chantorria. All that had changed now, of course, and so all the girls ran, still screaming, from the apartment and reconvened at Tinkerbell's, where they continued their party while Tinkerbell worked on Chantorria's groin.

Suddenly Trafford found himself alone apart from Caitlin Happymeal and, of course, Barbieheart.

'Well, Trafford,' said the moderator, 'it seems you're left holding the baby.'

'Yes, that's right,' said Trafford, inspecting Caitlin Happymeal's nappy.

'You won't mind if I join the girls, will you?' Barbieheart added, opening a tangerine-flavoured alcopop.

'No, no. Of course not. You have fun.'

Barbieheart's voice went silent and Trafford could see her turning to refocus on a different screen, clearly joining the party at Tinkerbell's. He finished changing his daughter and poured himself a large glass of passion-fruit alcopop. So much was happening so quickly.

He had been *on the news*.

What would Cassius, with his well-known aversion to people who made themselves conspicuous, make of that? Fortunately Trafford had not featured prominently in the piece, which had been very much a mother-and-daughter affair. Nonetheless the item had contained one most unwelcome shot, an image of him reading, the voiceover noting with approval that Trafford was clearly a responsible family man, who was always absorbed in some self-improvement manual or other. Trafford had watched this image in a state of shock because while it may have appeared that he was reading *Health and Wealth: How to Look Great and Get Rich*, he had in fact been reading *The Outsider* by Albert Camus. It was a terrifying thought: he had been seen, *on the news*, reading an existentialist novel.

If people were ever to discover the truth, the consequences would be too awful to imagine.

Trafford knew exactly what Cassius would say. The first rule of the Humanist movement was never to draw attention to oneself. On the other hand, Trafford reflected, Cassius had always insisted that the best form of deception was a bold front and you could not get much bolder than being the unwitting star of an infotainment loop. Besides which, being in the favour of the Temple could hardly be a bad thing. He had been able to use his new status to defend Sandra Dee at work and so bring her into the movement, and who knew what other opportunities might arise for him to put his spiritually elevated position to good use?

This thought (and another alcopop) brought Trafford's mind uncomfortably round to Confessor Bailey and his obvious interest in Chantorria. Suddenly he was angry; furious even. Not jealous, or at least he didn't think it was jealousy. After all, he was in love with Sandra Dee, and under normal circumstances nothing would have been more convenient than for Chantorria to develop an attraction elsewhere. Trafford was angry with Bailey's sudden interest because it was so stupid. Clearly Bailey wanted Chantorria because he had convinced himself that she was holy, a spiritually blessed woman, favoured by God, the mother of a miracle angel. Elders of the Temple always reserved the best of everything for themselves and that usually included the pick of the local women (for those who were not confirmed bachelors).

Bailey was pursuing Chantorria because she was his due.

Just then Chantorria returned from Tinkerbell's flat. Trafford was by then halfway through his third drink but the alcohol was not helping to lighten his mood. Chantorria was wearing a matching bra and thong in virginal white which, she explained, the girls had given her as a present to celebrate being on the news.

'Sweet, isn't it?' Chantorria said, taking up her clutch bag. 'Really, really tasteful. I think it hits the right note for a private audience with my Confessor.'

'Chantorria,' Trafford replied angrily, 'he's only interested in you because of Caitlin. You know that, don't you?'

'Well, what's wrong with that?' Chantorria snapped back. 'I'm the mother of a miracle angel; of course my Confessor's interested in me.'

Trafford moved discreetly to mute their webcast.

'Caitlin Happymeal is *not* a miracle angel,' he hissed.

'She is! She's alive, isn't she? Isn't that a miracle? Don't you think it's a miracle that our baby is the only survivor of the plagues?'

'Epidemics.'

'*Plagues*. Our baby is alive. That's all we know and it's a miracle whichever way you look at it.'

'Chantorria, you know very well that—'

'I know that God moves in mysterious ways, Trafford,' Chantorria said. 'Who made that . . . that *thing* you say you gave to her? God did.'

'Men did, Chantorria. Men using their intellect who—'

'And who made the men? Who made their intellect?'

286

'Well, who made this precious God of yours then? Another God, a bigger one? And who made him?'

'I am not discussing this any more, Trafford,' said Chantorria, turning up the sound again. 'All I know is that we have been blessed. We are the luckiest family in London. You think the blessing came one way, I think it came another, but either way it's a blessing and blessings come from God. Can't you understand that? What's not to understand? I'll see you at the Spirit House. Don't you dare be late.'

Chantorria, carrying her little bag, tottered towards the door. She was wearing a pair of stiletto heels that she also seemed recently to have acquired. No doubt another gift from Tinkerbell. Trafford watched her as she went. From the back she was almost totally naked. The only clothing that could be seen was her thin bra strap and the tiny piece of lace that emerged from between her buttocks.

'Aren't you going to say goodbye to the miracle angel?' he said with a sneer.

Chantorria turned and looked at him once more. 'Goodness, Trafford, I do believe you're jealous.' Then she tottered over to Caitlin Happymeal's cot. 'Bye, angel. Don't mind Daddy, he never wanted to give Mummy a seeing-to anyway so I don't know what his problem is now.'

After that she went out, leaving Trafford very clear in his mind what his problem was. He felt terrible. He was a committed Humanist and yet it seemed that he had by his own actions made a major contribution to the 'evidence' of God's mysterious ways.

Having Caitlin Happymeal inoculated had of course been the best thing he had ever done, but the unexpected consequence of people loudly giving the Lord the credit was deeply depressing. The fact that his own wife, who actually *knew the truth*, believed it was doubly depressing. And it was getting worse. Trafford had never dreamed they would end up on the news and the fact that Confessor Bailey was entering into spiritual communion with Chantorria would make things worse again. Endorsement from a Confessor of the Temple would further confirm people's conviction that Chantorria was blessed and that Caitlin had survived as a result of divine intervention. Trafford cursed the horrible irony that his private subversion, which had been motivated by pure reason, had been spun so as to entrench religious superstition.

Trafford turned to his computer with a new sense of urgency. His search program was almost completed. Within a few days he would be in a position to instruct the DegSep engine to create for him a virtual network of potential revolutionaries. Trafford intended to begin sending out messages to this anonymous community immediately. Cassius had promised to furnish him with the first, which, it had been agreed, would be a brief illustrated article on the theory of evolution. The second would be about the flood itself, explaining that the rise in sea levels had in fact been the unfortunate and preventable result of unrestricted burning of fossil fuels.

Trafford intended that the mail shots should be self-generating, an automated message cycle, triggered by a single code word which, once sent, would create an unstoppable avalanche of seditious spam that would continue even if the people who wrote it had been caught. Each message would have a title that he hoped would convince the recipient to read what had been sent. Trafford had been working on these titles also, as had Cassius and the others. Trafford's favourite had been suggested by Connor Newbury.

If God is so clever why does he choose such arseholes to run his Temple? Ever take a really critical look at your Confessor? Trafford smiled. If he received an email with a title like that he knew that he would open it.

You are not alone in wanting to be alone! That had been Cassius's suggestion, as had *Ever thought about thinking for yourself?*

So far, apart from *Can you keep a secret?* Trafford had not come up with a title, but now he wrote down the word *evolve.*

All the time he had been working on the program Trafford had been wondering what should be done with this virtual community, should he ever succeed in establishing it. After all, it was one thing to encourage people to think for themselves, but if all they did was think and took no action then the Temple had nothing to fear. For Trafford thinking wasn't enough; he despised the way his fellow Humanists were content to protest simply by their existence. Something physical had to be done. Revolutions in the head could only be the beginning.

A sign was needed, a secret sign. A single word perhaps,

something by which each freethinker might recognize another. A single word that said it all.

And Trafford knew that the word must be *evolve*.

Because 'evolve' was more than a word. It was a call to arms. A simple instruction to rise out of the swamp, to become a sophisticated organism, a creature capable of independent thought.

But the word 'evolve' dripped with heretical connotations. It could never be displayed openly, never be held up as a sign.

Trafford typed it out backwards and with a sudden surge of excitement noticed that it spelt *evlove*.

Ev Love. He had heard that phrase before.

'Let me hear you say Love! . . . Let me hear you say Everlasting Love! . . . Let me hear you say Ev Love!'

One of those shorthand phrases that the Temple had coined to describe their God was the reverse of the word which they feared most.

Ev Love. That would be his key. That would be the code to trigger the program and the term he would include in all communications. The term by which each recipient might display their faith, for if challenged they could claim it was simply a reduction of Everlasting Love.

Ev Love. It even sounded like Evolve.

He could not wait to tell Cassius.

Show the words Ev Love, Trafford wrote. *By these words shall you be known*.

32

At eight o'clock that evening Trafford, holding Caitlin Happymeal in his arms, presented himself at Confessor Bailey's house and was ushered by a servant into the same luxuriously appointed room in which he and Chantorria had sat discussing their now cancelled divorce. Chantorria was already there of course, sitting on a stool at Bailey's feet. She was reading from a book, a big, jewel-encrusted leather-bound volume entitled *Bible Stories and Other Inspirational Writings*.

Trafford thought that she looked rather flushed.

The Confessor raised a hand to indicate that Trafford should wait in the doorway until the reading was finished. Trafford was therefore forced to hover in silence while his wife completed the lines of doggerel with which she had been engaged and Confessor Bailey sat with his eyes closed and a rapturous expression on his face. He was stroking Chantorria's hair.

'Love is love and the Lord whom we call the Love is love,' Chantorria read in tones of deepest sincerity. 'Without the Lord who is the Love we have no love and since we have love, we have the Lord who is the Love, for the two are one, immortal and indivisible. It is so now, was so in the beginning and shall be so evermore. The Lord and the Love is kind and he is merciful and whosoever doubteth that shall be wiped from the face of the Earth and suffer hellish torment for all eternity. Such are the ways of the Love.'

'Thank you, child,' the Confessor said as Chantorria closed the book. 'That was beautiful. It eases my troubled and weary soul to hear the sweet voice of a righteous woman speak the Lord's truth.'

'I'm honoured to be your comfort, Holy Confessor,' Chantorria replied.

Only now did Confessor Bailey look at Trafford.

'Take a seat beside your wife,' he ordered. 'The Bishop Confessor is a busy man. I don't imagine that he will be long.'

Indeed Trafford had scarcely had a moment to sit down and acknowledge Chantorria's nervous smile when the loud banging of a staff on the front door announced the arrival of the great man. This knocking was followed by the frantic scuttling of servants in the hallway and suddenly Solomon Kentucky himself strode into the room, accompanied by four large security guards.

'I have come!' he said, almost as if he was the Lord himself paying a visit instead of merely one of his senior representatives on Earth.

Confessor Bailey, Trafford and Chantorria dropped immediately to their knees.

'My house is not worthy, Bishop Confessor, and nor am I,' Confessor Bailey replied.

'Damn right about that, Bailey,' the Bishop Confessor replied, laughing hugely. 'But then none of us is worthy in the eyes of the Lord, yet we all hope one day to stand naked before him. If I visited only with those who were worthy I'd have a damn small social circle! Ha! Ha! Ha! Am I right? Of course I'm right. Kiss my rings.'

He offered his huge, soft, podgy right hand for Confessor Bailey to approach. Upon each finger and the thumb were great sparkling rings. Confessor Bailey shuffled forward on his knees and kissed each one. Then the great man transferred the flashing neon mitre that he was holding in his other hand, and presented a second set of jewel-encrusted fingers to be worshipped and adored. Trafford and Chantorria of course said nothing in the presence of such eminence.

'So this is the family!' Solomon Kentucky thundered. 'I would know them were I to have met them among a thousand families! The blessing of the Love is upon them. I feel the Love.'

'Hallelujah!' shouted Confessor Bailey.

'Hallelujah!' echoed Chantorria.

'Stand, child,' Solomon Kentucky said to her. 'Gather

up your angel baby and stand. Do not be afraid.'

Chantorria took Caitlin Happymeal from Trafford's arms and stood before the Bishop Confessor. Trafford was disgusted to note that there was already a look of transported rapture on her face, and he wondered if she was about to begin speaking in tongues.

'You, child, are blessed in the favour of the Lord and the Love,' Solomon Kentucky intoned, 'and in his wisdom he has designed for you a purpose. There is work for you and your family to do!! Let me hear you say Yeah!'

'Yeah!' said Chantorria.

Trafford did not know whether the Bishop Confessor had meant him also. He decided it was safer to say nothing, not wishing to draw attention to himself. Solomon Kentucky didn't seem to notice either way. He was only interested in the mother and child. Handing his mitre to one of his guards, he laid a hand on each of their brows.

'I feel it!' he shouted. 'I feel it! I feel the blessing of the Love! This child is truly holy. Her mother is blessed. Let me hear you say All Right!'

'All right!' Chantorria shouted.

'All right!' Trafford echoed meekly, having been kicked by Confessor Bailey.

'This kiddie will inspire the faithful!' Solomon Kentucky went on. 'There has been great suffering of late. Many righteous people have lost a kiddie, two kiddies or more! The faithful need a sign. The people need a symbol! The honest, Love-fearing men and women of this great country of faith need hope! Let me hear you say A'come on!'

'A'come on!' Chantorria and Trafford shouted.

'A'come on, a'come on, a'come on – *on*!' Kentucky shouted.

'A'come on, a'come on, a'come on – *on*!' Chantorria and Trafford echoed.

'This kiddie, little Caitlin Happymeal, will be that sign. That symbol. That hope! In the name of the Lord and the Love. The Creator of all things and many things more. In the name of his holy mother Mary and his saintly daughter Diana. In the name of Jesus, Abraham, Elvis and Moses. In the name of the twenty-eight Apostles of the Gospel and the Fifteen Pillars of the Faith. In the name of the stars that guide us and the numbers that foretell that which only he can know and which for us is mystery. In the name of all the prophets and elders of the Temple. In the name of this tiny kiddie Caitlin Happymeal. I say Let his will be done. Amen!'

'Amen!' Confessor Bailey shouted.

'Amen!' said Chantorria and Trafford. Chantorria by this time was shaking and twitching, her lip quivering with ecstasy. Solomon Kentucky, on the other hand, suddenly dispensed with his evangelical posturing altogether and called for a chair that he might get down to business.

'As you know,' he said, accepting a large glass of sweet sherry and a chocolate eclair from a servant, 'these recent epidemics have been particularly severe and the suffering has been truly terrible. Yours is not the only community that has been devastated, although certainly the plagues that visited themselves upon this particular district were mighty indeed. Now little Caitlin Happymeal is, as we can see, highly telegenic and it has not gone unnoticed in the councils of the Temple that her Heaven-sent good fortune has struck a particular chord among the faithful of this parish and indeed, since she featured on the infotainment news earlier today, increasingly in the wider community. People are thirsting for good news and right now Caitlin Happymeal is it. She's a lively, pretty little thing and of course Chantorria here is more than easy on the eye and there is nothing like a hot momma with big healthy naturals and a cutesome kiddie to put a sunnier spin on things. Our PR people had in fact been looking for just such a combination to head up a post-plague feel-good campaign and, having checked out a considerable sample of surviving kiddies, we've fixed on Caitlin Happymeal to be our Face of Hope. We have decided to make this little child a poster girl for the Lord's divine mercy.' Kentucky helped himself to another cake before adding grandly, 'Your heavenly poppet is going to be a big, big star.'

Then the Bishop Confessor snapped his fingers and one of his grim, silent security guards inserted a memory stick in Confessor Bailey's computer. Immediately there appeared on the screen a series of adverts featuring Caitlin's face.

'This is just rough work,' Solomon Kentucky said, 'but you'll get the idea and I think you're going to love it.'

There was Caitlin Happymeal, smiling and gurgling and cooing in a video poster format, beneath the banner headline *Miracles Do Happen*.

'That's the shout line we're running with,' Solomon Kentucky explained. '*Miracles Do Happen*. Pretty good, huh? Short, clear, to the point. We want to say to people, "Don't despair. If the Love can save this child, he can save them all. In fact he *has* saved them all for he has gathered them to him." '

'Isn't that rather a mixed message?' Trafford said before he could stop himself. Confessor Bailey turned on him in fury.

'The Bishop Confessor is *speaking*,' Bailey snapped.

'No, no,' Solomon Kentucky insisted, 'this is the father. Let's hear him out. Mixed message, you suggest, young man? How so?'

'Well,' Trafford began nervously, 'is it our daughter who's been saved by *not* dying or all the dead children who've been saved *by* dying and then going to Heaven?'

Solomon Kentucky thought for a moment.

'Both,' he said finally. 'And in the beautiful eyes of Caitlin Happymeal all the parents whose kiddies are in Heaven will see the eyes of their own children and they will know that the Lord loves them.'

'Oh . . .' Trafford said. 'I see.'

'This little baby,' the Bishop Confessor continued, 'is to be the central image in a huge post-plague media campaign. She will carry the *Miracles Do Happen* message into every dwelling and workplace in the country. There will be video posters, commercials, a number-one hit song and above all your family will be the key figures of testification at a Wembley Faith Concert.'

'Oh my God,' Chantorria burst out, 'a Faith Concert! Us! Oh – my – God.'

Confessor Bailey turned sternly towards her because it was not her place to volunteer comment, but Solomon Kentucky gave her an indulgent smile.

'Yes, my child. Yes. You and your family are to be the centrepiece of the massive service of celebration that the Temple is planning, to mark the passing of the two great plagues. We intend to pack Wembley with grieving parents: one hundred and twenty-five thousand recently bereaved couples will be ticketed by lottery and then invited to a party to give thanks, not only for their own children's ascension to Heaven but also for the Love's mercy in delivering Caitlin Happymeal that she might be a child to all of them. All around the country via webcast and live video link-up the population will rejoice in the miracle of Caitlin's survival, which will lend hope and succour to everyone. You three will stand together alongside all the elders of the Temple plus every major celebrity in the land and give thanks for Caitlin and the clear, living, breathing evidence that *Miracles Do Happen*.'

Chantorria was weeping openly with happiness. Confessor Bailey put his arm around her for comfort. Both of them ignored Trafford.

'Your child,' said Solomon Kentucky, taking up his mitre

once more, 'will be a beacon! A messiah of faith! A light in the darkness of loss. Caitlin Happymeal will give hope back to the people!'

'Oh thank you, Bishop Confessor,' Chantorria stuttered through her tears. 'Thank you. Thank you.'

Trafford said nothing. He was thinking.

33

The campaign that Solomon Kentucky had described began almost immediately. The Temple understood its congregation and knew that it needed to act urgently to channel the devastated population into the correct emotional reactions. The nightmare that the nation had gone through with two virulent plagues following one after the other in quick succession had left people genuinely traumatized. People were used to the pain of bereavement, but each natural holocaust seemed to grow in scale and the dull horror that had settled on the nation had been in danger of turning to sullen anger. There was no question of people openly doubting their faith; the grip of the Temple and the fear of its Inquisition were too strong for that. Nonetheless, as each child died the blind acceptance of the spiritual status quo had received a tiny dent, and it was these dents that the Temple intended to hammer out with its message that *Miracles Do Happen*.

There were songs, concerts, fêtes, fun runs and endless services, all aimed at remembering and celebrating the lost children while looking with hope to the future, a future which was of course personified in the smiling, laughing, innocently uplifting image of Caitlin Happymeal. The Temple knew its business and somehow this focusing of the community's sight on God's love for this one child diverted attention from the unspoken question of his purpose in killing so many others. No doubt there were many parents who secretly asked the Love why *their* child could not have been chosen to be saved, but if they thought it they did not say it, for Caitlin's face had instantly become the symbol of future redemption and nobody wanted to risk the wrath of the Temple or of the Love himself by questioning it.

The equation was simple. The Lord sent the plagues because he was terrible and wrathful but the Lord saved Caitlin Happymeal because he was gentle and loving. 'What,' as Confessor Bailey thundered from his pulpit, 'was not to understand?'

As her fame increased, Chantorria became a woman possessed. She began playing the part of the mother of a miracle to the hilt, because she had convinced herself that it was true. There were no more parties at her and Trafford's apartment. As the madonna who gave birth to an angel baby, Chantorria felt her spiritual obligations keenly and began to spend more and more time either praying at the local Temple or at the house of Confessor Bailey. She took to wearing only white and carried a cross inscribed with a Gaia symbol. She bought an expensive pendant that featured all the signs of the zodiac and a rhinestone halo which was supported on a wire headpiece. She also dyed her hair golden.

Emboldened by the favour of the Confessor, she began to treat Tinkerbell and her other new best mates more as handmaidens than friends. She sent them on errands and gracefully 'allowed' them to wax her and apply her make-up. They scurried about to do her bidding but Trafford could see that they were resentful of her arrogance and her sudden piety. After all, most of them had lost children and it seemed hard that Chantorria, who had been alone in the tenement in not losing her baby, should then also become so exalted a figure.

If Chantorria sensed their resentment it only made her throw her weight about all the more. Perhaps it was the years of being downtrodden but she made no secret now of the fact that she considered herself a substantial cut above the rest. After all, had she not been chosen?

Trafford of course knew very well that she had *not* been chosen and he grew more and more furious. It was clear to him that she had been flattered into *believing* that she was a chosen one and he found his wife's naivety almost unbearably depressing and ridiculous. In fact he found the whole situation unbearably depressing and ridiculous; here was a child who owed her survival entirely to a science which the Temple despised, and she was being used to further the cause of blind superstition. Every time Trafford saw his daughter's face smiling out at him from a video hoarding he felt more angry.

Slowly, relentlessly, an idea was growing in his mind which could certainly in the short term prove an even more effective tool of revolution than his planned Ev Love campaign. It was to Sandra Dee that he first told his idea. Trafford was later to reflect that it was her romantic rejection of him which made him speak so recklessly, which made him suddenly anxious to *act* so recklessly.

They were together on her little boat. It was the first time she had agreed to their meeting alone since he had introduced her to the Humanists and Trafford had immediately taken the opportunity to tell her once again that he loved her.

'Don't love me, Trafford,' was her reply. 'I don't want you to love me.'

'Love isn't something you choose,' he said. 'I would have thought you'd read enough stories by now to understand that.'

'This isn't a story, Trafford. It's real life,' she said, 'crappy, shitty real life and I don't want you to love me.'

'I can't help it.'

'Well, I don't love you,' she said, adopting her most matter-of-fact voice. 'Really, Trafford, I don't love you at all. I like you. I like you a lot . . .'

'Well then . . .'

'And if I'm honest I'll admit that perhaps I *could* love you. But I don't and that's the end of it.'

'How can you say that!' Trafford protested. 'How can you be sure?'

'Because I've decided not to.'

'Decided! You can't just *decide* about—'

'Yes, you can, Trafford,' Sandra Dee interrupted. 'That's the whole point. You *can* decide. You *have* to decide. In this world you have to decide about everything, if you want to stay safe. If you want to stay *sane*, you have to decide. Love is a risk. Sharing is a risk. Two people are exactly twice as likely to give themselves away as one and to me those are unacceptable odds, which is why I made my decision a long, long time ago that I would never fall in love with anyone and that includes you.'

'Why did you make love to me then that one time,' he protested, 'if you knew you felt this way?'

'Would you rather I hadn't?'

Trafford avoided the question.

'But why did you?' he asked again.

'I felt like it. All that imaginary sex. It was hot. A girl can get excited without being in love, can't she?'

'So you were disappointed, is that it?' Trafford said angrily. 'You liked the fantasy stuff but I didn't live up to my descriptive powers, right?'

'Oh please, Trafford,' she snapped, 'don't bring male ego into it. We had sex, it's done. I never intended for a moment that it would lead to anything further. You know I'm a single girl. I've worked very hard to be one.'

'And you knew what I felt for you. How could you let me make love to you knowing that I was *in* love with you and that you didn't care at all?'

'Like I said before, Trafford, would you have preferred that I didn't?'

Once more Trafford did not answer. Sandra Dee pressed her point.

'Come on, tell me the truth. If I had said to you, "Trafford, I don't love you and I don't want any kind of serious affair with you, but I will have sex with you this once," would you have refused? Would you have said, "Oh no, I can't do that, not if you don't love me. It would be just too painful afterwards"? No. Of course not. You would have fucked me just the same. Admit it.'

The answer was obvious but Trafford would not admit it. Instead he did what many unrequited lovers have done and announced instead a grand gesture of self-sacrifice. Perhaps she would be sorry when he was gone.

'Well,' he said, 'it doesn't matter anyway because I don't think I shall be around much longer.'

'Oh? Are you planning to go away?'

'No. I'm planning to start a revolution.'

Sandra Dee was so surprised she laughed.

'What are you talking about?' she asked. 'What revolution?'

'The Temple wants my daughter to be a beacon. Well, all right, let her be a beacon. I will make her a beacon but not a beacon of blind faith. A beacon of reason.'

Sandra Dee had stopped laughing.

'How do you intend to do that?' she asked.

'The emotional climax to the *Miracles Do Happen* campaign is to be a big Faith Festival at Wembley Stadium.'

'That doesn't surprise me. The Temple would have a Wembley Festival to give thanks for a new line at Burger King.'

'Yes but this is to be truly colossal, the centrepiece of a nationwide celebration for the passing of the measles and mumps plagues.'

'So?'

'My family is to be at the heart of it. Chantorria and I are to present Caitlin Happymeal to the nation, live. They're actually planning to rechristen her Angel, dedicating her life to God. Think of it: they want to turn her into a baby nun. They want Chantorria and me to hand our baby over to God.'

'And what is it you plan to do?' Sandra Dee asked and the worried look on her face suggested that she had guessed where Trafford's thoughts were leading.

'At that moment when I'm called upon to testify to Caitlin's deliverance, and before anyone can stop me, I'm going to tell the entire nation that Caitlin is alive because I had her vaccinated.'

Sandra Dee looked stunned. After all, what Trafford was suggesting might very well be suicide.

'They will kill you on the spot,' she said.

'Well, revolutions are risky business,' Trafford replied. Despite the seriousness of what he was planning, he was also enjoying the drama of the moment and the effect his words were having on Sandra Dee.

'What if they kill Caitlin?' she asked.

'Why would they? It wasn't her sin, she's an innocent and I don't think even a Wembley crowd would stomach Confessors killing little babies. I imagine she'll be quietly fostered.'

'And Chantorria?'

'I'll tell them that she knew nothing about it.'

'What if they don't believe you?'

'She'll have to take her chances. Sandra Dee, don't you see what this could mean? It's a unique opportunity to do something truly extraordinary. To sow the seeds of doubt in the minds of millions of people. The Temple itself has made Caitlin famous with their ridiculous *Miracles* message. I can turn that message on its head! An opportunity like this won't come again.'

'An opportunity to make yourself a martyr! Trafford, you're asking to get killed! Why?'

'Why did anyone ever sacrifice themselves for a cause they believed in? I think it's my duty.'

'You're doing your duty just by being a Humanist. You're a living archive, an enlightened person who seeks to enlighten others. That's your calling. That's your duty.'

'I have the opportunity to enlighten millions!'

'They won't listen anyway.'

'They will. I'll make them listen. I'll make them wonder if their children couldn't have been saved too. I reckon if I'm careful with the way I approach it on stage and don't show my hand too early I'll get a good few minutes to speak. I'll lure them in by talking about how wonderful it is that Caitlin's alive. I'll even thank the Love and then, before they twig what I'm on about, I'll tell them about the vaccination. I might even credit God for that as well; that'll confuse them. Think about it, Sandra Dee! What Humanist has ever had such an opportunity to expose the madness of the Temple?'

'And what Humanists will be left after you've done it?' Sandra Dee asked angrily. 'They won't just kill you, they'll torture everything out of you first. What about the library? What about the others?'

'They'll never hear about the library because they'll be looking for a Vaccinator, not a Humanist. I'll tell them everything about the vaccination immediately. I'll hide nothing. I'll give them every detail. I'll give it proudly, as if to prove my point. Why would they look further?'

'You'll give them Cassius?'

'Well, I'll warn him first, obviously. He'll have to disappear. If he's careful he'll survive, he's a resourceful guy. Anyway I'm sure he'll agree that this will be worth the risk. This is a chance in a lifetime to turn the Temple's spin machine on itself.'

'What about me? We've been alone together. What if they find that out?'

'Why would they? How could they?'

'There are CCTV cameras at the marina. There are CCTV cameras everywhere.'

'Why would they pick up on that? We always arrive in crowds. Nobody notices us down here. Besides, they won't

308

be *looking*, I tell you. They don't know about the Humanists, they don't know about us. They'll be looking for a Vaccinator and I will hand them a Vaccinator. I'll guide them through my meetings with Cassius right up until the trip to Heathrow when he did it. All that will be on CCTV too. They'll be looking for Cassius all right.'

'And you will probably be burned.'

'Yes. I imagine I will be.'

Sandra Dee did not speak again for a long time. They sat together, lost in their own thoughts, as the boat rocked on its anchor.

'You really do intend to go through with this?' Sandra Dee asked at last.

'Yes. Absolutely. I believe I have no other course in life.'

'If I'd loved you, would you still be doing this?'

'I . . . don't know. Yes. In the long run, yes, I think I would. I have been ordered to stand on that stage at Wembley and credit divine intervention with Caitlin's survival. To give thanks to a stupid, vicious, capricious, illogical, immoral, maniacal deity who clearly exists only in the imaginations of idiots and bullies. I truly believe it would be better to die than do that.'

'In that case,' Sandra Dee replied, 'perhaps we should make love.'

'A farewell gift?'

'If you like.'

'Well, yes then. I do like.'

34

Once more Trafford and Cassius made the journey to Hampstead and found themselves in Connor Newbury's splendid reception room, where again Trafford addressed the Humanist Senate. He explained to them his idea of using Ev Love as the unifying symbol and reported that the first mail shot had been prepared and the trigger mechanism put in place.

'The DegSep search engine has identified our target audience,' he told them, 'and we are ready to reach out and make contact.'

'How many of them are there?' Billy Macallan enquired.

'Twelve million,' Trafford replied.

The big man nearly dropped the teacup he was holding.

'Twelve *million*?' he spluttered. 'Strewth, that's half the population!'

'I know,' Trafford agreed. 'I tried running a number of

different searches and the results were even more staggering. For instance, when I asked the computer to find those who had been blogged as sometimes avoiding Gr'ugs the figures went up to fourteen million. My belief, based on this evidence, is that the majority of people in this country are privately discontented and harbouring a secret self who is frustrated, unfulfilled and unhappy.'

'Well then,' Cassius observed, 'if our search profile is right then the Temple's house is indeed built upon shifting sand.'

'Absolutely,' Trafford said eagerly. 'If we can tempt people into displaying the Ev Love symbol then they will find their courage in numbers! My idea is that once we have begun the mail shots the next thing we do is start giving out times and locations and see if people turn up. If we've got our psychology right, pretty soon we'll be able to gather enough people to issue a Wembley Law!'

The idea was huge, so big that the room fell quiet for a moment.

'Well,' Professor Taylor observed, 'it's possible, I suppose. Most revolutions appear hopeless until they begin. A year before the Russian Revolution Lenin was a fringe exile with only a handful of followers. Christianity itself went from underground cult to official religion of the Roman Empire in scarcely a generation.'

'Exactly!' said Trafford eagerly. 'And I believe we have the perfect trigger with which to start our revolution. We should send our emails on the eve of the next Faith Festival, the one at which the Temple plans to display my daughter as evidence of the mercy of the Love.'

Trafford then told the Senate the plan which he had already outlined to Sandra Dee. 'I intend to confess to having had Caitlin Happymeal vaccinated but before that I shall lead the crowd in the Ev Love chant. I shall be wearing a shirt with the words "Ev Love" printed on it. Every one of the millions who have received our email will recognize that sign! By then some of them will have read our digest of the theory of evolution, and then they will see a person wearing the evolution slogan and explaining how science, not faith, can save children and that the Temple is preventing it from doing so. We will never get such a great chance to make so persuasive a beginning.'

They were understandably nervous. Trafford could see that their little movement had been static for so long that so radical an idea was hard for them to absorb.

'It sounds dangerous to me,' Newbury said nervously.

'Well, Newbury,' said Cassius, 'after Trafford himself, the person in the most danger from this plan is me and personally I think it's brilliant.'

'I'm telling you,' Trafford exclaimed, 'the need is out there! The *hunger*. Our profile search proves it. The people are a ticking time bomb and we have the chance to explode it right in the Temple's face.'

35

Trafford convinced the Senate of his plan and left the meeting in a state of high excitement. His job now was to begin working on the speech he would make at Wembley. It was clear that this must be planned with enormous care, beginning innocently, revealing its agenda subtly and delivering its bombshell so surprisingly that by the time people realized what had been said it would be too late for any Temple elder to intervene. Everything depended on the moment in which he explained why Caitlin Happymeal was still alive: that was the key.

Sadly, however, Trafford was never to be called upon to offer an explanation as to why his daughter was alive because, on the very morning after his meeting with the Humanist Senate, poor little Caitlin Happymeal developed severe diarrhoea and vomiting. Something had got into the water supply at Inspiration Towers and the whole building succumbed to a dose of cholera-plus. Everybody was extremely sick but there was only one fatality: the building's sole remaining infant. Caitlin Happymeal wasn't a miracle baby after all.

The Temple moved swiftly to limit the damage to its credibility. Within twenty-four hours of the child's death, all traces of the *Miracles Do Happen* campaign had disappeared from the streets and from cyberspace. The tragedy was not even reported on the news. Now that Caitlin had died, it was suddenly as if she'd never lived.

Trafford and Chantorria were so blinded by grief that for a few days they did not notice the radical change in their position in the community. They kept to their apartment, numb with shock, struggling to come to terms with the empty cot and the baby clothes and the toys which would never be played with again. If they noticed that there had been no callers and that nobody seemed inclined to stream in for a web chat, they put it down to people's embarrassment and reluctance to deal with the scale of their grief.

On the fourth day Chantorria went out. Her pain was not receding but growing and she had decided to visit Confessor Bailey. Surely he would be able to find some words of comfort to help her through the torment of bereavement. But the girl who only the previous week had been privileged to anoint the Confessor's feet with precious oils now got no further than his front door. There at the entrance a servant who had previously bowed and scraped before her informed her brutally that she was no longer loved by the Love, and that if she wished to see the Confessor she could do so at the Community Confession like everybody else. What was more, she was never, repeat never, to approach the Spirit House uninvited again.

Chantorria was an embarrassment to Confessor Bailey. He had bigged her up from the pulpit and now she was an affront to his credibility. She had made him look fallible and he wanted nothing more to do with her. She turned away and began slowly to make her way home. She was recognized on the route and people sneered and whispered and pointed. Some laughed.

On the steps of Inspiration Towers she met Tinkerbell.

'So Caitlin's dead then, is she?' Tinkerbell said bluntly without bothering even to say hello. 'Well, you'll have plenty of time on your hands now, won't you? Perhaps you could run a few errands for me.'

Still dazed with grief, Chantorria did not immediately comprehend the scale of animosity that her brief period as an exalted Temple favourite had provoked. Surely Tinks, her bestest mate, was not like all the rest?

'It's very lonely in our apartment now,' Chantorria said weakly.

'Is it really?' Tinkerbell said with heavy sarcasm.

'Trafford and I don't know what to say to each other.'

'Well, he always was a bit of an arsehole, wasn't he?'

'Could you pop down for coffee some time or a glass of wine, Tinks? I don't really know how I'm going to cope at the moment.'

'Coffee and a glass of wine?' Tinkerbell repeated coldly.

'Yes, or anything really.'

Tinkerbell shoved her face up close to Chantorria's and spat out her reply.

'Now you listen here, you stuck-up bitch,' she hissed. 'You were all high and mighty when you thought you were God's bloody favourite, weren't you?'

'No! No, I wasn't . . .' Chantorria protested.

'Yes, you fucking were. You had the whole bloody building running round after you. Well, now it turns out you're no better than anybody else. The Lord and the Love doesn't give a shit about you. And he didn't give a shit about your little brat either, did he? Because she's dead, isn't she? Just like the rest of our kiddies. Except at least none of us went around claiming our kiddies was saints. We never thought we was the Virgin fucking Mary and our kiddies was Jesus fucking Christ. No! But you! You, Chantorria, and your precious little Caitlin fucking Happymeal, you was the chosen ones, wasn't you? Well, not any more, *babes*. So deal with it!'

'Please don't!' Chantorria pleaded, tears running down her face.

'Just because the Confessor was sorting you out you thought the sun shined out of your arse. Well, you know now, don't you! So just you keep out of my way, all right? Because you made a fool of us, you did. I even had my Lexus running round trying to fix your shower. I even spruced up your scrawny manky muff for you. Well, you're on your own now, because you've brought disgrace on the whole of Inspiration Towers, you have. You've made fools of us and everybody wishes you'd just do what your kid did and fuck off and die.'

Chantorria ran weeping from her tormentor. When she entered her apartment there was no respite. Barbieheart was waiting for her, on the wall.

'Well, well, if it isn't the Holy Mother of God herself,' Barbieheart sneered.

'Barbieheart, please,' Chantorria pleaded, 'why is everybody being so cruel? I just lost my baby!'

'They all lost their babies, love, but they didn't use it to claim they was special like you, did they?' Barbieheart replied, twisting the truth without a thought. 'They didn't turn our building into a laughing stock by claiming that their snotty kiddie was the bloody new Messiah. No, love, you did that, didn't you? You made your precious bed and now you've got to lie on it because nobody wants to know you any more.'

With that, Barbieheart muted her sound and on the screen made an exaggerated performance of turning away – or at least as far away as her vast, stationary bulk would allow.

'Please, Barbieheart, please!' Chantorria wept, shouting at the camera, but Barbieheart opened a sack of cheesy fried corn snacks and ignored her.

Chantorria sank to the floor, crying uncontrollably. Trafford did not look at her either. He was sitting beside Caitlin Happymeal's empty cot, where he had sat for most of the previous four days. When he spoke he addressed empty space.

'Let the stupid bitch go, Chantorria,' he said. 'Who cares what Barbieheart thinks? Who cares what anybody thinks? It doesn't matter. Nothing matters.'

Chantorria looked up and began to stare at Trafford. For fully a minute she stared in silence until finally Trafford raised his face to hers.

'What?' he said.

'You.' Her voice was filled with bitterness. 'You. You bastard. This is all your fault.'

Trafford was astonished. He had not thought he was capable of feelings of any kind that day but Chantorria's accusation stunned him.

'What the hell do you mean?'

'Everything started to go wrong when you did what you did!'

'It started to go wrong when you began to believe that you were the chosen one. If we're a target now it's because you made a spectacle of yourself, because you chose to believe that God had saved Caitlin.'

Chantorria flew at him.

'Well, you certainly didn't save her, did you, you bastard!' she screamed. 'Your precious vaccination didn't save her!'

'It saved her from measles and mumps! She died of *cholera*, Chantorria. She wasn't vaccinated against cholera. A vaccination isn't magic, it's not like your bloody Temple, it's a scientific process that—'

'Shut up! Shut up! I don't want to hear! I tell you it all started to go wrong when you did what you did. We were all right till then!'

She was trying to beat her fists on his chest; he was forced to hold her off.

'Caitlin is dead!' he shouted into her face. 'Nothing else matters, not you, not me, certainly not those imbeciles out there' – he made a gesture to the webcam. 'Caitlin is dead and there is nothing we can do about it. She wasn't a miracle angel but she was *our* angel and she's dead.'

Slowly Chantorria's violent anger subsided. She sank back down to the floor and they did not speak to each other again that evening. Eventually, as the gloom gathered in the room, Chantorria went to lie on the bed, leaving Trafford still sitting beside Caitlin's cot. Neither of them slept; they simply began the process of enduring the night, separate and alone, locked in grief.

About two in the morning there was a sudden blast of noise and light as Tinkerbell and some of her girls exploded on to the wallscreen. They were all drunk, their faces flushed and ugly, and they had decided to drop in for a web chat.

'Hi, Chantorria,' Tinkerbell shouted, as usual leading the pack. 'Are you saying your prayers? Me and the girls were wondering what a saint does at night. Not much by the look of it, eh? Won't get another little kiddie with you in bed and him in the kitchen, will you? Or at least, if you do, that one really *will* be a miracle!'

The girls shrieked with laughter, clustered around Tinkerbell's webcam.

'Will you come and bless us, Chantorria?' another of the gang sneered. 'Why don't you put that halo on and come up and sing us a hymn!'

Trafford sat with his eyes closed listening to the laughter and the shrieking, which seemed to go on for hours. He did not even have the energy to reach over to the control and mute the sound. Bullied or not bullied, it was all the same to him now that Caitlin Happymeal was gone. Chantorria lay silently also, too devastated, it seemed, even to beg for mercy.

Eventually the pack tired of failing to get a reaction and lost interest in their fun. Peace returned but it did not bring rest. For yet another night Trafford did not sleep at all and from the sound of sobbing in the bedroom he knew that Chantorria was not sleeping either.

The following day was a Fizzy Coff and so Trafford was forced to get up, eat something and prepare for work. Bereavement was far too common an occurrence for it to be used as an excuse for absenteeism. Quite the opposite in fact; people were expected to seek out an audience with whom they could express their grief.

Chantorria was still lying on the bed as Trafford made ready to leave.

'Well, I'll see you later then,' he said as he began unlocking the door. 'I'll get some food and stuff on my way back, shall I? Unless you feel like doing some shopping?'

Chantorria turned to look at him, her eyes hollow. For a moment Trafford was taken aback. She did not look anything like she had ever looked before. She looked like a zombie.

'I mean,' Trafford continued, 'I don't mind doing it

myself. I just thought it might give you something to do, get you out of the apartment.'

Still Chantorria did not reply. More and more her face looked to Trafford like the face of a corpse.

'Well,' he said finally, 'I'll see you later then. Call me if you need anything.'

As his hand was on the latch she spoke.

'We deserve this, you know,' she said in a strange, deathly monotone.

'Please, Chantorria. Don't.'

'We tried to defy God.'

'We did *not* try to defy anyone . . .'

'He had a plan and we tried to cheat. Now he's punished us for it.'

For a moment Trafford thought about continuing to reason with her but one look at the lifeless, soulless, hopeless apparition that had previously been his wife and he realized it was pointless.

'I'll come straight back after work,' he said.

When Trafford arrived at the office, Princess Lovebud was lying in wait, clearly anxious to exact revenge for the brief period of self-assertion that Trafford had enjoyed during his time as a Temple favourite. He had been expecting unpleasantness but he was nonetheless surprised at the form which her initial attack took. She actually hit him. She marched across the room and slapped him in the face with all the strength that her elephantine arm could muster. The blow sent him reeling.

'You little shit,' she shouted at him. 'We're the joke of the whole of DegSep, we are. I must have had a thousand emails already! I told them we were blessed, I told them we had a prophet on our floor! Now what do I look like? Well, I'll tell you something right now, you little wanker. I'm watching you, I am, and when you put a foot wrong, which you will, you're dead.'

Trafford said nothing and went to his desk. He passed Cassius, who gave him a tiny nod of sympathy. Sandra Dee was nowhere to be seen.

Ever alert to weakness of any kind, Princess Lovebud noticed Trafford looking.

'Yes,' she sneered, 'I notice that ginger bitch you was sticking up for hasn't had the guts to show her face. No, because she knows I'm after her too. Well, let's face it, you're not a lot of use to her now, are you? Not now it turns out that the Lord and the Love don't care about you at all.'

Trafford was sorry that Sandra Dee was absent; he had been hoping to see her, hoping for a smile of encouragement to help him through the day. With his daughter gone his love for Sandra Dee was the only positive emotion he had left in his body. Not that it could ever fill the void left by Caitlin Happymeal and it was unreciprocated anyway, but he would have liked to see her.

He wondered where she could be.

Just then the lift doors opened and two policemen emerged, accompanied by an official of the Temple. They marched straight across the floor towards where Trafford was sitting but it was not until they were standing before him that he realized it was him they had come for.

'Trafford Sewell,' said the Temple official, 'you're under arrest for crimes against faith.'

Instinctively Trafford turned to look at Cassius. His face was frozen with fear.

36

After Trafford had left the building to go to work Chantorria had shaved her head. Then she had put on her whitest bikini and the halo of which she had previously been so proud, but which she now wore upside down. She had then gone to Dirty Sexy Filthy Bitch and bought a small cat-o'-nine-tails from their S&M range. With this she had begun walking through the district whipping herself and shrieking at the top of her voice that the Lord and the Love should smite her down for the sinner that she was. Eventually, with her back lacerated and bloody, she arrived at the Spirit House to which she had been denied entry the previous day.

Once more she stood on the step and begged to see the Confessor. Once more she was refused but this time she screamed and shouted at such a pitch that Confessor Bailey came to the door and threatened to call the police if she did not leave.

'Punishment is all I deserve,' Chantorria protested. 'There can be no forgiveness for me. I want to confess.'

'Confess then and clear off,' Confessor Bailey replied.

'My husband had our baby vaccinated while I stood by and did nothing!' Chantorria screamed. 'Now the Love has taken Caitlin away from me as punishment for defying him.'

This was a very much more significant confession than Bailey had been expecting and he immediately had Chantorria brought into the house and taken down to the cellar while the Community Inquisitor was summoned. During the wait Bailey, unable to contain his horror at Chantorria's crime, took up his whip and flogged the weeping woman as she lay writhing on the wet stone floor. All the servants of the house were called to witness the punishment and the largest and strongest of them took up the lash when the Confessor tired.

Bailey had just called for cakes and wine to give him strength and ordered his men to chain Chantorria to a rough wooden table when Brother Redemption arrived. The Community Inquisitor was rarely seen in daytime; he was a creature of darkened rooms, gloomy cells and the night. Unlike most officers of the Temple, he was thin, but such flesh as he had was covered in tattoos. His body was a tableau of occult symbols and hellish nightmares in which various devilish creatures performed acts of sex and torture on sinners. On his forehead the legend *Ask not for whom the bell tolls. It tolls for thee* was written in Gothic script. Brother Redemption travelled about the parish in a rickshaw drawn by four convicted felons. Inside the rickshaw he kept his instruments of torture, and these were carried in when he swept into Bailey's Spirit House demanding to be shown the wretched sinner who had poisoned her baby. No screws and clamps were necessary to force a confession because Chantorria was only too anxious to unburden herself.

'I am a sinner! I deserve my punishment,' she sobbed from the table on which she lay in chains. 'My husband set our family on the path of defying the Lord!'

'Bring her up to the street,' Brother Redemption ordered.

'Perhaps, Brother,' the Confessor protested, his face red and his lips wet, 'I should keep the girl here for now. I know the wretched woman and it may be that more would be learned if I were to deal with her personally.'

Confessor Bailey was standing at the foot of the table on which Chantorria had been spread. He had divested himself of his magnificent cloak and golden thong and was naked apart from his white thigh boots and the bejewelled piercings that adorned his private parts. These flashed and glinted in the dim cellar light.

'Bring her up to the street,' Brother Redemption repeated and turned on his heel.

Confessor Bailey was furious to be dismissed in such a manner but the Inquisition was not an organization that even he could cross. Chantorria was dragged back up from the cellar and out into the street, where a jeering crowd had assembled. There she was bound by her wrists to the back of the rickshaw and forced to run behind it as Brother Redemption whipped up his four convicts and drove away.

37

Trafford was taken from his desk at DegSep then by boat to the headquarters of the Lake London Inquisition. This was a truly terrifying edifice, spoken of only in whispers, and it occupied the great dome of what had once been the city's foremost cathedral. Known to all as the Booby, in shape it reminded people of a surgically enhanced breast.

The lower section of the cathedral was unoccupied as it was at the mercy of the capricious Thames flood tides. A reinforced concrete floor had been installed at the base of the dome, some sixty feet above the waterline, and on this floor a labyrinth of cells and offices had been constructed. Even though the great half-ball of space had been partially filled, it still retained something of its former acoustic qualities and as Trafford entered he could hear the groans and screams of tortured souls echoing around the building.

Having been marched about halfway round the vast circle, past cell after cell containing a broken, whimpering object of human misery, Trafford was thrust into what he immediately saw was a torture chamber. There were racks, chains, hooks and cages, a glowing brazier that housed branding irons, knives, clubs, spikes, pincers, skewers, pliers and any number of objects, the terrifying uses of which Trafford could only guess at.

Six people were already present in the chamber: a guard, a large man who worked the bellows that heated the brazier, a man at either wheel of the rack, a hooded Inquisitor and, finally, a shaven-headed woman hanging unconscious from a rusty iron grid, naked but clothed in a crimson bodysuit of congealing blood. Trafford recognized her with a shudder. It was Chantorria.

'Good afternoon, Trafford,' said the Inquisitor, removing his hood. 'My name is Brother Redemption and I am the Temple-appointed Inquisitor for your district. On my face you will see written *Ask not for whom the bell tolls. It tolls for thee*, and no face ever displayed a truer sentiment. Your wife has told us that you like abusing children.'

Trafford tried to block out the horrifying scene that lay before him and to think. When they had arrested him they had not told him what crime of faith he was accused of, but since they had also arrested Chantorria and the Inquisitor had mentioned abusing children it seemed a fair guess that his arrest concerned the vaccination of Caitlin Happymeal.

Despite the terror churning in his stomach, Trafford saw

in this a glimmer of hope, because it meant that possibly they knew nothing as yet about his Humanist activities. Certainly they would execute him for having his child vaccinated but with Caitlin Happymeal gone Trafford did not fear death. Pain certainly, but not death. All Trafford cared about now was Sandra Dee, whom he loved, and his fervent belief in Humanism and the redeeming power of reason. For Trafford, his only duty left on Earth was to protect these things and so in that moment he conceived a plan. If they knew about the vaccination then their purpose would be to discover how it had been achieved, or at least by whom. Trafford therefore resolved to avoid giving them Cassius's name for as long as he could physically stand it, in the hope that Brother Redemption would assume that this was his only secret and would neglect to pursue other lines of investigation.

'Whatever I did I did alone,' Trafford replied. 'Neither my wife nor anyone else had anything to do with it.'

'And what did you do, Trafford?' the Inquisitor enquired.

'I have nothing to say to you.'

'Ah, so it's a secret, is it?' said Brother Redemption. 'Chantorria tells me that you are a keen keeper of secrets. Is that true?'

'I can't tell you. It's a secret,' said Trafford and a second later he lay sprawled on the concrete floor, his jaw aching from the guard's punch.

'Did you arrange to have your daughter vaccinated?' Brother Redemption asked.

'What does it matter now?' Trafford gasped. 'She's dead anyway.'

'The appropriate response to a question is an answer, Trafford.'

Trafford received a vicious kick from behind. He did not look up from where he lay with his cheek pressed against the wet concrete. He watched sideways as Brother Redemption's boots crossed the floor and stopped at the foot of the grid from which Chantorria was hanging. Trafford heard the harsh clang of metal against metal and then, with a grim, soggy kind of thud, Chantorria's limp, beaten body fell into Trafford's line of vision, her bruised face scarcely three feet from his own. He had thought she was unconscious but now her eyes opened and they stared at each other across the concrete.

'I'm sorry,' Trafford said.

Chantorria struggled to reply.

'I deserve this,' she whispered, her lips fat and crusted with blood. 'We both do. We defied God.'

'If God approves of the way you've been treated then he *should* be defied,' Trafford answered. 'He's no better than the Devil.'

He must have been kicked in the head at this point for he lost consciousness, and when he regained it he found himself chained to the same grid from which Chantorria had fallen. His face was pressed hard against the metal. His naked body was dripping with icy water and through the bars he could see the guard standing with an empty bucket in his hands.

'The prisoner is awake, Inquisitor,' the man said.

Trafford listened as footsteps walked round the grid behind him until once more Brother Redemption came into sight.

'Your wife tells me that you posted a birthing video that was not your own. Is that so?'

'Yes, I did do that.'

'Might one ask why?'

'Because I believe that a person has a right to privacy.'

'Weren't you proud of your birthing video?'

'Why should I be proud of a natural event for which I can take no credit?'

'Because the Temple urges you to be proud of every single aspect of yourself, Trafford – your size, your colour, your opinions, your choice of body jewellery. Unless of course you have something to hide. Do you have something to hide?'

'I have nothing of which I'm ashamed, if that's what you mean.'

'I'm fascinated then. If you had nothing to be ashamed of, why on Earth would you desire privacy?'

Trafford thought for a moment.

'Because I consider it fundamental to my sense of self.'

'Or perhaps it's because you're a pervert and a heretic.'

Trafford did not reply.

'Perhaps,' the Inquisitor continued, 'you desire privacy in order that you may pursue your reading? What is this, Trafford?'

Trafford's heart sank as the Inquisitor produced a copy

of *The Origin of Species*, which Trafford had last seen underneath his bed and wrapped in the cover of a celebrity magazine headlined *When bum lifts go wrong. Celeb saggy arses at the beach.*

'It's a book about natural history . . . I like natural history.'

'Trafford, reading the work of the Antichrist Darwin is a crime against faith.'

'I know that. I am a faith criminal.'

'Where did you get this rubbish, Trafford?'

'I found it. I often find books. I keep my eyes open all the time. There's quite a few still around if you look. In the attics of derelict buildings mainly and rotting in landfills of course. All sorts of things come to the surface when the water table rises.'

Trafford could see the Inquisitor's face through the bars and tried to read on it whether he was being believed. But the watery blue eyes into which he stared gave nothing away.

'I read a page or two,' Brother Redemption said. 'It seemed like absolute shit to me.'

'I expect that's because you're as stupid as you look, Brother.'

'Five,' said Brother Redemption. Trafford heard a snap and a rush of air and instantly his back was split open with a pain such as he had never before experienced. Four more lashes followed and when the whipping was done he was weeping and screaming for mercy.

'Earlier today,' the Inquisitor went on, 'your wife Chantorria went to her Confessor and told him that you had Caitlin Happymeal inoculated. Is that true?'

'Yes, it is.'

And despite the pain he was in, Trafford drew strength from the fact that the Inquisitor seemed to have moved on from his interest in books.

'She said that you acted against her wishes,' Brother Redemption said. 'Is that also true?'

'Yes, it is. She told me not to do it. She begged me.'

'Then perhaps she will be spared. That will be a matter for Solomon Kentucky and the will of the people.'

Trafford saw Brother Redemption's attention turning back to the copy of *The Origin of Species* that he was holding. The Inquisitor's eyes glanced downwards and he began idly flicking through it. Trafford struggled to think of something to say to divert his attention.

'If Chantorria confessed all this voluntarily,' Trafford asked, trying to keep his voice steady, 'why was it necessary for you to beat her?'

To his relief the Inquisitor snapped the book shut with a grunt of contempt and hurled it into the brazier.

'It was necessary to discover whether she was telling the truth or not,' he replied. 'She is clearly a witch and witches are cunning.'

'She is not a witch.'

'She allowed the good people of her community to believe that she was holy when in fact she was harbouring a heretic and a devil baby. Doesn't that seem like the work of a witch?'

Trafford did not answer. His strength was bleeding out of him from the deep wounds on his back.

'Who vaccinated your child, Trafford?' the Inquisitor asked in the most casual of voices, and with that question Trafford knew that the true ordeal was about to begin.

'I shall never betray him,' Trafford replied. 'He tried to save my baby. I'll never tell you.'

'You will, Trafford.'

'Never.'

'Ten,' said the Inquisitor.

Ten more lashes followed, by the end of which Trafford was semi-conscious. Next they branded the word 'heretic' on his stomach and his buttocks and stretched him on the rack.

All through this agony Trafford kept the face of Sandra Dee in the forefront of his mind. It was for her that he was holding out. Cassius was the diversion that would lead Brother Redemption away from the secret of the library. If they discovered that, Sandra Dee would be caught. Trafford even began to hope that he might die before he gave way and then the secret would be truly safe.

As they stretched him they applied electricity to his genitals and began to remove his fingernails.

It was then that Trafford's strength finally deserted him.

'Enough,' he cried. 'The name you are looking for is—'

'Cassius,' said the Inquisitor.

Trafford was shocked. He struggled to find some clarity in the crimson confusion of his thoughts.

'I don't understand,' he whispered finally.

'What's not to understand?' Brother Redemption asked. 'It was your colleague Cassius who pushed the poisoned

334

needle into Caitlin Happymeal. I've known from the start. All the pain you have been through has been for nothing. I was just curious to see how long you'd hold out. Call it professional interest.'

'But . . .'

'Trafford, *of course* we knew. You *knew* we knew, if only you'd bothered to think about it instead of trying to be a hero. When you first told Chantorria that you had been approached by a Vaccinator it was on the day of a Fizzy Coff, and you said it was a colleague who had come to you. You told her, she told us. From there it was the simplest process of elimination to alight on Cassius. Unfortunately, unlike you, he was a little too quick for us.'

'He escaped?'

'He's dead.'

'You killed him?'

'He killed himself. Straight after you were arrested. Went to the men's bath and rest room comfort area and took poison. He knew which way the wind was blowing.'

Trafford said nothing but deep inside himself, despite the terrible pain, his soul was flying. Cassius was a hero! If he'd been caught and tortured the secrets of so many would have been revealed: Vaccinators, Humanists and Sandra Dee most certainly. But he had protected them all; he had silenced himself before he could be made to speak.

'So, as I say,' Brother Redemption went on, 'your agony and the loss of those three fingernails were for nothing. I must say, you held out remarkably. In fact I had very nearly decided to stop. We don't want you dead, after all.'

'Why would you care? You knew my secret anyway. Does it really matter if you kill me now rather than later?'

'Of course it matters, you bloody fool,' said Brother Redemption. 'The Temple needs you. You and your wife have made fools of the elders. They trumpeted your brat as a miracle baby and then she died. Now we know why she died.'

'From cholera.'

'Sent by the Love because you defied him. Now it's your job to confess your sins to the nation that they might understand the full story of the cursed child Caitlin Happymeal.'

38

The great show trial was to be held a week later. It was to take place at Wembley on the very night that had originally been scheduled as the climax of the *Miracles Do Happen* campaign.

Trafford was to get his moment in the spotlight after all.

In order that the trial might be seen to be legal and to observe due process, the Temple allowed Trafford some medical treatment in his cell and also assigned him a lawyer. Her name was Parisian Poledance and she visited him on the evening before the great day.

'I understand that, unlike your wife, you decline to repent or even to take responsibility for Caitlin's death?' Parisian Poledance stated in a clipped and officious tone. She wore the silver wig, black bra and thick, substantial knickers of her profession and seemed to Trafford to be every bit as cold and efficient as her uniform suggested.

'Of course I don't take responsibility,' Trafford replied. 'She died of cholera. I didn't make the water in our tenement.'

'No, obviously not. God did. The question the law must ask is why did God make the infected water? Do you accept that the Lord and the Love visited cholera upon your tenement in retribution for your efforts to circumnavigate his will?'

'No, I do not.'

'Trafford, if you take responsibility for your actions, we may gain a lighter sentence.'

'I do take responsibility for my actions. That's the point. It seems that I am the only person who does. Unlike the law, I don't blame God and I don't credit God. I saved my daughter from mumps and measles. Then she died of cholera. I do not believe that I or God had anything to do with it. It was the Temple who denied me access to a cholera vaccine.'

Parisian Poledance tapped at her computer in an impatient manner. Clearly she did not appreciate having to waste her time with deluded people who refused to accept basic legal principles such as that God had everything to do with everything.

'Right then,' she said tartly, 'let us get down to first cases. Do you admit that you had Caitlin vaccinated?'

'Yes, I do.'

'Is there anyone or anything on to which you can shift some of the blame?'

'I don't understand.'

Parisian Poledance made no effort to disguise her

frustration at what she clearly thought was wilful obstruction on Trafford's part.

'The law recognizes victim status as a plea in mitigation,' she snapped. 'If you can establish grounds for claiming that you yourself are a victim, the judges will be obliged to take that into account in their summing up. For instance, did your parents fail to big you up as a child, thus leaving you with crippling esteem issues?'

'No.'

'Are you an addictive personality? Are you struggling with inner demons or a reliance on prescription drugs? Have size issues and negative self-image led to your failing to fulfil your enormous potential as a proud, strong person?'

'No.'

'Have you been subjected to disrespect by those who refuse to recognize your legitimate pride in who and what you are?'

'No! None of those things. I'm not looking for a plea in mitigation. I loved my daughter and I acted as I did in her best interests, that's all.'

Parisian Poledance looked at her watch, clearly desperate to be done with this pointless and unrewarding brief.

'Trafford, I have been appointed by the Temple as your legal counsel. It is my duty to inform you that "acting in your child's best interests" is not a defence for having her vaccinated.'

'I don't need a lawyer to tell me the law is insane, Ms Poledance. I was not offering it as a defence, merely as an explanation.'

'So you have no defence?'

'I do have a defence.'

'I mean a legal one,' Parisian Poledance snapped, 'under the law of the land and of the Temple. Not some time-wasting foolishness.'

'I have a defence.'

'You realize that you are to stand trial on two counts: that you are a Vaccinator and an Evolutionist, neither of which you deny?'

'Yes and my defence will be the same on both counts.'

Parisian Poledance gave him a weary look.

'Have you studied eight years at the bar, Trafford?'

'No. I haven't.'

'I have. And since then I have had another ten years' experience in court. I confidently expect one day to be a Temple counsellor.'

'Congratulations.'

'And yet while I can see no defence for a confessed Vaccinator and Evolutionist under the law, you can?'

'Yes.'

'What is it?'

'My faith.'

'Your faith?'

'The law of the Temple states that a person's faith is inalienable. To deny a person's faith is incitement to religious hatred. Well, I believe in vaccination. I believe in evolution! I believe in an understanding of the physical universe based on empirical evidence and deduction, not a supernatural controlling being. That is my faith! My God

340

is called Natural Selection. Natural Selection made me! The law guarantees me my right to faith.'

For a moment Parisian Poledance was silent. Briefly, she seemed lost for words.

'On what basis do you call your belief in the delusions of the monkey men a faith?' she asked finally.

'Because I believe in them absolutely with all my heart.'

'Believing in something does not make it a faith,' Poledance answered pompously. 'I believe in sweet wine and ginger biscuits. I believe in rats and cockroaches, but none of those things are my faith.'

'Biscuits are physical objects. Rats are natural creatures like ourselves. Evolution is a mental concept, something we understand in our minds, just like God.'

Parisian Poledance thought for a moment. It seemed to Trafford that she was actually taking an interest in his argument.

'You say that evolutionary theory is a faith because you believe it.' She wore a sly expression. 'Why do you believe it?'

'Because it's beautiful, it's logical and it can be proved. It is the only, and I mean the *only*, satisfactory explanation for the emergence of complex life on Earth! Every shred of evidence thus far discovered on Earth fits it, while not one shred of evidence has been found to show that the universe was made in a week and man in a day. Man did not emerge in a day! Whatever it was that brought him about, be it God or some cosmic coincidence that can be called God, it did *not* happen in a day! It happened over millions and millions of years.'

'So you say that the ideas of the monkey men can be proved?' the lawyer asked.

'Yes, if not absolutely then certainly beyond reasonable doubt.'

'Ah ha!' Poledance cried triumphantly. 'Then it cannot be a faith!'

'What?'

'A faith is something in which a man must *believe*. Something in which he must put his trust, his *faith*. If it can be proved then it's fact and a fact requires no *faith* to believe in it. Thus your ideas have no protection under the law.'

'Because they're true?'

'Because you claim that they can be proved by evidence. No faith can be proved by evidence, that's what makes it a faith. Either your monkey men ideas have no basis in science, in which case you can call them a faith, or else they are based on scientific proof, in which case they are not a faith and the law offers them no protection. Which is it to be? Can vaccination be *proved* to work or do you merely have *faith* in it? Is your evolution based on solid evidence or do you follow it through pious conviction?'

'Vaccination can be proved and evolution is based on solid evidence.'

'Then these things have nothing to do with faith and you will be convicted of heresy.'

Trafford actually found himself gently smiling.

'Well,' he conceded, 'I did not really expect to convince you.'

Parisian Poledance looked relieved. She turned to the webcam on her computer. 'Let the record show that the defendant did not wish to offer up a defence or a plea in mitigation.'

She rose to leave. She had done her duty and clearly had no desire to linger any longer. At the door she turned once more to face Trafford.

'You do realize that they will almost certainly burn you, don't you?'

'My daughter is dead,' Trafford replied.

'Oh, get over yourself,' said Parisian Poledance.

The cell door clanged behind her as she left.

39

When Trafford met Chantorria backstage at Wembley
Stadium, it was the first time that he had seen her since
she had lain bleeding on the cell floor in front of him.
Since then they had cleaned her up considerably and
applied body make-up to her cuts and bruises. She looked
much better, although her near-shaven head gave her a
somewhat wild appearance, particularly coupled with the
strange, faraway look in her eye.

'Hello,' said Trafford.

'We are sinners. We deserve this,' was her only reply.

They had been brought up the equipment ramp and
were standing with their guards behind a massive bank of
speakers. Out on the stage a song was just finishing. It was
followed by a deafening roar and then the muffled voice of
the singer could be heard addressing the crowd. Due to the
directional nature of the sound system, Trafford could not

make out what he was saying but it was no doubt an injunction to dream the dream and be whatever they wanted to be.

Trafford looked at Chantorria. He wondered if she was recalling the last time they had been at the stadium, when they had been a part of the cheering multitude and not, as now, terrifyingly, an event on the bill. It was so little time ago and yet they had come such a long way since then. That had been the night when for the second time he had raised the idea of vaccinating Caitlin. It was fitting, he thought, that their journey should end here.

Trafford was surprised to notice within himself a strange sense of calm. He supposed that when you knew that you were shortly to be burned at the stake, preparing to speak heresy to a crowd of a quarter of a million people held no fears.

Up until this point the Faith Festival had been progressing along the usual lines. The regular announcement had been made that this was the biggest festival ever, easily surpassing in scale and significance the previous week's record-breaking gathering. The interchangeable sequence of stars had informed the crowd that all the problems of the world would disappear if only they wanted them to, that poverty, disease and injustice would very soon be a thing of the past if only they would all put their hands in the air and sing. Girls had been hoisted briefly on to sagging shoulders and banners had been waved. Hundreds of thousands of burgers and doughnuts had been consumed and now the evening was moving towards its usual climax, which would be a mass grieving for the dead kiddies.

This climax, however, was going to be different. Tonight there was to be a grand trial for heresy and Trafford and Chantorria were the co-defendants. They stood, naked and in chains, in the wings of the great concert platform as the last band of the evening bade their farewells to the crowd and left the stage with their dancers, roadies, hangers-on and the popular comedian who had introduced them. Then Bishop Confessor Solomon Kentucky strode past them without a glance, and was guided around the great speaker stacks by his security staff and out on to the stage in order to explain the significance of what was about to happen.

'People of faith!' Trafford heard him shout. Such was the quality of Kentucky's diction that Trafford could make out his words despite the backstage distortion. 'Tonight, as always, we assemble to worship the Love and give thanks for the deliverance of our tiny innocents into Heaven. Let me hear you say Amen!'

'Amen,' came the thunderous response.

'Amen,' Trafford heard Chantorria whisper under her breath.

'Now, on the subject of tiny innocents,' Solomon Kentucky continued, 'I have words to say to you. Tonight we expose a grievous crime against faith! A crime perpetrated by two wicked sinners. A crime so corrupt and duplicitous that it deceived even the all-seeing eye of the Temple. Let me hear you say Love!'

'Love!' the crowd roared.

'I said let me hear you say Love!' Solomon Kentucky shouted.

'LOVE!' came the even louder response.

'Ev Love,' Trafford whispered under his breath as a sound technician bustled up to him.

'All right if I mike you up now?' the technician asked and without waiting for a reply proceeded to hang a radio pack over Trafford and Chantorria's shoulders.

'All right if I tape it to the chains?' he asked, carrying on with his job, gaffer-taping little microphones to the chains that hung around their necks.

A second technician bustled up to join the first.

'When they come off,' he said, 'we need those mikes for the finale.'

'I *know*,' the first technician replied irritably, 'I have read the running order.'

On stage the Bishop Confessor continued his introduction.

'You recall this child!' he said. And on the vast screens all round the stadium could be seen the picture of Caitlin Happymeal that had been central to the *Miracles Do Happen* campaign. Trafford and Chantorria saw it too on the backstage monitors and separately they wept.

'You recall that this child survived *measles*,' Solomon Kentucky went on. 'This child survived *mumps*. This child survived the most virulent plagues that have so far been sent by the Love to blight our fair city on a lake. People, I say to you that it was a miracle! Let me hear you say Oh yeah!'

'Oh yeah!' they shouted.

'The Temple loved this child! We saw in this miracle baby a symbol of hope! A symbol of the Lord and the Love's faith in the future of all mankind! We celebrated her survival at our places of worship and on the net. We raised up the child's mother as a paragon of virtue before the eyes of all women! Let me hear you say Yes we did!'

'Yes we did!' they shouted.

'Let me hear you say YES WE DID!' Kentucky repeated.

'YES WE DID,' the crowd echoed dutifully.

'But then, people! . . . Then, O my people!'

And now Kentucky's voice shook with passion and sorrow. Trafford watched him on the backstage monitors as he began to twitch and to fidget, like a man possessed.

'Then, people, the miracle child died! She died, people! Ah, let me hear you say Woe is me!'

'Woe is me,' the crowd shouted.

'That's *right*, people, woe is you! Because get ready for this, my children! I said get ready for this. I say *go figure*! Because it turned out this miracle child wasn't a miracle child at all. Right after she survived the mumps, just as we were saluting an angel among us, a common cholera came and gathered this sorry child up. It took her straight to Heaven and, let me tell you, there's nothing miraculous about that. It happens every day. And let me tell you something else, people! When I heard that news my heart was heavy. My heart was confused. *Why* had the Lord and the Love saved this child only then to take her? Why had he taunted us so? Let me hear you say Why!'

'Why!' the crowd roared.

'Why!' Solomon Kentucky roared back.

'Why!' was once more the thunderous response.

'Why?' Chantorria whispered as she stood backstage in chains.

'I'll tell you why!' the Bishop Confessor shouted. 'Punishment! That's why! Punishment for sin! Bring forth the sinners!'

Music played and Trafford and Chantorria were pushed out into the dazzling glare of the spotlights, whipped from behind as they tripped and stumbled, dragging their chains over the coils of cables, guitar stands and leads, drum kits and endless plastic bottles that littered the stage. As they approached the Bishop Confessor, the music grew in huge crashing chords, a choir sang doom-laden snatches of opera and blood-red fireworks lit up the sky.

'Behold the sinners, the parents of the child!' Solomon Kentucky shouted. 'Bring forward the woman!'

Chantorria was then thrust centre stage, where she collapsed at Solomon Kentucky's feet.

'Chantorria!' he cried. 'Tell the people why the Love took your baby from you!'

'Because we defied God's will,' Chantorria wept. 'My husband had our child vaccinated and I stood by.'

There was a moment's hush from the crowd. This was a serious crime indeed.

'What did you say?' the Bishop Confessor roared.

'I said my husband had our child vaccinated.'

'Beat her!' Solomon Kentucky instructed and guards

stepped forward with whips to lash Chantorria as she grovelled on her knees.

The crowd, thus treated to the thrilling punishment of a chained and naked woman, screamed their hatred and called for heavier blows until finally the Bishop Confessor raised his hand for silence.

'Chantorria,' he said solemnly, 'did your husband allow witches to push poisoned needles into your child in an effort to cheat the Lord? Did your husband say unto himself, other children may be gathered unto Heaven but not mine, for I will pervert the Love's purpose with witchcraft?'

'Yes, yes, he did!' shrieked Chantorria, bleeding terribly from the blows she had sustained.

'And were you punished for it!'

'Yes! The Lord took my baby!'

'Beat her!' Kentucky instructed once more and again the crowd screamed for blood as this time Chantorria was beaten into unconsciousness.

'Bring forward the man witch!' the Bishop Confessor shouted and now it was Trafford's turn to be thrust to the centre of the stage.

'Your baby died,' cried Solomon Kentucky.

Trafford struggled to focus. He knew he would have only one chance to make his point. There could be no room now to cajole the crowd with subtlety as once he had planned: brevity and clarity were all that mattered.

'Yes, Bishop Confessor! She died. But not of measles or mumps, which she had been vaccinated against. The vaccines worked! She died of cholera. There is a vaccine for cholera also, but unfortunately I could not get it for my daughter.'

'Silence!' shouted Solomon Kentucky.

'The vaccines worked! They gave my daughter a resistance to the diseases for which they were designed. Listen to me, people!'

'Beat him!' cried Kentucky and the blows began.

'Demand vaccinations for your children!' Trafford shouted as he tried to shield himself from the blows. 'People here today, demand vaccines for your children!'

'The Lord and the Love will not be denied!' cried Kentucky.

'Any God who kills a child to punish its parents is not worth worshipping!'

At that point, through the crunching of blows Trafford realized that the tone of his voice had changed and he knew that his microphone had been turned off. He heard the Bishop Confessor screaming 'Witch and heretic!' at him and demanding that he be beaten harder. But for a moment, before he lost consciousness, he thought he felt a silence from the crowd – as if some of them might even have understood what he had to say.

40

When he came round he was back in his cell. It took a long time for him to work this out as his eyes were glued together with blood, his ribs felt broken and his muscles were too smashed up for him to move.

And yet, as he lay there, immobile, his body racked with pain, facing the certainty of an agonizing death, he felt a sort of contentment.

In a way, he'd won. He had made a protest. He had spoken out, forming two or three whole sentences of truth in a world where truth was illegal. Not only that but he had done it in the middle of a Wembley Faith Festival! A quarter of a million people had heard him live and many millions more would have seen and heard it on an infotainment loop. The Temple had designed his confession as a major event and briefly he had hijacked it. Nobody had ever done that before. Nobody had ever spoken the truth at Wembley and he doubted that anyone ever would again. In a society where everybody was 'proud' to be an individual but was in fact one of so many sheep in a vast herd, he was unique. And who knew? Perhaps somebody had listened. Perhaps one or two in that multitude had heard his point and had begun to think. Even if he had planted a single seed of doubt in one person's head, he had made a difference. He had scored a victory against the Temple. Who else could say as much?

But more than that. Much, much more than that. He had held on to all his precious secrets. They would kill him while actually knowing almost nothing about him. They knew that he had had his child vaccinated but that was a secret he was proud to advertise. They knew nothing about his secret world, his studies in science and history, fiction and the power of the imagination. He doubted whether their imaginations, brutish and stunted as they were, would even understand it if they did.

He had told them nothing about the Humanists, not a word! The fools had not even known enough to guess that a man who had had his child vaccinated might pursue other subversive activities. The network was safe. Cassius was dead but the library would remain open, and other libraries would one day be formed. For the time being at least they were safe. Macallan and Taylor were safe. Connor Newbury was safe. Above all, Sandra Dee was safe! His silence, and Cassius's courage in taking his own life, had saved them all.

And they knew nothing of his love. His most painful

and precious secret. They did not know that he was in love with Sandra Dee and that he had given her the gift of books so she would for evermore be free to travel to better worlds than the one the Temple had made. Sandra Dee would be proud of him; right now, he imagined, she would be terrified, fearful that his capture would lead them to her. But as weeks went by and no arrest came she would understand that she was safe. She would return to the library. She would induct others to the cause. And who knew, perhaps one day the world would be free of blind faith.

Doctors arrived and inspected his wounds.

'Have to have you fit enough to mount the bonfire' was all they would say when he enquired about his condition.

The following day he was brought a Zimmer frame and told that he must take some exercise.

'Your execution is in less than a week,' the doctor said. 'If you can't walk to it unaided then it's us who'll answer for it. In my view, if they want their prisoners fit enough to be properly executed then they shouldn't beat them so hard in the first place – but nobody listens to me.'

Trafford was helped off his bed and out of his cell. He was made to limp along the great circular corridor and towards the centre of the dome, where he found himself suddenly beneath the great vaulted ceiling. The middle part of the floor that had been laid at the base of the dome had not been built upon, so it was open to the roof far above. This was clearly the exercise yard, for it was filled with other figures just like Trafford, bruised and broken, supported by frames and walking sticks, taking their exercise in preparation for their execution.

'Walk,' the guard said.

Trafford joined the shuffling crowd, his thoughts fixed mainly on Sandra Dee. Sometimes, of course, his mind turned to Caitlin Happymeal and from there to Phoenix Rising, his other lost child, but he did his best not to dwell on such sadness.

'I forgive you,' he heard a voice say. It was a strange voice, inflicted with some form of impediment, and at first Trafford did not realize that it was directed at him. Then the same voice addressed him by name.

'I forgive you, Trafford.'

Looking round, Trafford saw a swollen face, purple with bruising, both eyes blackened and almost closed. Peering into it, he realized with a chill of horror that he knew this person. The last time he had seen him he had been wearing thick glasses and guarding the entrance to his precious library.

'They . . . caught you?' Trafford asked.

'Of course they did,' the Owl said in his strange new voice. 'I presume you talked. It doesn't matter. We'll all talk in the end. Me too, I'm sure. I tried to bite my tongue out when they came for me but I made a half-arsed job of it and they sewed it back. Fortunately I have very little for them. I never knew the names of most of the people Cassius brought to us. Except for the troublemakers, like you.'

'I didn't betray you,' Trafford replied.

'Whatever,' the Owl replied, 'to use a phrase which I personally abhor.'

'Keep walking!' a guard barked and the Owl moved on, leaving Trafford to shuffle in the opposite direction.

After this Trafford saw Macallan and then Taylor, and Connor Newbury, shockingly reduced from his former glory. There were others also that he recognized from the library and Trafford realized with an anguished heart that somehow or other the Inquisition had penetrated the resistance after all. He started looking about, desperately searching for Sandra Dee, hoping against hope that he would not find her. Why had she been so impatient? Why had she insisted on joining the library so soon? If only she had waited she might have avoided this terrible round-up.

Then he saw her. She was standing by the door through which he had entered the exercise yard and staring back at him. He began to hobble towards her but she did not move. Nor was she bruised or injured in any way. She was dressed, as always, prettily but modestly and she looked fresh and clean. Beside her stood Brother Redemption. Trafford stopped. Then he watched as Sandra Dee said something to the Inquisitor, as if giving him an order. Then Brother Redemption began walking towards him.

41

Trafford was ordered to follow Sandra Dee back to his cell. Head bowed, he watched the gentle sway of her light cotton dress as she walked. It was a dress he had last seen spread out around her as she sat nearly naked on the bench of her boat, listening to his sexual fantasies.

'Leave us,' Sandra Dee said to Brother Redemption as they entered Trafford's cell.

'But—' the Inquisitor began to protest.

'He's been beaten half to death,' Sandra Dee snapped. 'I don't think he's likely to give me any trouble. Leave us.'

'Very well, ma'am,' the previously all-powerful figure said and left without further protest. The door closed behind him and Sandra Dee and Trafford were alone.

'You work for the Inquisition?' Trafford asked. Somehow he felt calm; the calm of the already dead.

'Well, not exactly,' Sandra Dee replied. 'I'm a government

employee, like you. A policewoman, a spy really, but effectively we all work for the Temple, don't we?'

Trafford might have felt strangely calm but that did not prevent him from being totally confused.

'You came to work in our office . . . to spy on us?'

'Yes.'

'Do the police have a spy in every office?'

'Of course not.'

'Why ours?'

'We were looking for a Vaccinator,' she explained. 'You're wrong about all the data NatDat collects being useless, by the way. We use it all the time, particularly Degrees of Separation. That's how we knew that in the last few years our dead friend Cassius had been around colleagues whose children seemed to be bucking the plague trends. Simple link: find a parent whose child survives a plague, key in all known contacts, keep doing it until you find a common factor. In this case, Cassius. That's how we usually catch Vaccinators. Using DegSep.'

There were so many things that Trafford wanted to ask, so many accusations that he wished to hurl into the face of this woman who was a spy.

'But . . . if you catch Vaccinators by tracing healthy children' – Trafford's voice shook with outrage – 'you must accept that vaccination *works*!'

'Obviously, Trafford. That's why the police are not the Inquisition. They are obliged by their faith to deny it. We are not bound by such strict codes of piety. We catch the Vaccinators because we know that vaccination works and then they burn them because they know that it doesn't.'

Suddenly Trafford lunged at her, his fist clenched, his face snarling. He did not get halfway across the floor before his wounded body gave out.

'Please, Trafford,' said Sandra Dee, 'don't be ridiculous.'

'By arresting Vaccinators you murder children!' he shouted.

'I'm a policewoman, Trafford. My job is to uphold the law.'

'Why? Why are you a policewoman?'

'For all the reasons that you became a Humanist. For all the reasons that first attracted you to me and . . .' here she seemed momentarily to hestitate, 'and me to you.'

'Don't be insane.'

'I'm serious. I am everything you are except I have mastered my conscience. Working undercover allows me as many secrets as I want. Only I know who I am. The false blog you uncovered gets selected and uploaded for me by a clerk in my department. I've never even looked at it. I think that the world is as shitty as you do, Trafford, but by working for it I get to opt out. I don't even have to have a fucking boob job. My body's my own and my soul is my own. I live an entirely secret life and the Temple means nothing to me. And what's more, in the course of my duties I get to meet the most interesting people. People like you, Trafford. And the other Humanists. We had only guessed at their existence before you brought me to them. We had absolutely no idea they were so organized, and while I was pursuing you I got to read all those wonderful books. I shall keep mine. That's why I'm a cop, Trafford. Drug cops take drugs, vice cops look at illegal porn and I get to read *Pride and Prejudice*.'

'You filthy, selfish bitch . . .'

'Trafford, selfish is the *only way to be*. Why shouldn't I be selfish? When you consider what humanity is, what a useless, fucked-up tribe of sadistic, pig-ignorant fools we really are, you see that selfishness is actually the only moral course. Why sacrifice yourself for other people? They're all utter shits. If you have the character to *make* a sacrifice, you're already too good for the arseholes you want to save. Look at the world they built.'

'Am I a shit? Was Cassius a shit?'

She looked at him for a moment before replying.

'No. You're not a shit, Trafford. You're a fine man and I liked you. There are exceptions, of course, but not enough to be worth martyring yourself for. Humanity had it all and threw it away. If it had it all again it would throw it away again. History is one long proof that the human race does not deserve the brains it was born with. We're a rotten useless breed and in the long run the only thing to do is to look after number one.'

Trafford was still lying on the floor where he had fallen. She pulled him to his feet and helped him back to his bed. He was surprised how strong she was.

'Think about it, Trafford,' Sandra Dee continued, 'and you'll see I'm right.'

'Why would you care what I think?' he asked.

'Because you're clever and good at keeping secrets,' she replied. 'We need people like you.'

For a moment Trafford did not understand what she was saying.

'What do you mean?' he stuttered.

'I mean that it's time for you to grow up. You wanted to be an individual, then *be* an individual. Your child is dead; your wife has denounced you. You're a non-person now, so you can pretend to be anybody we choose. Join us, become a spy. We can change your face, place you in a community and you'll get to keep all your secrets while you ferret out other people's. We could even see each other occasionally to swap books or . . . whatever. It's that or burn, Trafford.'

'I'd rather burn.'

'I suggest you need to think about it.'

'Thinking about it will change nothing. I'd rather burn for ever than become what you are, Sandra Dee.'

'And what's that?'

'Inhuman.'

'Then I'm proud to be inhuman because humanity is shit.'

'It isn't and you know it. You've read enough books to understand that. Humanity encompasses the highest and the lowest that nature has to offer. I'd rather die still believing in the highest than become what you are. You're the lowest, far lower than a bully like Princess Lovebud; compared to you, she's an angel.'

Sandra Dee got up without another word and went to the door. Then she turned.

'We killed Caitlin Happymeal, by the way,' she said.

Trafford was white with shock.

'You . . . killed her?'

'Yes. Didn't you think it was a bit of a coincidence that she died just before you planned to use the climax of the *Miracles Do Happen* campaign to announce that Caitlin had survived not through the work of the Lord but through being vaccinated? You never should have told me the plan, Trafford. The moment you did that, I knew she would have to die. I reported what you'd told me to my superiors and they got our chemical people to introduce the cholera virus into your building. We killed Caitlin Happymeal to prevent you using her as a tool against the Temple. So you see, her death is really your fault.'

Even as Trafford's head swam with the horror of what she was telling him, a final idea was growing in his mind. One last plan.

'I loved you,' he said.

'I didn't ask you to,' she replied.

'But you made love to me.'

'I had sex with you.'

'Do you think you know what love is?'

'I think so.'

'I don't think you do.'

'Well, we'll never know, will we? At least you won't.'

'I wanted to tell you . . . To tell you what love is . . . I wrote you a letter. I wrote it to you at work on the morning I was arrested. I think perhaps I sensed that something was going to happen.'

'Sensed? Trafford,' Sandra Dee said with a smile, 'I thought you dealt only in reason?'

'It's filed under Ev Love.'

'Ev Love?'

'Yes. Everlasting Love.'

Despite the coldness which she was working so hard to portray, something in Sandra Dee's manner changed at this.

'Everlasting love?' she asked, and Trafford thought he detected in her voice the tiniest of cracks.

'Yes,' he replied. 'Everlasting love.'

Sandra Dee resumed her defiant smile, her defences once more intact.

'Always the romantic, eh, Trafford?' she said. Then she was gone.

Trafford was left alone, wondering. Would she look? She was a police spy after all; she was interested in people and naturally curious. Also, despite what she had said, Trafford knew that she had loved him a little. In her own inhuman way. He thought she would look. He believed that she would look and if she did, if she went to Trafford's folder at DegSep and opened the Ev Love file, the emails would be sent. Emails which contained the message of evolution. Emails which from that point on would be self-generating.

42

On the morning scheduled for Trafford's public execution the news loops were filled with the story that the heretic of Wembley, the man who had openly boasted of poisoning his child, was also a member of a sinister sect, a secret, subversive terrorist organization. Worse even than the suicide-bombing teenagers of the Other Faith, these people, the news reported, sought to revive the dreadful lies of the monkey men through study and teaching. Their sworn aim was to bring back the very delusions that had caused the Love to send down his terrible flood in the first place.

The route to the funeral pyre along which Trafford was whipped was therefore lined with many thousands of outraged citizens, a great crowd blind with fury over the heretic pervert who enjoyed poisoning children and who believed his great-grandfather was a monkey.

At the place of execution the other members of the sect had already been crucified and were hanging, still alive, from the crosses to which they had been nailed. The crowd hurled mud and stones at them as some begged for mercy and offered to repent while others stayed silent. Trafford noticed that Connor Newbury did not plead. Trafford was surprised; he had not credited him with such character.

Chantorria was there too, naked and in the stocks, a willing object of scorn, her mind half gone with grief and fear, babbling that only through her suffering might her baby one day find her way to Heaven.

Trafford mounted the steps from which he was to be put on to the fire. With a chill of anguish he saw that the pyre was made of books and he realized this was the contents of the library that had brought him so much happiness.

Confessor Bailey was already in place when Trafford reached the top of the steps. As his Confessor, it was Bailey's job to demand of Trafford that he recant and deny his beliefs prior to his execution.

'Trafford Sewell,' he intoned solemnly into the microphone, clearly relishing his moment in the spotlight, 'do you confess to being a Vaccinator and a reader of books and a believer in the so-called "science" of the monkey men?'

'I do,' Trafford replied loudly, 'and proudly!'

The crowd shrieked its derision. Looking down, Trafford saw that Princess Lovebud and Tinkerbell had somehow forced themselves to the front of the crowd. Their faces were ugly with spite.

'Will you recant your sins?' Confessor Bailey called. 'Will you deny that vaccination is a science and that man evolved rather than being created in one day by God?'

'No. Never.'

'Then you must be burned alive.'

'A faith which has to be extorted is worthless!'

'Burn him!'

Trafford had never dreamed that he would have the strength to die rather than recant but now he found it. As they bound him to the stake, he stared down into the faces of the crowd. A microphone was pointed in his direction in readiness for his screams.

'Everlasting Love!' he called out suddenly. 'Everlasting love! *Ev Love! Ev Love! Ev Love!*'

For a moment there was quiet in the crowd, everybody anxious to hear what last blasphemy the heretic had decided to deliver.

'Don't look forward into ignorance!' Trafford cried. 'Look *backwards* to enlightenment. Look *backwards*. Ev Love, backwards I tell you. Ev Love! *Ev Love backwards*.'

And in that moment, as the hooded executioner advanced with his burning torch to light the pyre, Trafford saw a waving hand in the crowd. He turned to look, expecting a familiar face, but the man who caught his eye was a stranger. As Trafford looked, the man pointed at his vest. On it were written the words *Ev (erlasting) Love!*

The man nodded steadily at Trafford.

Looking round the crowd, Trafford caught sight of a girl on her boyfriend's shoulders. She carried a banner. The banner said *Ev Love*. The girl was not cheering but merely staring intently towards Trafford, her boyfriend staring too.

Sandra Dee had taken his bait and gone looking for evidence of his love! For whatever reason – curiosity, sentiment or mere psychological interest – she had entered Trafford's folder on the DegSep computer and opened the Ev Love file. He had tricked her in the end and caused her to release his viral email. Millions of people had received the first Humanist mail shot.

Trafford was placed on the bonfire and the fire was lit. But as the flames from the burning books began to lick about his feet, he found one last moment to smile, for he knew in his heart of hearts that one day the Temple would be defeated. *Reason* dictated it. Reason and the theory of evolution. For no society based on nothing more constructive than fear and brutish ignorance could survive for ever. No people who raised up the least inventive, the least challenging, the least *interesting* of their number while crushing individual curiosity and endeavour could prosper for long. Trafford knew that natural selection would save the world, as it had done before when other tyrants had tried to crush the human spirit, and that one day the Confessors of the Temple would be extinct.

THE END

Also by Ben Elton:
DEAD FAMOUS

One house, ten contestants, thirty cameras, forty microphones, one murder . . . and no evidence.

Dead Famous is a killer read from Ben Elton – Reality TV as you've never seen it before.

'ONE OF THE BEST WHODUNNITS I HAVE EVER READ . . . A FUNNY, GRIPPING, HUGELY ENTERTAINING THRILLER'
Sunday Telegraph

9780552999458

PAST MORTEM

In romantic desperation, mild mannered detective Edward Newson logs on to the Friends Reunited website in the search of the girlfriends of his youth. As a reunion of the class of '88 is planned, the years slip away and old feuds and passions burn hot once more. And as history begins to repeat itself, the past crashes headlong into the present. Neither will ever be the same again.

'A WRITER WHO PROVOKES ALMOST AS MUCH AS HE ENTERTAINS'
Daily Mail

9780552771238

THE FIRST CASUALTY

Douglas Kingsley is sent to Flanders in 1917 to investigate the murder of a British officer. Forced to conduct his investigations amidst the hell of the Third Battle of Ypres, Kingsley soon discovers that both the evidence and the witnesses he needs are quite literally disappearing into the mud that surrounds him.

'RIVETING ACTION SCENES BRISTLE WITH A QUEASY ENERGY . . .UNPUTDOWNABLE AND DISGUSTINGLY REALISTIC'
Sunday Telegraph

9780552771306